"There is something you can do to prevent them from moving Bailey Ann to that foster home in Sheridan," Genevieve said.

He waited, but she didn't continue. She just stared down into the sink, as if she was worried that it was a suggestion that he wasn't going to like.

"What is it?" he asked. "I've already pushed her release date from the hospital. And I've signed a contract with the hospital, so I can't just quit—"

"I'm not suggesting you quit," she assured him. "Or that you lie about her medical condition..."

"Then what are you suggesting?" he asked. "What can I do to keep Bailey Ann with me?"

She drew in a deep breath as if she needed to brace herself just to tell him her proposal...

Dear Reader,

You are cordially invited to a wedding—or maybe two—in Willow Creek, Wyoming. Maybe there'll be one at Ranch Haven, home of the legendary Sadie March Haven. She was already a legend for often retold stories of her fighting off wolves and breaking a car window to rescue a certain feisty Chihuahua. Now the multi-hyphenate (mother/grandmother/ great-grandmother) is a legend for all the matchmaking she's been doing. But she worries her latest match between her grandson Dr. Colton Cassidy and lawyer Genevieve Porter has worked a little too fast and that people are going to get hurt. But with as much pain as the family has endured, they've also had joy and love. So it's no wonder that even though it isn't Valentine's Day in Willow Creek, Sadie has instigated a Valentine's Day in August to have the town decorated with hearts and flowers for another wedding she has planned...

I hope you've been enjoying all of Sadie's shenanigans as much as I've enjoyed writing about them. Sadie is one of my favorite characters. I'm not sure if she reminds me of someone or if she's who I will become in thirty years. She's definitely meddled with me as much as she has her family, stealing so many of the scenes I've written and my heart, and hopefully yours, too!

Happy Reading!

Lisa Childs

HEARTWARMING

The Doc's Instant Family

—

Lisa Childs

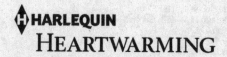

HARLEQUIN®
HEARTWARMING™

ISBN-13: 978-1-335-47562-6

The Doc's Instant Family

Copyright © 2024 by Lisa Childs

For questions and comments about the quality of this book, please contact us at CustomerService@Harlequin.com.

Harlequin Enterprises ULC
22 Adelaide St. West, 41st Floor
Toronto, Ontario M5H 4E3, Canada
www.Harlequin.com

Printed in U.S.A.

Recycling programs for this product may not exist in your area.

New York Times and *USA TODAY* bestselling, award-winning author **Lisa Childs** has written more than eighty-five novels. Published in twenty countries, she's also appeared on the *Publishers Weekly*, Barnes & Noble and Nielsen Top 100 bestseller lists. Lisa writes contemporary romance, romantic suspense, paranormal and women's fiction. She's a wife, mom, bonus mom, avid reader and less avid runner. Readers can reach her through Facebook or her website, lisachilds.com.

Books by Lisa Childs

Harlequin Heartwarming

Bachelor Cowboys

A Rancher's Promise
The Cowboy's Unlikely Match
The Bronc Rider's Twin Surprise
The Cowboy's Ranch Rescue
The Firefighter's Family Secret

Harlequin Romantic Suspense

Hotshot Heroes

Hotshot Hero Under Fire
Hotshot Hero on the Edge
Hotshot Heroes Under Threat
Hotshot Hero in Disguise
Hotshot Hero for the Holidays

Visit the Author Profile page
at Harlequin.com for more titles.

With great appreciation for my editor, Adrienne MacIntosh, for her great insight and support and her incredible spreadsheets that keep me on track with all my deadlines! Adrienne, you've made my busy schedule stress-free and fun. I can't wait to write many, many more books with you!

CHAPTER ONE

COLLIN CASSIDY DROPPED heavily into the chair behind his desk, more from shock than exhaustion. He felt like he'd been sucker punched. A fist hadn't delivered the blow, though. The voice emanating from his cell phone speaker had. This wasn't the first hit he'd taken over the past couple of weeks, but it definitely struck him the hardest.

"Dr. Cassidy, did you hear me? Are you there?"

"Um… I…" Maybe he hadn't heard the social worker correctly. "Can you repeat that?"

"I found a foster family that will take Bailey Ann. Unfortunately they're in Sheridan."

That was more than an hour from Willow Creek, Wyoming—more than an hour from Collin.

"But that might be a good thing," Mrs. Finch continued. "It'll be close to the children's hospital where she had her heart transplant, and she'll be able to go back to seeing her doctors there."

And not him.

"Are you sure the foster family can handle her health care?" he asked. "If she doesn't get her meds…" Her little body could reject the heart that she'd waited so long to receive, the heart she'd nearly rejected once when another family hadn't been able to handle her care plan. That was why the seven-year-old was in the hospital now.

That was one of the reasons he didn't want her to go. The other…

"I've been wanting to talk to you about fostering or adopting Bailey Ann myself," he admitted.

A sigh drifted out of his cell speaker. "You've just recently moved to the area," she said. "And you've just started your job at the hospital. Are you sure now is a good time for you to be considering adoption or even fostering? Especially a child who has special needs like Bailey Ann?"

"That's why I want to do it," he said. Because she was so very special.

"So you have a home with space for Bailey Ann? Child care arranged for her while you're working what must be very long hours? Child care qualified to handle a child with her medical issues? You could do this with your schedule?" Mrs. Finch asked. "Because this other family is ready now to take her. They're a little older, so they've only agreed to a short-term placement."

He was losing her, just like he'd lost so many other people and places who mattered to him. "She's still regaining her strength after that last foster family didn't give her the antirejection meds correctly. She needs to be monitored for a week or maybe two yet at the hospital."

"I will make sure this family gets the proper training over the next two weeks," the social worker assured him.

A couple of weeks.

Was that enough time for him to prove himself capable and worthy of caring for her?

"We all want what's best for Bailey Ann," she said with that gentle tone that women had used when they'd broken up with him in the past. That whole "it's not you, it's me" thing when they were both well aware that it was really him, that because of his hectic schedule, he wasn't as available or attentive as they needed him to be. He wasn't enough for them.

He wasn't enough for Bailey Ann either. He wasn't ready. Just as he hadn't been ready to help his own parents. He hadn't been able to take care of them, to save them. His mom hadn't survived. His dad had, but because of other doctors and surgeons and someone else who had unknowingly made the ultimate sacrifice.

That was how Collin felt about Bailey Ann, how hard he'd fallen for her. He was willing to make whatever sacrifices were necessary to be enough for her. Before he could say anything else to the social worker, to make his intentions clear, Mrs. Finch ended the call, as if the matter was settled.

Would she even give him a chance?

Knuckles tapped against wood, drawing his attention to the man standing in the doorway to his office. Looking at Colton was like looking into a mirror; they had the same dark eyes and dark hair, the same facial features and tall build. Colton, a firefighter, was a little more muscular than Collin, not that he would ever admit it to his twin.

And they weren't the only ones in the family who shared a striking resemblance. In addition to their older brother Marsh, they'd recently discovered they had cousins who looked almost as much like them as he and Colton looked like each other.

Colton's brow was furrowed beneath the brim of his black cowboy hat. He wasn't wearing his firefighter gear or his paramedic uniform. So, not at the hospital for work. At that moment, their expressions were probably alike: troubled.

They'd had a lot of troubles in the past few weeks, and it wasn't surprising that his brother was less upbeat than usual. The family ranch house had burned down, but they'd been about to sell it anyway. And fortunately nobody had been hurt in the fire. But what they'd learned after it…

All the family secrets their father had kept from them: a grandmother and cousins they'd never known about. Even their last name. It wasn't Cassidy; it was Haven.

Collin was reeling, too, but he'd decided to focus on Bailey Ann, on making sure she was not alone. Like he usually felt.

"Hey, everything okay?" Colton asked him. "You look like you lost your best friend. And I know that's not possible since I'm right here."

They were identical twins, but they were really nothing alike. If they weren't brothers, they might not even be friends. Colton was easygoing and charming while Collin was intense and focused, so focused that he'd never really taken time to make friends. So Colton probably was his best friend.

"I just got bad news about Bailey Ann," he admitted.

Colton pressed his hand to his chest as if he felt the ache that Collin was feeling. "Oh, no, is her body rejecting her new heart again?"

A pang struck Collin, too. "No. She's actually improving a lot." She'd be ready to leave the hospital as soon as Mrs. Finch trained this other family in how to look after her.

He sighed. "I just got off the phone with her social worker. She found a placement for her."

Colton stepped farther into Collin's office and peered at his face, his dark eyes questioning. "That's a good thing, right?" he asked.

With his emotion choking him, Collin could only shake his head.

"Are you worried they can't handle her medical care, like her last foster family?"

He sucked in a breath and nodded. "But that's only part of it."

Colton's mouth curved into a slight grin, and he nodded, too. "You've fallen for her. *You* want her."

He nodded again, then released a shaky sigh. "But what can I really offer her?"

"Love," Colton said. "You love her. That's all that little girl wants. Someone who loves her and who will always be there for her."

Tears stung Collin's eyes, and he had to close them. "But I'm not ready. I would need a house and child care help for when I'm working, and I don't have enough time…" He hadn't had enough time to save his mom or help his dad. He'd had to get through school first and undergrad and med school and his residencies and fellowships. Everything took too long.

"We have somebody in our lives now who knows how to get things done," Colton said with a grin. "Sadie."

A grin tugged at Collin's mouth, too. Their indomitable grandmother that they hadn't even known they had. "She is a force of nature."

But because of that, Collin had actually been trying to avoid her. The old woman was intent on matchmaking, and he had no plans to get swept up in her schemes like his cousins and now even his twin had.

He cleared his throat and asked, "Are you here to see Livvy?" That was probably why Colton had showed up at the hospital in his casual clothes, looking more like a cowboy than the firefighter and paramedic he was.

Colton's whole face lit up with love at the mention of the ER doctor for whom he'd fallen so hard. But then his grin slipped away and he shook his head. "I actually came to see you."

"About what?" Collin asked.

Colton stood there for a moment, his hands shoved deep in the pockets of his jeans. Then he shook his head. "Never mind. It can wait. You need to focus on Bailey Ann so you can prove to the social worker that you're the right family for her."

Collin wasn't even sure where to start. Sadie? She really was good at getting things done, like setting up his twin and her friend's granddaughter so they couldn't help falling in love. Not that that was a bad thing, though, since Colton was happier than he'd ever been. But even with his happiness, something was weighing on him.

"I know something's been bothering you," Collin said. He'd been trying to get his twin to tell him what it was for the past couple of weeks. "So spill it."

Colton shook his head again. "Don't worry about it. It can wait. Bailey Ann can't. You need to focus on her. Get Grandma to help you."

Collin's stomach knotted at the risk of reaching out to Sadie Haven. "She's going to use it as an opportunity to set me up with whoever she has picked out for me. I don't have time for that when I have to focus on Bailey Ann."

Colton chuckled. "You think she has some kind of master plan for all of us? Like she's arranged a marriage for each of us?"

"Don't you?" Collin asked. "She had Katie for Jake. Emily for Ben. She brought Melanie back to Dusty after he lost her. And then Taye for Baker."

"Yeah, because she knows all of them really well. She raised them." Their cousins hadn't had easy childhoods either. They were young when their dad died, younger than Collin and his brothers had been when they lost their mom. "She didn't think Dad had even survived after he ran away all those years ago, and she had no idea we existed until a few weeks ago."

Collin continued as if his twin hadn't interrupted. "And she found Livvy for you."

Colton laughed and shook his head. "No, she didn't. We found each other right here at the hospital."

Collin snorted. "Yeah, so you think. But how'd you wind up working out of this hospital?"

"I got transferred to Willow Creek Fire Department from Moss Valley."

"And you know very well that Sadie was behind that transfer," Collin reminded him. "Just like we figured out she was behind Marsh getting the position of interim sheriff of Willow Creek when the sheriff suddenly decided to retire. Why do you think she wanted you to work here?"

"So that we would all be closer to Ranch Haven. She wanted to get to know us, to spend more time with us," Colton said.

Collin nodded. "To spend more time with us and to get us involved with whoever she's picked out for us."

Colton shook his head again but slower, more tentatively, and he murmured, "No…"

"That's why I've been staying away from her," Collin admitted. Marriage wasn't for him. He'd already lost too many people in his life, and he had no intention of ever risking his heart. And even if he thought it was safe to fall in love, with all his student loans to pay off yet, he was in no position to get married. These were all reasons that he should let Bailey Ann go to that foster home, but letting go of her was one more loss he wasn't sure he could handle. He had started treating her during his internal medicine residency. Despite all of her health struggles and all of the people who'd abandoned her because of them— her biological parents and numerous foster families—she was still so affectionate and optimistic. She was an inspiration for him.

He would have to do everything he could to get custody of her, even swallow his concerns and ask his grandmother for help. He'd simply be firm about not being able to give his heart away. He couldn't handle another heartbreak.

And it would break anyway if Bailey Ann was sent away. So right now, he had nothing left to lose.

GENEVIEVE PORTER HAD lost everything that had ever mattered to her—some things and people before she'd even realized they had mattered. She'd made so many mistakes in her life that had cost her dearly. The biggest mistake was in not realizing how short life could be for some.

Too short.

The second biggest mistake was in trusting people she shouldn't have. One was her ex-husband. The other...

"I'm sorry," Sue Masters said as she settled heavily into a chair across from Genevieve's desk. The gray-haired woman worked as a nurse in the Emergency Department at Willow Creek Memorial. "I thought that you wanted to make sure that your nephews were all right. That they were safe."

"Yes, but I just wanted you to let me know what you heard around town or if they had to go to the hospital," Genevieve said, with a pang of regret. "I didn't expect you to call Child Protective Services on the Havens."

After one of the boys had been injured in an accident, Sue had called CPS to investigate the children's safety with their current guardians. The case had, fortunately, been closed quickly, with the Havens being cleared.

Tears shimmered in Sue's usually frosty blue eyes. "I know. I made a terrible mistake."

"The mistake was mine," Genevieve said. Along with so many others she'd made over the years. "I should have been clearer about my intentions." The problem was that she wasn't even sure what her intentions were.

Not anymore.

Sue reached across the desk and patted Genevieve's clenched hand. "I can't imagine how you must feel over all of this. The fact that the Havens didn't even let you know…"

They had probably contacted her mother or at least tried, but Genevieve doubted Sue would believe that. Clearly she remembered Genevieve's mother as the sweet little girl she'd grown up with, not the bitter woman she'd become. Given the way Sue's face usually had a pinched look to it, like she'd just sucked a lemon, Genevieve's mother probably wasn't the only one who'd become bitter over the years.

Genevieve didn't want to become like either of these women, though she worried she had without even realizing it. "They may have tried to." Genevieve defended the Havens. "I've moved a lot over the years. And Mother and Father have as well."

"But surely there would have been a way to get them the news about the crash and…" Sue murmured.

"Have you talked to Mother lately?" Genevieve asked.

The older woman's face flushed. "No. But I know they're out of the country a lot."

Genevieve suspected the woman hadn't spoken to her old school friend in years. Once her parents had moved away from Willow Creek, they'd cut all ties to their hometown and had never looked back. Not even now…

Unlike Genevieve who, when she'd finally learned of her loss, had returned. But once she'd arrived in Willow Creek, just the thought of contacting the Havens had made her stomach clench. Her life had been one painful loss after another, and she couldn't face opening herself up to that again. So she'd done what she always did and had thrown herself into work. She'd joined a local law firm, the same one at which Ben Haven had worked before becoming deputy mayor of Willow Creek and now mayor. She didn't want to follow his political path, but she'd thought that he might come around the office from time to time.

He hadn't. And now she hoped he didn't. After the debacle with CPS, Genevieve hoped she didn't encounter any of the Havens. But her heart ached to meet seven-year-old Miller, five-year-old Ian and the toddler, Jacob. Her nephews.

SADIE MARCH HAVEN, soon to be Lemmon, was falling in love all over again with the little girl lying in the hospital bed. She understood now why Bailey Ann was Collin's favorite patient, and why Colton, who'd shared that tidbit with her, also spent so much time visiting the little girl. He must have been by today because the child was wearing his black cowboy hat. Since he was rarely without it, the little girl must have either charmed or manipulated him into letting her borrow it. The hat was so big it kept slipping down over her face so she pulled it off. With her sparkling dark eyes and dimpled smile, Bailey Ann was beautiful, but she was more than that. She radiated goodness, sweetness and hope.

All the things that Sadie, after all the tragedies in her eighty years of life, had learned to embrace, to hold on to with all her might.

"May I give you a hug?" she asked the little girl.

Bailey Ann threw back her covers and scrambled across her bed to wrap her arms around Sadie's neck. She patted Sadie's long hair. "You're pretty," the little girl said.

Sadie laughed. Nobody had called her that in a long time. If ever…

Not even her late husband.

Her fiancé, that old fool Lem Lemmon, said sweet things, and the way he looked at her made her feel pretty. Made her feel like a young girl again instead of the old woman that she was.

"You're the pretty one," she told Bailey Ann as she pulled back and cupped the child's cheek in her hand.

Something about the child reminded Sadie of Jenny. And moisture filled her eyes at the thought of the granddaughter-in-law she'd lost in the car accident months ago with her beloved grandson Dale. Gone, like so many other people she'd loved.

Bailey Ann's hands were in Sadie's hair, her fingers running through the long white strands. "Your hair is so pretty. You look like Mrs. Claus."

Sadie laughed again. "I guess I will be soon," she admitted.

Every year Lem dressed up like Santa Claus. He'd had white hair and a white beard for as long as most people could remember, and for the month leading up to Christmas, he wore his Santa suit and sat in a sleigh in the Willow Creek town square. Kids stood in line for hours to tell him what they wanted to find under the tree. And Sadie knew that if he didn't think their parents could afford to give them presents, he would make sure they got something to open on Christmas morning himself. Lem Lemmon was a good man. Once it would have killed Sadie to admit that, but now...

She wasn't sure that she could live without him. This was love. This was what she wanted for all her grandsons.

"Are you psychic?" a deep voice asked.

"No, Dr. Cass, she's Mrs. Claus," Bailey Ann said.

Sadie chuckled and turned her head to grin at her grandson who stood in the doorway. He arched a brow over one of his dark eyes, and a pang struck her heart again at how much he looked like his grandfather and his father. She'd lost his grandfather a dozen years ago, and she'd thought his dad was dead longer than that.

But, despite all the odds, Jessup was alive. He'd been living as JJ Cassidy on a ranch just an hour away from Ranch Haven.

"I haven't married him yet," Sadie said. But they couldn't wait much longer, not at their ages and not with the way they felt about each other. She leaned closer to the little girl and whispered, "And you have to keep it secret who he really is…" She pressed a finger against her lips.

Bailey Ann gave her a solemn nod before moving her fingers across her mouth like she was zipping her lips and throwing away the key.

Sadie couldn't resist. She had to hug the child again. "You are just precious," she said.

"Yes, she is…" Collin murmured, his voice gruff with emotion.

Clearly this grandson already knew something about love—a father's love for a child. This little girl wasn't biologically his. Colton had told her that whatever family she'd had once had abandoned her because she'd always been so sick. But Collin was sticking by her.

"Bailey Ann," he said. "Did you know that your visitor here is my grandmother, Sadie Haven?"

"Hi," Bailey Ann whispered.

"You seem to already know about Bailey Ann," he said to Sadie. "How did you…"

"I have sources everywhere," she said. Or at least she tried. But she wasn't always successful at getting the information she wanted. Collin's father was a good example. He'd taken off after high school and she hadn't been able to track him down. She hadn't even known where to look. That was because he hadn't wanted to be found. He'd been so sick, and he'd stayed away to avoid her overprotectiveness—and to avoid breaking her heart if he died.

Now that they were back in touch, she knew how much he regretted staying away. He understood well what she'd gone through because his oldest son, Collin's brother Cash, had disappeared after high school, too.

"My twin has a big mouth," Collin said.

"A family shouldn't have secrets," she said. Collin snorted derisively. "Hmm… I wonder what my cousins would say if they heard you make that claim?"

Heat rushed to her face. She had kept secrets from his cousins—or at least one big secret. The cousins had no idea they had an uncle, and none of them, including her, had known about Jessup's sons. Cash, Marsh, Collin and Colton. The Cassidys.

"Well, a family *shouldn't* have secrets," she repeated. "That doesn't mean that they don't." She suspected his twin was keeping a secret, that something was bothering him. But now she could see that something was bothering Collin even more.

With the way he was staring at the little girl, with such longing and loss, it was clear what it was. "I'm not psychic," she said. "But I can tell that you need me."

Collin chuckled softly. "And I bet you love that."

"I love you," she said. "I want you to be happy."

And maybe that would excuse what she was about to do...

CHAPTER TWO

Collin hadn't been entirely joking when he'd accused his grandmother of being psychic. He and Colton had just been talking about her that morning and then a few hours later, there she was before he'd even had the chance to reach out to her.

But she wasn't psychic. She just had her sources, specifically his twin, and that was why she was so aware of what was going on in Collin's life. He hadn't even had to ask for her help.

She'd offered it anyway, in the form of a business card for a lawyer who specialized in family law, including adoptions. Genevieve Porter.

The woman worked out of a law firm on Main Street where too many people might see Collin walking into the two-story brick building. As a doctor just establishing himself in Willow Creek, he couldn't afford gossip about a visit to a law firm. He didn't need anyone wondering if he was hiring someone to represent him for malpractice.

So he helped himself to the black cowboy hat that his brother had left with Bailey Ann. She was all too happy to lend it, thinking it was hilarious that he could "dress up as" his brother.

He doubted the townsfolk would bat an eye over Colton visiting a law office. The firefighter was a hero without an enemy in the world. And no problems…

At least not until the last few weeks when he'd begun acting as if something was weighing on him. Maybe Colton did have a reason to see a lawyer himself. Once Collin found out if he even had a chance of fostering, let alone adopting Bailey Ann, he would get his twin to tell him what was going on with him.

On his break, Collin put his plan in motion. Doctor's coat off, cowboy hat on, he headed to see Genevieve Porter.

For a moment, he wondered if she was part of his grandmother's matchmaking scheme. But no, he didn't believe Sadie would jeopardize a child's future. He had to trust that this Porter woman was a good adoption lawyer.

Once he stepped inside the reception area, with its exposed brick walls and high, coffered ceiling, he told the silver-haired receptionist his name and with whom he had an appointment.

The woman flashed him a smile and picked up her phone. "Dr. Cassidy is here for you," she said.

Given the short notice with which he'd gotten this appointment, he expected to have to take a seat and wait while the lawyer worked him in, but a door opened and a woman's voice called out. "Dr. Cassidy? You can come right back."

The silver-haired receptionist pointed to the open door just off the reception area. He assumed he was being pointed toward Ms. Porter's secretary or paralegal.

His patients often complained about the medical assistant and nurse asking them questions only to have him ask them again. Maybe lawyers were like doctors in that respect: they wanted to know the client's reason for showing up before they saw them. He hadn't really said much when he'd made the appointment, just that he needed to see her as soon as possible for some legal advice.

And he was lucky enough to get in late that afternoon.

He walked through the open door and found himself staring in awe at the woman waiting for him. With pale blond hair, bright blue eyes and delicate features, she was beautiful, but she also had an energy about her that would have been impossible to ignore. Intelligence radiated from her bright eyes, and she moved with such grace as she closed the door behind him and walked toward the desk.

The office was big with bookshelves lining the three interior walls and blinds covering the tall windows on the brick exterior wall. Most of the light came from the lamp on the big, mahogany desk behind which the woman took a seat after waving him toward one of the chairs in front of it.

"What can I help you with, Dr. Cassidy?" she asked.

"You're Ms. Porter?" he asked, just to confirm what he already suspected: her identity and the reason his grandmother had referred him here. As a setup…

She nodded and smiled. "Sorry. I didn't introduce myself. I must be getting used to how relaxed things are in Willow Creek."

"You're not from here?" he asked.

Color flushed her pale skin, and she looked away from him, as if she was uncomfortable. "Let's talk about you and your reason for needing my advice."

He'd vowed to focus only on Bailey Ann right now, even over his own twin. But something about her made him so curious that, despite Sadie's scheming, he was tempted to ask her more questions about herself.

But clearly she was more comfortable asking rather than answering questions. She picked up a pen and poised it over the legal pad on her desk. "What can I help you with?"

He settled into one of the leather chairs and clasped his hands together. The skin on them was still a little pink from the burns he'd sustained in the fire three weeks ago.

He and his family had lost their house that day. But they'd lost more than that. They'd lost even more than their material possessions and mementos. They'd lost their identities, too, and their family history as they'd known it.

"Dr. Cassidy?" Ms. Porter prodded him. "Are you all right?" She was staring at his hands as well, her blue eyes clouded with concern.

"I am," he said. But he wouldn't be if he lost Bailey Ann like he'd lost so much else.

GENEVIEVE WASN'T SURE why the doctor had wanted to see her. She wasn't a malpractice lawyer. Though she wondered, from the damaged skin on his hands, if he'd been the victim instead of the perpetrator of malpractice. Hilda, the receptionist, hadn't gotten any information out of him when she'd made the appointment. She'd probably figured Genevieve should just be grateful that she had a client, any client, given that business for her had been light since she'd moved to town a month ago.

"Dr. Cassidy?" she prodded him when he remained curiously quiet as he stared at his hands. "Are you sure you're all right?"

He leaned back in the chair and expelled a ragged sigh. "No. I'm not sure of anything anymore..."

"I know the feeling," she muttered softly enough that she hoped he didn't hear.

But he leaned forward again and stared at

her with those strangely intense dark eyes. "Ms. Porter?"

"Genevieve," she said. That was something she liked about Willow Creek; it was so much more casual and informal than DC. "Call me Genevieve."

"I'm Collin," he said.

Collin Cassidy. He sounded and looked—with his black cowboy hat and dark eyes and long, lanky body—like he should be a rodeo star or country singer. But he was a doctor.

"Collin, then." She gave him a warm smile. "I hope I can help you, but if it's in regard to your job, I don't have any experience with malpractice claims."

"Fortunately neither do I," he said. "I was referred to you because you specialize in adoptions."

A cold chill rushed down her spine despite the suit jacket she wore over her sleeveless sweater. She'd only made that claim to one other person—a lawyer with another firm.

"Who…" Her voice cracked, and she cleared it before continuing, "Who referred you to me?"

"Sadie Haven," he said.

She should have known…

This was all going to blow up in her face, like so much of her life had. If only she'd been honest from the start.

She drew in a deep breath and resolved to tell him the truth. Or at least some of it. "While I have some experience with family law and have handled some adoptions, I mostly do estate planning now." That seemed to be the biggest need in Willow Creek. She'd specialized in other areas in DC.

He emitted a soft groan of disappointment or maybe frustration. "Oh, I should have known what she was up to," he muttered.

"She?"

"Sadie," he said again. "You know her, right?"

She shook her head. "I've never met Sadie Haven."

"Oh, I'm sorry then. I must have misunderstood," he said, his face flushing. "I was really hoping you could help me."

For some reason she wished she could as well. "Do you and your wife want to adopt?" she asked.

"No—yes," he answered with a slight head shake.

"Which is it?" she asked with a smile.

"*I* want to adopt. I don't have a wife."

She felt a strange rush of relief and nearly shook her head at herself. She had no business being attracted to anyone right now, least of all a client. Especially a client Sadie Haven had referred to her...

What was that about?

"Would it be easier if I had one?" he asked.

"One what?" she asked, and she glanced down at the blank page of her legal pad. She needed to start taking notes, needed to figure out what was going on...

"A wife," he replied. "Would it be easier for me to adopt if I was married?"

"Not necessarily..." She was intrigued now.

Dr. Cassidy shook his head. "It doesn't matter. It's not like I could find someone to marry me in two weeks anyway."

"Two weeks?" she repeated. "I don't understand."

"The little girl I want to adopt, my patient, is going to be leaving the hospital in two weeks," he said. "Her social worker found her a foster home, but it's only short term. I want to foster her instead and then adopt her to give her a home without any further disruption to her life."

"You can certainly petition to adopt her," she assured him.

"Her social worker wants to place her in foster care in Sheridan," he said. "She'll be so far away, and if this home is like the last one, and they don't follow her medical orders…" His deep voice got so gruff, he stopped and cleared his throat. "I just don't want to risk anyone else taking care of her. I don't want to lose her."

He wasn't talking about just losing custody or contact but of his patient losing her life. That struck her heart, and she felt concern for the child that she hadn't even met. "Are one or both of her parents alive? If so, we could see if they'll grant you legal custody," she said. That would be the easiest way.

But if they weren't alive…

Genevieve knew all too well the problems that could cause.

"No idea. They signed off their rights to her before I met her," he said. "She's a ward of the state and has been frequently moved from foster home to foster home because no one can handle her medical issues."

"What are those?" she asked.

"She was born with an enlarged heart, which

eventually caused congestive heart failure, and she's just recently had a heart transplant," he said. "She's only seven years old."

That pang struck Genevieve's heart again. "Oh, that's so sad…"

But for some reason, Collin Cassidy smiled. "She's the happiest, sweetest little girl despite all the challenges she's had. And I want to give her a home that's safe and consistent."

"Do you have a foster care license?" she asked. "Because the adoption could take some time, but if you were licensed for foster care, we could get her placed with you while we filed the paperwork for adoption."

He shook his head again. "I didn't think… There's so much going on… I'm not ready…"

She bit her lip. "Okay. You said you're not married. You're right—that can be a barrier but it's not unworkable. Tell me about your home situation."

He glanced at his hands again and shook his head. "My family home burned down a few weeks ago, and we're all staying at someone's house here in Willow Creek."

While she was sympathetic to him, she also had to think of the child. "Are you sure then that she would be better off with you than the other foster family?"

He sucked in a breath as if she'd slapped him. "That other family isn't even trained yet in how to care for her and they don't want her long term," he said. "She's been my patient all through my residency and fellowship in Sheridan, which is most of her life. I know her. And I love her."

More than a pang struck her heart now; it was as if someone squeezed it. She could hear the love in his voice and see it on his handsome face.

"I…I would like to talk to her," Genevieve said. "I'd like to see what she'd like…"

"I don't want to get her hopes up," Collin said. "In case this isn't possible, in case I can't get licensed as a foster home or qualify to adopt her…"

"I understand," Genevieve said, and his consideration for the child increased her estimation of him. "But I'd still like to meet her."

"I don't want to get my hopes up either," he admitted. "Do you…" He stopped and cleared his throat again. "Do you think you can help me?"

She leaned back in her chair for a moment

and studied him across her desk. He was so good-looking and obviously smart since he was apparently a cardiologist. But she'd learned the hard way to protect herself from handsome, intelligent men who were used to getting what they wanted. Like Bradford, her ex-husband, who had wanted biological children more than he'd wanted her. When she hadn't been able to give him those children, he hadn't wanted her at all anymore. Thoughts of her marriage usually hurt, but somehow, the pain didn't come.

Maybe she was over him. Or maybe she was as dead inside as Bradford had accused her of being, except that she was moved by the care this handsome doctor had for a little girl he wanted to make his own.

"I want to help *her*," she said. She wasn't sure if that would help him or not. It depended on what was best for the child.

Instead of being offended, he grinned and nodded. "Thank you…" Then he muttered, "Sadie strikes again…"

She was pretty sure she wasn't meant to hear that. The chill rushed over her again, reminding her who had brought him to her specifically.

Why had Sadie referred this man to her? Was she sending a message to Genevieve that she knew she was here? Maybe that she knew what Genevieve had done, or at least caused…?

BEN HAD BEEN expecting and dreading this visit. While he loved his grandmother, he also knew that when she was on the warpath, there could be collateral damage. He didn't even know Genevieve Porter, but he felt a pang of sympathy for her that she was in Sadie Haven's sights.

He also felt a twinge of regret that he'd shared her name with his grandmother. But he'd been concerned that this lawyer had been asking questions about his nephews and who now had legal custody of them.

Why had she asked? Had she intended to challenge that custody for a client or for…?

He had a feeling he was about to find out. Since Ms. Porter worked out of his old law firm, Grandmother would probably have him investigate her.

His door opened, and he rose from behind his desk as Sadie walked in. She used to storm this office when Lem had been mayor. She'd loved giving him grief over how he managed the town. She only took Ben to task occasionally, usually when he deserved it like when he'd meddled in her love life like she kept meddling in everyone else's.

But she looked happy now, her face aglow with a bright smile.

And he tensed with suspicion. She'd been so upset over the lawyer call and most especially over that complaint to CPS.

"What's going on?" he asked, studying her through narrowed eyes.

"What do you mean?"

"You're not mad."

"Should I be mad?" she asked. "Have you done something to upset me?"

A smile tugged at his lips now. "When have I ever upset you? Did I upset you by bringing Lem around the ranch for dinner?" he asked.

She sighed. "Yes, you did, Benjamin Haven, and you know it. You upset my entire lonely, solitary life."

"You two really are getting married." He was still stunned at the success of his matchmaking. But maybe he shouldn't have been surprised; as everyone said, he was the most like Sadie.

Other people said it as if it was a bad thing, but he knew the truth.

She nodded. "Yes. Very soon. We're too old to wait."

He snorted his derision at her claim.

His grandmother and his deputy mayor were more vital at eighty than most people were in their thirties, which was another reason he was glad he took after her.

"So when's the happy day?" he asked.

"Soon," she said. "But I need your help."

"You want me to be your wedding planner?" Like he didn't have enough to do with running the town and helping his family with his nephews and the ranch. And with school starting soon, he wouldn't see as much of his fiancée as he wished either. Emily, as a teacher, would be back in the classroom instead of spending so much of her time at Ranch Haven which was an hour from town.

She snorted now. "I know how to plan a wedding," she said.

He chuckled. "I guess you do. You've been planning all of ours since you hired Katie, Emily, Melanie and Taye to help out at the ranch."

While her match making had worked out

for him and his brothers, Ben wondered how his cousins were going to handle her meddling. She'd already been messing with their lives more than they might have realized.

Though thinking back to some of their visits to the ranch, he suspected they were well aware of her antics.

"Since we've had and are going to have so many weddings, I have a proposal for you," she said.

He chuckled. "I've already accepted Emily's proposal," he reminded her.

She reached out and smacked his shoulder. "I'm taken, too, thanks to you," she said. "To get everybody into the mood for romance, I propose that the town decorate for Valentine's Day, bringing out all the hearts and flowers and pink and red…"

"It's August," Ben said.

"So? We have Christmas in July. Let's have Valentine's Day in August."

"*We* don't promote Christmas in July," he said. "Retailers do to bump up their sales. What are you trying to sell, Grandma?"

"You have to ask?" she asked with a sigh of disappointment.

And he groaned. She was trying to sell romance, and since he and his brothers had already taken her bait, she must have come up with this plan to guide his cousins into falling in love.

"I thought you were going to be too busy for your matchmaking with everything going on with the boys."

"CPS closed the case," she said. "Lem's lovely granddaughter made certain of that."

Dr. Livvy Lemmon hadn't appreciated someone saying that she'd failed to report when five-year-old Ian had come into the ER with bruises. She'd known that his falling in the barn had caused those bruises, not any abuse or neglect, and she'd made certain the CPS investigator had known that as well.

No wonder Ben's cousin Colton had fallen so hard and fast for the doctor. Still, his cousins Marsh and Collin were single yet...

And maybe his cousin Cash, but Ben hadn't met him. He'd figured Sadie would be looking for her runaway grandson even more intently than she'd looked for her runaway son.

She'd found Jessup, alive and with sons of his own, which was part of the reason she was so happy. Lem was the other part.

"What about Genevieve Porter?" he asked.

"Don't you want to find out more about her?" Once the question slipped out, he bit the inside of his cheek. He'd probably fallen right into her plan for him to investigate the lawyer.

But she just smiled. "I have Collin handling that."

He wondered if Collin knew he was "handling" that. But before he could ask anything else, she was patting his cheek as she so often did.

"Just get those decorations up as soon as possible," she said. "I always wanted a Valentine's Day theme for my wedding."

He snorted again at the thought of Sadie wanting anything to do with hearts and flowers. But then her smile slipped a bit, and he wondered if she was thinking about her recent heart attack. He felt a twinge of regret.

Or maybe she really was a romantic. Maybe that was the reason for all her meddling—that she loved love as much as she loved all her grandsons.

Or maybe she just loved meddling…

CHAPTER THREE

COLLIN STEPPED OUT of the law office into the late afternoon sun, squinting like he'd just woken up. But he couldn't wake up from this nightmare, just like he'd never been able to as a kid.

He didn't want Bailey Ann growing up like he had, with so much uncertainty about his life. His dad had had so many flare-ups with lupus that his organs had been affected. First his kidneys and then his heart. Collin had gone to bed every night worrying that his dad would be dead when Collin woke up again. The irony was that he hadn't worried about his mom, and then she was the one he'd lost to breast cancer.

Bailey Ann had already lost both her parents, not to death but to abandonment. And then there had been so many foster homes that had put her back into the system because the doctor's appointments, hospital stays and medications had been too much for those families to handle.

He'd been the most constant person in her life; she couldn't lose him any more than he could lose her. Had he made that clear to Genevieve Porter? Did she understand that this wasn't just about what he wanted?

He glanced over his shoulder at the law office, wondering if he should go back inside and try to explain it to her more clearly. But no, she'd had another client coming in, and she'd agreed to meet Bailey Ann after that appointment at the hospital.

She would talk to her and find out what the child wanted. He breathed a slight sigh of relief. Bailey Ann would want to stay with him. He was certain of it.

But how was he going to make that happen? Even if Genevieve Porter filed paperwork with the court for him, he still wasn't ready. He slept in the den at the property where his dad was staying until the insurance claim was settled on their burned house. He needed a place that was big enough for him and Bailey Ann and a live-in nanny who had experience caring for a child with medical challenges. And he'd need to accomplish all of that within two weeks and hope that Genevieve Porter agreed to help him, too.

He tugged down the brim of Colton's hat, blocking the sun, and as he could see more clearly, his eyes settled on Becca Calder's real estate office across the street. If anyone could find him a house on short notice, it would be Becca. Intent on talking to her, he stepped off the curb.

And a horn blared. Tires squealed. He stepped back and grimaced over his mistake. The truck hadn't been close, but Collin had upset the driver. The truck's box was piled high with plastic totes, and the driver pulled to the curb where he was standing.

He didn't have time to deal with an irate driver. But the guy just waved at him, motioning him to pass in front of his truck. Collin waved back, looked both ways this time and hurried across the street.

He didn't have an appointment, so chances were Becca would be too busy to see him. Or she might not even be in the office at all. But when he pulled open the door, she was right there in front of him in the reception area.

Collin hadn't seen her in years. He was struck by how different she looked than the girl who used to hang out in the barn with his older brother Cash.

Gone was the long, tangled hair; she wore the black tresses in a sleek cut that just skimmed her chin. And instead of worn jeans and an oversize sweatshirt, she wore a suit much like the one Genevieve Porter had been wearing, with a lightweight jacket, pencil skirt and heels.

While he was happy to see her, she did not seem as thrilled. She groaned and said, "Colton, stop badgering me. I am not getting into the middle of you and Cash and whatever has you so anxious to see him right now."

She'd mistaken him for his twin. The cowboy hat. He reached up and touched the brim again, pushing it back with slightly shaking fingers.

She focused on his hand, and her dark blue eyes narrowed. Then she groaned again. "You're not Colton."

His hands were definitely a giveaway. While Collin had sustained burns in the fire, Colton had been one of the responders, wearing his protective gear as he and the other firefighters fought to save the family home.

"No, I'm not Colton," Collin said.

Becca closed her eyes and sighed. "Forget what I said…"

"You and I both know that's not going to happen," he said. "What's going on with Colton and Cash? And do you still see him?"

"Colton's been by the office a couple of times," Becca said.

Collin shook his head. "You know I'm talking about Cash, not my twin."

"Collin…" she murmured.

"Yes, Becca," he said. "It's me." After mistaking him for Colton, she must have considered that he could have been Marsh, too.

"I heard you were in Willow Creek. That you're all in Willow Creek now," she said.

"Does that include Cash?" he asked.

Pink color flushed her pale skin. "Like I've been telling your twin, I'm not getting in the middle of that…"

"Of what?" Collin asked. "I still don't know why Cash took off like he did. Why he was so mad at Dad…" But he trailed off as he realized what his oldest brother's reason might have been. Maybe he'd learned the truth long before his brothers had. Maybe he'd found out about Sadie and the rest of their family that Dad had kept secret from them.

He bristled a bit as anger nagged at him. But as he'd done every time it had threatened to erupt before this, he reminded himself that all that mattered was that Dad was alive. He was doing well.

He needed to focus on that, on making sure that Dad kept doing well, which he might not if his sons expressed how angry they were with him.

Was that why Colton had come around Becca's office? Looking for Cash because he'd figured out why their oldest brother might have left?

But just as Collin needed to focus on Dad staying well, he needed to focus on making sure that Bailey Ann did, too. "I'm not here about Cash," he assured Becca. "I need your help with something else."

Becca's blue eyes narrowed as she studied his face with apparent skepticism. "My help?"

"I need a house," he said.

She groaned again.

"What's wrong now?" he asked.

She stepped back and waved him into her office. An older woman was standing up behind her desk, peering at them.

"Which one is this?"

"This is Collin. Dr. Cassidy," Becca said. "Collin, this is my mom. Phyllis Calder."

Phyllis smiled at him. "You look just like your brother."

"It's the hat," Collin said, pointing to the brim.

Mother and daughter both chuckled.

"Yeah, it's the hat," Becca teased. And it felt like they were kids again for a moment. But Cash had been gone seventeen years now.

And Collin wasn't certain they'd ever been kids, not growing up as they had with that constant worry and helplessness. Maybe that was why Cash had left and never looked back.

Collin couldn't really blame him. Even though he wanted to.

"So you want to buy a house?" Becca asked.

He nodded. "I need to. It has to be at least a three bedroom. And I need it within two weeks."

She chuckled again. "You must be joking."

That urgency he'd been feeling turned to panic now. Just as he'd already begun to suspect, he didn't have enough time to do what he needed to…to be able to keep Bailey Ann.

He was going to lose her, too.

ONCE HER CLIENT LEFT, Genevieve opened her desk drawer and pulled out the family portrait. The young couple, obviously so in love as they beamed at each other, the three little boys gathered around them on the bales of hay in a barn. This wasn't her family.

Genevieve had thrown it away just like her parents had because she hadn't agreed with her younger sister's decision to get married right out of high school to start this beautiful family that she'd had. Embarrassed that her daughter was marrying so young and worried that the town would think it was because she had to, Mother had insisted on moving away from Willow Creek.

Maybe she'd been worried that the town would compare Jenny to her and remember how she'd had a child while she was in high school: Genevieve. She'd always wondered if that was why her mom and stepdad had named her sister Jennifer, like she was supposed to be a do-over of Genevieve, whose name was French for Jennifer. Like she was the legitimate daughter and Genevieve had been the mistake. But then that had given Jenny no room to make any mistakes, and that was what Mother and Jenny's father had been convinced she'd been doing. So they had sold everything and moved away and had never returned.

It had been even easier for Genevieve to cut off contact. She'd been in law school on the other side of the country, and as busy as she'd been, she'd barely talked to her sister. Jenny had been six years younger than Genevieve, so they'd never been in the same school at the same time or had the same friends. And feeling like she'd been the mistake and Jenny had been the wanted child, Genevieve had resented her a bit through no fault of Jenny's. And she'd avoided her so much, burying herself in her books, that they hadn't had much of a relationship growing up.

She touched her sister's beautiful face. She'd still looked like a teenager in that picture despite eleven years having passed since her high school graduation. She'd also looked so happy, happier than Genevieve had ever been.

So who had made the mistakes?

Not Jenny. She hadn't needed to get married; her oldest had been born four years after her high school graduation. She'd wanted to get married because she truly loved Dale

Haven. She'd made a beautiful family. Something Genevieve hadn't been able to do.

She put the picture back in the drawer and pushed it closed. She couldn't look at her sister without tears burning her eyes.

She hadn't even known Jenny had died until a few months after her tragic accident. Because of that, Genevieve hadn't been there for the funeral or for her nephews.

She'd failed them.

She couldn't fail any other children. So, like she'd told Dr. Cassidy, she needed to talk to his patient first. She needed to know what Bailey Ann wanted before she did anything else.

Drawing in a deep breath, she picked up her briefcase from the floor and headed toward the door. Hilda had already turned off the lights in the reception area, but the late afternoon sunshine streaked through the blinds.

At her former law practice in DC, people had often worked around the clock. Here in Willow Creek, they usually knocked off before five.

Genevieve usually stayed as late as she could because she didn't want to go home to the big empty house she'd bought when she'd first moved back to Willow Creek.

But this afternoon she didn't have to go home just yet; she was going to the hospital to meet Bailey Ann. She hoped Dr. Cassidy was the right choice for the little girl, that despite being unwanted by her parents and foster families, she was wanted now and forever, not just short term. Genevieve understood all too well how Bailey Ann might feel, how it felt to be unwanted. Her own mother had left Genevieve to be raised by her grandparents while she'd gone to college. Then her grandparents had simply given her back once Mother had her degree. The people who raised her hadn't even tried to fight to keep her.

And Mother had never let her forget that Genevieve was a mistake. They'd used her very existence as a case study for why her younger sister Jenny shouldn't marry out of high school.

Genevieve counted down the days until she could graduate from high school and leave Willow Creek far behind. She'd doubled up on credits, graduated early and left for college. And she'd never intended to return...

But here she was. Now she stepped outside the law office onto Main Street. In some ways, it looked like nothing had changed. But the town was bigger than she remembered. There were more shops and restaurants. New buildings had been erected and old ones had been renovated.

It was not just bigger but nicer than she remembered.

And warmer.

She lifted her face to the late afternoon sunshine, but a shadow fell across her instead. Collin Cassidy towered over her, his black hat blocking out the sun. He was bigger than she'd remembered, too, even though she'd just met him an hour ago. The man was so tall and broad. Was he nice?

He'd seemed so, but Genevieve knew to be cautious. Even nice guys could be incredibly selfish.

"Were you waiting for me?" she asked with some concern. She'd told him she would talk to Bailey Ann after work, but she knew how to find her own way to the hospital.

"I'm not stalking you," he assured her. He turned slightly and pointed across the street. "I was just over there, at the real estate office, talking to Becca Calder." His broad shoulders sagged now, and his head was bowed, as if she'd given him bad news.

She could imagine what that was. "Still low inventory?" she asked.

He nodded. "Yes."

"When I bought my house, that was the case then, too." She and Becca had looked all around Willow Creek for something when the big house near town had miraculously popped up.

"She said there's very little on the market," he said. "And even if something came up, I wouldn't be able to close on the property with a mortgage for more than a month...if I even qualify for financing because of all of my student loans."

He was definitely feeling defeated. Genevieve understood that feeling all too well.

"I'm going to meet Bailey Ann now before visiting hours are over," she said. "Do you want to go to the hospital with me?"

A smile curved his lips, but sadness lingered in his dark eyes with that defeat. "I always want to see her."

"Introduce us," she said. "And then leave me alone to talk to her."

"I don't know if that's a good idea anymore," he said.

"You don't want her?" she asked.

He tensed. "Of course I do. But if it's not possible, I don't want to get her hopes up."

"I'll be careful when I talk to her," she promised, wishing that she'd been careful when she'd first talked to Sue about her nephews.

Wishing that she'd done so many other things differently...like being able to face the Havens. Every time she'd gone to pick up the phone or drive out to the ranch, she'd been filled with dread. What if they hated her for how she'd failed Jenny? She couldn't blame them. How could a person turn their back on their own sister? To not be there when she was married or when she'd given birth to any of her three precious children? To not be there when Jenny died, when she was buried, when those three boys needed her the most?

And what had she been doing? Trying to make the perfect life for a man who'd left as soon as it was clear she couldn't give him his own children. Those tiny lives she hadn't been able to bring into the world.

She closed her eyes for a moment, struggling to contain her emotions. When she opened them, Collin was staring at her with deep emotions of his own in his dark eyes.

"I want to warn you that Bailey Ann is

in hospital in the first place because of her last foster family," Collin said. "They didn't give her the antirejection medication in the proper doses. And she'd started..." His voice cracked now as emotion overwhelmed him. "She was very sick. And she's still getting her strength back."

She blinked against tears, both for her own difficult past and for the brave little girl this doctor was fighting for. "I'll keep that in mind and won't tire her out. Thank you for trusting me."

They shared a smile, and the tense moment passed. She looked around to clear her thoughts. Several workers were on ladders, hanging things from the streetlights along Main Street. She narrowed her eyes and stared in disbelief. "Are they hanging hearts?"

He tipped back his head and looked up as well. "Yes..."

And around the base of each lamppost, red, white and pink flowers had been planted.

"I don't understand," she murmured. "Are they decorating for St. Valentine's Day?"

Before he could reply, a banner swung across the street, tethered to a light post on either side. It read: *Happy Valentine's Day!*

Collin chuckled, and the deep rumble of it raised goose bumps on Genevieve's skin despite the warmth of the summer day. "Okay…"

"Isn't it August?" Genevieve asked.

He chuckled again. "I'm new to Willow Creek," he said. "I don't know what all their traditions are, but apparently Valentine's Day in August might be one of them…"

He didn't sound any more convinced of that than she was, though.

"I wonder if Sadie has anything to do with this…" he muttered.

Sadie…

Why had Sadie referred him to her?

Jenny, in her letters, had always raved about her. She'd idolized and adored Sadie Haven. But Genevieve hadn't been gone so long that she'd forgotten about the reputation Sadie Haven had earned for being a formidable adversary. At least to the former mayor, Old Man Lemmon.

Did she know what Sue had done on Genevieve's behalf? Was Sadie her adversary now, too?

"GETTING OLD IS not for the faint of heart," Lem Lemmon mumbled to himself as he stared out his office window at the town square across the street. Balloon hearts and other heart-shaped decorations hung from every light pole, and flowers in pink, red and white were planted in every bed of the little park area.

"Oh, yeah?" Ben asked.

Lem turned around to find the mayor standing in his doorway. "I don't recommend it."

"You trying to tell me something?" Ben asked, arching a dark brow. "I'm just over thirty now, you know."

Lem chuckled. "And we both know I was talking about me."

"You're not old, Lem."

"I've been old a long time," he said. People had called him Old Man Lemmon for at least twenty years. Sadie had probably started it, as Sadie started most things. "I thought I was still pretty sharp, though, until I looked out my window and saw everything decorated for Valentine's Day. Isn't it August? Or have I missed the last six months passing?"

A pang of panic and regret struck him as he thought about his late wife and how much time she'd lost and forgotten. She'd forgotten everything in the end. Everything but him.

What would she think of him and Sadie?

Somehow, he thought she and Sadie's late husband, Big Jake, would be laughing.

They would have gotten quite a kick out of him falling for Sadie, and probably an even bigger kick out of Sadie falling for him. No. Getting old was tough work, but if you got lucky, you might get to take another shot at love.

Especially when you knew how precious and short life was.

"You missed Sadie," Ben said. "She stopped in earlier." He pointed toward the window and all those decorations. "That was her."

Lem chuckled. "Of course it was. And you went along with it."

Of all Sadie's grandchildren, Ben was the most like her, and the most able to handle her. For example, knowing it was best to mobilize the town gardening crew to put up Valentine's decorations at Sadie's request for them.

Ben nodded. "I figured maybe I can get Emily to the altar a little earlier. And maybe Sadie suggested this to get you to the altar a little earlier."

Lem grinned. "We're not going to waste any time. Not at our ages…" And not after Sadie's recent health scare. But Sadie wanted to make sure her great grandsons were all right. That there was no threat against them anymore, like that call to CPS and to her lawyer.

He glanced back out the window at those decorations. At all the hearts and flowers...

"She's up to something..." he murmured. She hadn't brought him in on this yet, unlike her other schemes where she'd enlisted him.

"When isn't she up to something?" Ben asked.

"True."

But what was she up to this time? And who did she really intend to send a message to with this whole Valentine's in August thing?

CHAPTER FOUR

As COLLIN AND Genevieve rode the elevator up to Bailey Ann's floor, his stomach was in knots. Not over Genevieve meeting the little girl. Bailey Ann loved company, and Genevieve had promised that she would be careful not to raise the child's hopes. The knots in his stomach were because he had raised his own hopes for a moment, thinking that Sadie could actually work her magic. That somehow he would be able to foster and then adopt the child he loved like his own.

But there wasn't enough time. She would definitely wind up going to that foster home in Sheridan, and he wasn't certain if that family would be equipped to handle her care with such little training. And if her body rejected her heart again, she might not make it.

"You're so quiet," Genevieve remarked. "Have you changed your mind?"

"No," he quickly replied. "Not at all. It's just… I don't see how…"

"We'll talk about that after I talk to Bailey Ann," she said.

She was going to wait until then to tell him he was beyond hope?

Collin had had to give out that news to patients before. That they'd done all they could and there was nothing more…

He empathized with them because he'd received that news himself. He'd lost his mother and, for so long, thought he was going to lose his dad, too.

But his dad had hung in there all these years, battling all the immune issues he'd had with lupus. Suffering through kidney failures and transplants and now his heart…

Collin barely noticed when the elevator dinged and the doors swished open. Genevieve touched his arm, and he felt a little jolt of awareness even through the material of his shirt.

"Are you okay?" she asked.

No. But not wanting to get into everything with her, he just nodded. "I appreciate you coming here to meet her," he said. "It's hard for her—not having any family to come see her—so she loves getting visitors."

Genevieve's long lashes fluttered for a moment as she blinked. "That's sad," she said, her voice cracking slightly.

"She's not sad, though," Collin said. "She's such a sweet, happy little girl. Here, you'll see." He reached out then, pressing his fingers against the small of her back to guide her in the direction of Bailey Ann's room. And again, even through her jacket, he felt that little jolt—a shock of awareness.

He couldn't remember the last time he'd reacted that way to anyone. He'd been so focused on becoming a doctor that the dates he'd gone on had never led anywhere serious. Everybody had wanted more time and attention from him than he'd had to give.

But things were different now. He was no longer a resident or a fellow. He was established. He would have more time for Bailey Ann. But could he convince her social worker and a family court judge of that?

Could Genevieve, if she agreed to help him?

His pace slowed as he neared the open door to Bailey Ann's room. And he lowered his head and his voice to whisper to her, "Just a short visit for now, okay? We don't want to tire her. Let me know if you need to speak with her again later."

"I understand," she said. "I won't stay too long." Genevieve nodded decisively, and he was touched at how seriously she was taking Bailey Ann's health before even meeting the little girl.

He hated leaving her alone in her room, hated leaving her at all. How would she handle leaving him? Would her foster parents tell her silly stories to help her go to sleep or hold her hand when she was scared? Or would she be alone again? He couldn't figure out a way for even the legendary Sadie Haven to stop her assignment to that foster home in Sheridan.

How was Genevieve Porter going to stop it? Would she even want to?

He drew in a deep breath as they neared the open door to Bailey Ann's room. Through it, he could hear the deep rumble of a voice that sounded eerily like his own. Colton...

He touched the brim of his hat. No doubt his twin had returned for that. Or more likely just to see Bailey Ann. Colton and his fiancée, Livvy, had started spending a lot of time with the little girl, too, at Collin's request. He hoped that his family would help her feel less alone.

Genevieve glanced up at him, her brow furrowed beneath the wispy strands of her pale blond hair. "She sounds an awful lot like you…"

"That's not—"

A high-pitched giggle cut him off. Then Bailey Ann's voice saying, "You're silly, Uncle Colton!" She sounded nothing like him, more like Tinker Bell.

"I thought she didn't have family," Genevieve said.

"She doesn't," Collin said. "That's my brother."

"Dr. Cass!" Bailey Ann called out; she must have heard him, too.

Warmth spread over him as it always did when she called for him with so much excitement and affection. He grinned. "How do you know it's me?" he asked as he gestured Genevieve into the room ahead of him. "I could be Uncle Colton." He pointed at the hat.

"So you're the one who took it," Colton said as he grabbed for it.

"Told you!" Bailey Ann said. "I didn't lose it!" But she looked away from him and his twin to focus on Genevieve. "Wow! You're so pretty! You look like one of my Barbie dolls."

With her pale blond hair and bright blue eyes, Genevieve really did resemble the doll that to some had represented unattainable perfection.

There was definitely something unattainable about the lawyer. Any time she'd seemed about to reveal something personal to Collin, she'd stopped herself and pulled back. Maybe she'd just been trying to remain professional, or maybe she was private. He'd been accused of being the same, though, so he wasn't about to judge her for it.

Except for Bailey Ann, Collin always tried to remain professional and a bit detached so that he could focus on his patients' care and not his own feelings. But it was impossible to stay detached from Bailey Ann.

Genevieve smiled at the little girl and said, "You are very sweet, just like Dr. Cassidy told me you are."

"Bailey Ann, this is my…" He didn't want to say lawyer, but he wasn't even sure if she would agree to represent him. To help him. "My friend, Genevieve Porter."

"I'm Dr. Cass's friend, too," Bailey Ann confided. She smiled warmly at Genevieve, then jumped up on her bed and threw her arms around Collin's neck. And as she did, Colton pulled off his hat.

"I'll take this back." He plopped it on his own head and turned toward Genevieve and held out his hand. "I'm Dr. Cass's far better-looking twin, Colton."

Genevieve shook his hand and smiled brightly up at Collin's brother. And for some reason Collin felt a little jab of something, but it couldn't be jealousy. Despite whatever Sadie's motives in referring him to Genevieve were, he wasn't interested in the lawyer for anything other than her legal help so he could foster and adopt Bailey Ann.

And he had to make certain that she was willing to help. Bailey Ann pulled away from him and reached for Genevieve. Instead of shaking her hand, she hugged her, too, wrapping her short arms around Genevieve's neck. And as she had with Sadie, she touched Genevieve's hair. "It's so pretty and soft…"

"I love your curls," Genevieve said.

"Did you come to visit me?" Bailey Ann asked as if awed. Maybe she thought Genevieve really was a doll come to life.

"Yes, I did," Genevieve said. "Is that okay with you?"

"Yes!" Bailey Ann exclaimed. "Do you want to play a game? I have Memory. And old maid. And checkers."

"And she cheats," Collin warned her. "So be careful with this one."

Genevieve gave him a slight nod.

She must have understood what he was really telling her: to be careful with Bailey Ann when talking with her as she tried to ascertain the little girl's wishes for her own future so she could decide whether or not she would help him. No. Help her. That was all she'd agreed to do, once she'd determined what was best for Bailey Ann. He doubted she could determine that with one conversation, though.

Time to leave them to it—which meant it was also a good time to grill Colton about what was going on.

"You've got your hat back, brother. Say good-bye to Bailey Ann, and I'll walk you to the elevator."

Colton leaned down and kissed the little girl's cheek. "You be nice to Dr. Cass's friend. No betting on Memory and taking all her money." Bailey Ann had spent enough time with Collin's twin to know he was teasing and she giggled. Then Colton smiled at Genevieve. "Nice to meet you, Ms. Porter."

"Genevieve," she said. "And nice to meet you, too."

Colton's grin widened, as if he was thinking about flirting with her. But because he was madly in love with Livvy Lemmon, he would only do that to irritate Collin. Like Collin had probably consciously irritated him a few times when he'd talked to Livvy before Colton had known which of them the beautiful ER doctor had fallen for...

Collin had never had any doubt it would be Colton. Colton was the fun, lighthearted twin. Collin had always been too focused and intense for people to feel comfortable around.

At the moment, he needed to find his focus, though. He tugged on Colton's sleeve, pulling him into the hall with him. "Let's get out of their way so they can get to know each other," he said.

Once they were out in the hall, Colton started firing the questions at him before he could light into his twin himself. "How did you make a friend? Especially one who looks like that? And why would you be introducing her to Bailey Ann already? What's going on?"

Collin glanced through the open doorway where Bailey Ann was setting up her checkerboard on her tray. He tugged Colton farther from the doorway and whispered, "She's a lawyer. Sadie recommended her."

"Oh, she did, did she?" Colton chuckled. "What?"

"Well, look at her. No, I don't have to tell you to do that. You haven't really taken your eyes off her." He chuckled again.

Collin felt himself flush. "Yeah, yeah, Sadie probably is scheming, but it's not going to work on me. My only interest in Genevieve Porter is her legal help so I can foster and adopt Bailey Ann."

Colton nodded, but there was still some skepticism in his dark eyes as he stared at Collin.

So Collin turned the tables on his brother. "So that's what's going on with me. What's going on with you?"

"What do you mean?"

"You wanted to tell me something earlier today," Collin reminded him. "I know it's about Cash."

Colton's dark eyes widened, and the color left his face. "How on earth—"

"I saw Becca today. She thought I was you."

"Because you were wearing my hat," Colton said in realization.

"Yep. What's your sudden interest in finding Cash?" he asked.

Colton shrugged. "You don't think he deserves to know what we just learned?"

"Are you sure he doesn't already know?" Collin asked.

Colton sucked in a breath. "You figure that's the reason he left?" He released the breath in a sigh. "I did consider that myself…"

"I don't know what to think," Collin admitted. About his family or about Genevieve Porter. "But I can't focus on anything but Bailey Ann right now. So I'll leave finding Cash up to you." And he would focus on trying to keep the little girl safe.

GENEVIEVE WAS GETTING her butt kicked by a seven-year-old. And she wasn't even letting Bailey Ann win. She was distracted though and kept glancing into the hall where the two men appeared to be having a serious discussion.

About Bailey Ann?

About her?

Collin's twin had certainly been curious about her, about their *friendship*. Obviously he knew they weren't friends.

"They look a lot alike, don't they?" Bailey Ann remarked as she slid her checker into a spot on Genevieve's side of the board.

"The checkers?" Genevieve asked, but she smiled to show she was joking. She knew the little girl had noticed her interest in the Cassidy twins.

Bailey Ann giggled. "No. Those mostly look like mine. Red."

"Yes," Genevieve agreed. "You're really good at checkers."

"Dr. Cass taught me," Bailey Ann said. "He's really smart. And funny."

"Funny?" Genevieve asked. She hadn't seen any hint of a sense of humor in him, but then he was incredibly worried about this young patient of his.

Bailey Ann giggled. "He tells really funny jokes. But the nurses and Uncle Colton call them silly dad jokes." Her smile turned wistful. "I wish he was my dad."

A little flutter moved through Genevieve's heart. "You would like for him to be your dad?"

Bailey Ann vigorously nodded, and her chocolate brown curls bounced around her shoulders. "Yes, he's like my dad because he's been around the most in my life. And he takes care of me. He reads books to me and tells me stories until I go to sleep. And he makes me feel better when I'm sick or scared."

That flutter was a pang of pain now. A doctor being the most constant person in the child's life was incredibly sad. But Bailey Ann didn't seem sad, just as Collin had told her.

Bailey Ann leaned closer and whispered, "That's why I call Colton 'uncle,' because he would be if Dr. Cass was my dad. I would have a big family if Dr. Cass was my dad because he has a grandma and brothers and cousins. I never had any family like that."

It was almost as if the little girl had figured out why Genevieve was there. Or maybe this was what she really wanted, and she told everybody. Or maybe she felt this instant connection with Genevieve that she felt with her.

"You really like Dr. Cass," Genevieve said.

"I love him," Bailey Ann said. "He takes the best care of me." Tears glistened in her big brown eyes. "I wouldn't be alive if it wasn't for him."

And now he wasn't just going to make her healthy but care for her as a father would his child. That was what she'd wanted to do for her nephews if their situation had been different.

"Is that why you love him?" Genevieve asked. "Because he takes care of you?" She might love all the nurses and surgeons, too.

But the little girl shook her head. "I love him because he's really nice and he spends time with me, playing games and watching TV, and when I'm scared he tells me this funny story about a bunch of little boys growing up on a ranch and doing silly things like playing tricks on each other with toads and grasshoppers. He asks me questions, and he really listens to what I tell him. Not like Mrs. Finch."

"And who is Mrs. Finch?" Genevieve asked.

Bailey Ann wrinkled her nose with distaste. "She's my social worker. She doesn't listen to what I want. She just puts me anywhere she thinks they'll take me." The little girl shuddered. "But those families are always so busy. And I'm just more work for them."

Parenting was a full-time, around-the-clock responsibility, but a child should never feel like a burden. And obviously this child felt like one.

Obviously Collin Cassidy didn't make Bailey Ann feel like a burden to him. Or had he coached her on what to tell Genevieve or the social worker?

Genevieve had learned at a young age, like Bailey Ann, to tell people what they wanted to hear. She'd wanted approval and acceptance but most of all, love, and so she'd tried to be what her mother had wanted, what her grandparents had, and her husband...

But she must have never said or done the right things because none of them had ever really loved her like Bailey Ann loved Dr. Cassidy.

And like he loved her.

He stood alone now in the doorway to Bailey Ann's room, his gaze on them, his body language tense. He was worried about losing the little girl. And not just to that foster family.

He was worried about losing her for another reason. For the big scar that peeked out of the top of her nightgown. The scar from her heart transplant.

DESPITE HAVING THE day off from the fire department, Colton had spent most of it around the hospital like he often did when he was working as a paramedic. Even after he took the elevator back down to the lobby level, he didn't leave. Instead he waited to see his fiancée, who was working in the ER.

Or waiting for a patient to come in as she hung out at the check-in desk. He grinned when he saw her, and warmth flooded his chest. He loved her so much.

"Hey, Doctor," he said. "I wonder if you could help me…"

"Are you feeling sick?" she asked with a smile because she knew he was flirting, as he always did with her.

"Lovesick," he teased.

A nearby door opened, and Nurse Sue poked her head through. He waved, which seemed to startle her. She quickly backed out.

His eyes narrowed. His family suspected that Sue had been the one who'd reported the Havens to CPS for an accident that had been Colton's fault. He should have been watching his young cousin better when five-year-old Ian had been in the barn at Ranch Haven with him. The little boy had let a wild horse out of its stall and it had knocked him over and momentarily knocked him out in the process.

It truly had been an accident. The boys were well cared for by Colton's family. But the unnecessary CPS investigation had upset the security the three little orphans had with their Uncle Baker and his bride-to-be, Taye, at the Haven ranch. They didn't know who it was, or what agenda the mystery person might have.

The boys were safe and loved. That was what mattered. Grandma had insisted that she would handle the matter of who had made that complaint to CPS, and he had no doubt she'd take care of things. Maybe he should tell her about Cash, too. Though he'd vowed to tell Collin first. But Collin was so worried about Bailey Ann that he really hadn't wanted to think about Cash.

And Colton couldn't stop thinking about him. He expelled a heavy sigh.

Livvy came around the desk to hug him. "Did you tell him?" she asked with concern.

He'd already shared with her what he'd found in the fire at his family ranch house. A family heirloom—his grandfather's silver lighter with the initials *CC* for Cornelius Cassidy etched in it. He'd last seen that lighter with Cash when he'd run away all those years ago.

But the lighter had turned up so Cash must have as well. To burn down the family ranch that his dad had finally agreed to sell?

"He knows I'm looking for Cash, but he didn't want any details. His total focus is on Bailey Ann right now," Colton said. "Her social worker found a temporary foster home for her."

Livvy waited, knowing him so well that she had to know there was more. And it wasn't the good news it should have been.

"In Sheridan," he finished.

And she gasped. "Collin must be so upset. And Bailey Ann…"

"She doesn't know yet," Colton said. And he hoped she never had to learn about it. "Grandma recommended a lawyer for Collin to contact, and she's upstairs with him and Bailey Ann right now."

"I hope she can help," Livvy said.

Colton hoped so, too.

CHAPTER FIVE

"DID YOU PREP HER?"

The question startled Collin, making him jolt like the elevator did as it started descending to the lobby. Prepping Bailey Ann in the past had entailed getting her ready for a surgery or a procedure, something no child should ever have to endure let alone all on her own.

"What do you mean?" he asked Genevieve.

"She told me all the right things, like a witness whose lawyer had prepared them to take the stand," she replied.

"I thought you were an estate lawyer," he said.

"I am now…"

She talked like she was an old hand at trial proceedings, so maybe she'd been a criminal lawyer or some other type.

He was curious but figured it probably wasn't worth it to ask. She wasn't as apt to answer questions as to ask them. Probably something else that came from being a lawyer.

"I had no idea you were going to want to talk to Bailey Ann today," he reminded her. "So I wouldn't have had the chance to prep her. I didn't even want to talk to her about this…if I can't actually foster or adopt her."

And he hadn't. But he wasn't sure what Bailey Ann and Genevieve had talked about alone, though when he'd rejoined them, she hadn't seemed upset.

Or overly hopeful.

She'd just seemed very happy and not just because she'd beaten the lawyer at checkers. She also seemed to like Genevieve.

"She wants you to adopt her," Genevieve said.

And he sucked in a breath. "You weren't supposed to put that thought in her head—"

"I didn't," she interjected. "It's already there. That's why she calls your brother uncle. She wants you to be her dad."

A warm rush of relief and love flooded Collin. He'd hoped that was what she wanted, too, but he hadn't been certain. And he hadn't wanted to bring it up to her.

"I didn't know for sure," he said. "I didn't know if she would be happier with a family. A couple and other kids…"

"She wants you and your family," Genevieve said. "But she shared that Mrs. Finch doesn't listen to her."

"She must not," Collin agreed. "Because Mrs. Finch has yet to say a word about any of this to me." And in one short conversation, Genevieve had learned how the little girl felt about him.

Collin knew she loved him, like he loved her, but he hadn't realized that she wanted to be his daughter as badly as he wanted to be her dad. His legs felt a little weak, and he took a moment to lean back against the elevator's mirrored wall. Then the doors began to slide open, but Collin didn't move.

"Are you all right?" Genevieve asked, and she touched his arm.

And he felt that little shiver of awareness again. He nodded. "Yes…" Then he shook his head. "No…"

Her lips curved into a smile. "This again. So which is it, Dr. Cassidy?"

"I'm happy that she feels that way, but it's going to be even harder now if I can't adopt her or even at least foster her," he admitted. It was going to rip out his heart. And now he knew that it would upset her, too.

The doors dinged again and began to close, but Genevieve reached out and pushed her arm between them. "Are you going back up to see her?" she asked.

"Not yet." Although he usually stayed with her until she fell asleep, he needed some time before going back to her room. He might give away how he felt, how much he wanted to adopt her. "I want to talk to you first. Do you have time?" At her nod, he glanced through those doors, over to where his brother leaned over the check-in desk. "But not here..."

They'd driven here in separate cars, so she suggested, "Come on, you can follow me home. We can talk in privacy."

If she could help him adopt Bailey Ann, he would follow her anywhere.

If this was DC, Genevieve wouldn't have told a man she'd just met to follow her home. But this was Willow Creek, and the man was a cardiologist who desperately wanted to adopt an abandoned child.

He'd gotten to her just like Bailey Ann had. They belonged together. She knew for certain now that it was what they both wanted. The timeline was going to be tricky, though.

While she could file all the necessary paperwork in this county and in Sheridan and hope that the case would move quickly through one of the family courts, she doubted she could stop that temporary foster home placement from going through. And if this foster family in Sheridan didn't take care of Bailey Ann any better than her last one had and her body started rejecting her heart again…

The little girl might not get her wish for the family she wanted. For Collin to officially become her father…

She might never get another wish.

Genevieve released a shaky sigh at the unfathomable thought. She had to do something. Then maybe she would stop feeling so helpless because of all the things she hadn't been able to do.

All the people she'd let down.

Her sister.

Her ex-husband.

Herself.

She had to help Bailey Ann and Collin Cassidy. While she'd been playing checkers with the little girl, she'd been strategizing about how to get the cardiologist set up as a foster parent. That was the first step toward keeping Bailey Ann here in Willow Creek with him. And then they could get the adoption process started...

That was why she wanted to talk to him alone. So there would be no other witnesses, like Hilda or his twin, to overhear the strategy she was about to suggest.

Unfortunately her drive home from the hospital was so short that she didn't have much time to come up with an idea of how to make the suggestion to Dr. Cassidy. A mile from Willow Creek Memorial, she turned onto a side street with big lots and mature trees and sprawling homes. As she slowed to turn into the driveway, one of the three garage doors began to open at the approach of her SUV.

The house was set up with all the smart technology features Genevieve had gotten used to during her marriage. Bradford had always had to have the latest and greatest.

The car the cardiologist drove, an older model economy vehicle, turned into the driveway behind her. She stepped out of her SUV, closed the garage door and walked through the interior door to the house.

Wait until she told him the plan she'd come up with...

Her face heated just thinking about it.

She headed to the side door to let him in, remembering Bailey Ann and how she didn't think her social worker listened to her. Genevieve wanted the little girl to know that *she* had listened to her, that she understood exactly what she wanted. She opened the side door of the mudroom and stepped out onto the driveway.

He was leaning against his car, waiting for her. His vehicle was almost too small for a man his size, while she drove that tank of a sport utility vehicle. But she'd thought she might need those three rows of seats if she had needed to take custody of her nephews.

That assumption had been a mistake, like so many others she'd made. She hoped this wasn't another. But if it kept a little girl safe and made her happy...

"I hope you're not worried that I lured you here to murder you," she said.

"I wasn't thinking that..." he said. "Until now...because of course, if you lured me here to murder me, you wouldn't want me to think that."

She smiled. "Maybe Bailey Ann is right. Maybe you are funny."

His mouth curved into a slight grin. "She's the only one who thinks that."

"She loves your dad jokes," she assured him. Because she wanted him to be her dad...

Because she loved him. And he loved her.

Genevieve couldn't imagine how it felt to be loved like that. Wistful at the thought, she emitted a shaky sigh.

"Are you sure you're comfortable with me being here?" he asked.

"Doctors have to promise to do no harm," she said. "So I'm not worried about you murdering me."

"I am no threat," he promised.

She wasn't so sure about that. If she suggested her strategy...

She would just have to remind herself the reason for it: Bailey Ann. She was doing this for the little girl, not for her handsome doctor.

"What about your husband?" Collin asked, with an arched brow, as if he was questioning if there was a husband. "Won't he mind you bringing your work home with you?"

"Not anymore," she said. "We're divorced."

"I'm sorry," he replied.

"I'm not," she said. Life was a whole lot easier, and her heart was a lot safer now that she didn't have to worry about disappointing someone she loved. She'd learned from the mistakes she'd made with Bradford, and she wasn't going to risk her heart again.

"Okay…" He glanced around at the house and the yard. "This is a kind of big place for just you. You have kids?"

A lump suddenly filled her throat, the one that always choked her whenever she thought of that, of the kids she hadn't been able to have. Even though she'd never had them, she missed them, or at least the idea of them, more than she missed Bradford. Swallowing hard, she could only shake her head. Then she turned back toward her house and held open the door for him.

He followed her inside the mudroom. He glanced around at the benches and lockers, washer and dryer, laundry sink and dog shower. "Should I take off my shoes?" he asked.

"Don't worry about it." She led the way into the kitchen, which had a large center island and granite countertops and windows that looked out onto the big backyard. A Crock-Pot sat next to the stove, the scent of chicken and garlic and lemon pepper waft-

ing out of it. She'd put it on this morning and
had nearly forgotten about it. "Are you hun-
gry?" she asked.

"I wasn't until I smelled that," he said.
"Smells a lot better than the hospital's cafeteria food."

"I'm not sure it'll taste any better," she said.
"I've been trying out new recipes." She'd actually been trying to figure out what she liked
since she'd gotten so used to making Bradford's favorites instead.

"I'm happy to be your guinea pig for this
recipe," he said. "But I don't think that's why
you had me follow you home."

"I really hate having too many leftovers,"
she said with a smile. She also wanted to stall
before she shared her strategy with him. So
she took her time making a salad and setting
the table and dishing out the food.

He didn't just sit there and watch like
Bradford used to, while sipping a drink and
talking about his day. Despite her protests
because of his still-healing hands, Collin insisted on helping her, taking care of washing,
peeling and slicing the vegetables. Maybe he
was stalling, too, with concern that she would

tell him it wasn't possible for him to foster and adopt.

Clearly, from what he'd already said to her, he knew that he wasn't ready. That he didn't have the house or the stability that was necessary.

But she did.

SADIE STILL COULDN'T believe her eyes when she saw her oldest son. She always felt as if she was just dreaming, as she often had over all those years he'd been missing, of seeing him again. Of him being alive…

But he was alive, and he was doing well. Better than she'd thought possible.

"When are you going to get used to seeing me?" Jessup asked.

And she realized she'd been staring at him silently since he'd opened the door. "I don't know if I will," she admitted. "But I don't care, just as long as I can see you."

"Are you here to try once again to get me to move out to the ranch?" he asked.

"No, Collin made it clear that you need to be close to the hospital. That you should have been before…"

But he'd stayed out at the Cassidy Ranch

until the house had burned down. He hadn't wanted to sell it, but with all his medical bills, he'd had no choice. She'd wanted to help him, had tried, but he'd refused.

Just like he'd refused to move back home.

"I should have been," he agreed. "Can't imagine where I got this stubbornness from."

She chuckled. "You come by that on both sides," she said. His father, Big Jake, had been stubborn, too, but not as bad as she'd been. As she sometimes still was.

"You don't often leave the ranch yourself," he said. "What are you doing in town?"

"I was at the hospital earlier—"

"Mom!" he exclaimed, and he reached out to grasp her shoulders. "Are you all right? I know you had that issue with your heart—"

"I was there to see Collin," she said. "And to meet that little patient of his that he's head over heels about…"

"Bailey Ann," Jessup said. "I need to meet her, too."

"She's a sweetheart," Sadie said, her voice a little gruff with the emotions rushing over her. A child shouldn't have to go through all the medical issues she had. And if that wasn't bad enough, she had no family. She'd had to do it all alone but for Collin. "Will be nice to have a little girl in the family with all the boys we already have."

Jessup's brow furrowed. "What do you mean?"

"Collin wants to adopt her."

"He what? I knew he was attached to her, but…how's he going to do that? He's so busy. And…" He trailed off as he focused on her and nodded. "*You*…you're going to help my son."

"Not me…" she murmured. But she hoped that the person to whom she'd referred him to would help him. And maybe that would help Genevieve Porter, too.

CHAPTER SIX

COLLIN WAS SURPRISED that he'd managed to eat, let alone enjoy it as much as he had. He was so on edge about the whole situation with Bailey Ann.

The sun was beginning to set outside now, leaving him one less day already in the two weeks he had left with her. He should have stayed at the hospital with her.

But if anyone could help him, he had a feeling that Genevieve Porter could. She was smart and empathetic, and clearly already cared about Bailey Ann.

While he didn't mind sharing a meal with her, he was worried that she was putting off talking about the situation. It probably meant that she couldn't help and she didn't want to disappoint him and now Bailey Ann, too. That the little girl wanted him to be her dad affected him so much, making him love her even more than he already had. He had to press his hand over his chest as if to hold it all inside him.

"Heartburn?" Genevieve asked. "I think I have some antacid."

"No, the food was delicious," he said. And meant it. "I usually eat at the hospital, so this was a real treat. I just… It's killing me not knowing if this is possible…" Something else hadn't even occurred to him until now. "And here you are feeding me and I haven't even given you a retainer yet. How much do I owe you for your time today?"

She waved a hand at him from over the sink where she'd been washing out the crock part of her Crock-Pot. He'd wanted to help her, but she'd only let him load the dishwasher. "Consider this a free consultation," she said.

His heart, that had been so full just moments ago, felt as if it deflated, and he sucked in a breath. "So it's not possible, is it?" he asked. "There's no way I can get approved as a foster home let alone adopt Bailey Ann before the two weeks is up…"

He'd known it was a long shot, but when Sadie had recommended Genevieve, he'd thought that long shot might pay off.

"No," she said. "There's no way *you* can

get approved in that amount of time. It took me more than a month here."

"You're a licensed foster home?" he asked. That might explain why she had such a big place for herself. And the SUV was big, too, with three rows of seats.

She'd said she had no husband anymore and no kids, but maybe she just meant she had no kids at the moment.

"Yes," she said, and that strange expression came over her beautiful face again, as if she was withdrawing behind some wall. "I was registered as a foster parent before I moved here. When I bought this house, I did it with kids in mind."

"I know Mrs. Finch is going to make sure that the foster placement she found for her has medical training but…" The thought of her being out of his care, out of his supervision, sickened him. Maybe he would need that antacid.

"You're worried," she said.

"She got so sick last time," he said. "And her body nearly rejected her heart, and she waited so long for one that would match, that would fit…" Emotion choked him, but he fought it, as he always had to when he thought about how much that little girl had already endured. "She can't go through that again."

"So let's keep her here," she said.

"In Willow Creek? Mrs. Finch said there were no suitable foster homes here…" But he glanced around her large kitchen. "But you said you're approved…"

"I just got approved here," she said. "I was approved in DC, too. But I haven't actually taken care of any kids yet, so I doubt that Mrs. Finch would consider me suitable for Bailey Ann."

"Then how… What chance do I have to take care of and adopt her?" he asked. "Just tell me how it is. I need to know what I can do, if there's anything I can do…"

"I do think there's something you can do to prevent them from moving her to that foster home in Sheridan," Genevieve said.

He waited, but she didn't continue. She just stared down into the sink, as if she was worried that it was a suggestion that he wasn't going to like.

"What is it?" he asked. "I've signed a contract with the hospital so I can't just quit—"

"I'm not suggesting you quit," she interjected to assure him.

"Then what are you suggesting?" he asked. "What can I do to keep Bailey Ann with me?"

She drew in a deep breath as if she needed to brace herself just to tell him.

And knowing that, he suspected her suggestion was going to be something he didn't like. "If this will help me keep Bailey Ann, I'll do it," he said. "I don't care what it is…" That little girl's health and her life were far more important to him than anything else.

Even himself…

"Please tell me," he urged her. But just in case he needed to brace himself, too, he drew in a deep breath as well.

Finally she released hers, but her voice was so soft and raspy when she spoke that he wasn't sure he'd heard her correctly. Because it sounded a lot like, "Marry me."

SHE'D JUST WHISPERED the words, but her throat felt raw as if she'd shouted them at him. And he looked like she had, or that she'd struck him so hard that he'd lost his breath.

The expression on his face, how utterly appalled he seemed to be, made her laugh out loud. "I don't have any designs on you," she assured him. "I just want to help you. No, not you. I want to help Bailey Ann get what she wants. I want to show her that *I* listened to her. She wants to stay with you, and I think this is the fastest way to make that happen and so that she doesn't get moved to Sheridan."

"Marrying you is the fastest way to do that?" he asked, his dark eyes clouded with either skepticism or confusion.

"I already have a foster care license," she reminded him. "So you wouldn't have to start that whole process to get approved…" She didn't want to be insensitive, but he had to face the reality, so she continued, "…*if* you could even get approved."

He sighed. "Mrs. Finch made it clear that I would need my own house. And there's no way I can manage that within two weeks. Becca made that clear."

"I have a house," Genevieve said. "One that's already licensed for foster care."

"Why did you get that license?" he asked, his brow furrowing with confusion. "You said you haven't taken care of any kids yet, so what was your reason for…"

Tears stung her eyes, and she had to close them for a moment, to clear them, before she opened them again. "I…I wanted to foster…"

"But your husband didn't?"

"Ex-husband," she reminded him. "And no…but…" There was so much more to the story. To her story…about how hard she'd tried to get pregnant, the babies she'd lost and the kids out there who needed a home. She'd wanted some of those kids.

But this wasn't about her. This was about a little girl who had no one else in her life.

"Let's focus on Bailey Ann," she said.

"You do that every time you start to reveal something personal," he remarked. "You step back and shut down."

She flinched at the term Bradford had often used to describe how she'd dealt with all the disappointments they'd had, all those failed fertility treatments and rounds of IVF. And even in the ones that hadn't failed…

"You came to me for help," she said. "Not for my life story."

"I came to you for legal advice," he said. "I didn't expect this…" He gestured around the kitchen.

"Are you talking about dinner or…"

"What do you think?" he asked with the stunned expression he'd had since she'd uttered those two words.

She chuckled. "Oh, you're talking about the marriage proposal?"

"Are you the funny one?" he asked. "Is this all a joke?"

She could have used that excuse to save face. *I was just kidding...*

But she couldn't forget what Bailey Ann had told her. She shook her head. "No. I really want to show that little girl that I listened to her."

"She asked you to marry me?" Collin asked, his brow still furrowed with confusion.

"No. She wants to stay with you, though. She wants you to be her dad. I don't think we can get her into your care in two weeks, and even if that foster family takes good care of her, that could still be a problem. They might change their mind about caring for her short term and file to adopt her, too. And if they're already caring for her, that would give them the advantage with the judge."

Collin groaned.

"That's why we need to keep her here, with you," she said. "But if you marry me, then we can move Bailey Ann in here with us, into a foster care licensed home. And if her cardiologist is living here, always available to handle her medication care, how can her social worker refuse to place her in this home?"

"Because she would be placing her with two strangers who just got married in order to get custody of her."

"She can't prove we're strangers. I doubt she would think strangers would marry to foster a child with special medical needs," she said. "And if she does have doubts, we'll figure out how to deal with whatever questions she might have. Bailey Ann is the priority."

Collin nodded in agreement. "She is for me. But you just met her. And while I know how easy it is to fall for her, I still don't understand why you would do this."

She didn't know how to explain it to herself, so she wasn't sure she could explain it to him. "I want to help her," she said.

And maybe, in some small way, it would make her feel better about all the people she hadn't been able to help. The people she'd failed…

She didn't want Bailey Ann to be one of them.

"Again, you just met her," Collin said. "She's as much of a stranger to you as I am."

But was she? That little girl had had a heart

replacement three or four months ago. Could it be her sister's heart?

No. Jenny had been an adult, albeit a petite one. Her heart wouldn't have gone to a child. But it didn't matter to Genevieve whose heart the little girl had.

"Bailey Ann needs help," Genevieve said. "And she doesn't have any family. She just has you."

Collin muttered something beneath his breath, something that sounded a lot like, "And I'm not enough…"

But maybe she just imagined that was what he'd said because she'd felt that way so many times herself. That she wasn't enough.

"If her social worker is wrong about this family like she was wrong about the last one, Bailey Ann could be in danger," Genevieve pointed out. "And if something happened to her, it would haunt me…"

Just like all the other mistakes she'd made haunted her.

JESSUP HAD BEEN uneasy ever since his mother had left. She was up to something. He'd known it even before Marsh came home laughing about all the Valentine's decorations hanging around town.

"In August?" Jessup asked.

Marsh nodded, then pushed up the brim of his white Stetson. "Yes, I asked Ben and Old Man Lemmon what was going on, and they both answered me with just one word."

"Sadie," Jessup said before Marsh could.

Marsh chuckled and nodded again. "Yup…"

Jessup groaned. "What is she up to now?"

"Hearts and flowers all over town, more than half her grandsons coupled up…" Marsh chuckled again. "I don't have to be interim sheriff to figure out that she's playing matchmaker again."

Tension gripped Jessup. While he loved his mother and was happy to be reunited with her, he was all too well aware of how overbearing she could be. That was why he ran away from her all those years ago.

Because he'd known that her desperate efforts to fight his disease would have hurt them both emotionally and mentally. Was she going to do the same thing with his sons that she'd done with him?

Drive them away?

He'd already lost one. He couldn't lose any more of them.

"Don't let her get to you," he advised his second oldest son. "Don't let her bother you."

Marsh chuckled again. "She doesn't bother me," he assured his dad.

Marsh was the most like Jessup's younger brother. Michael had never let Sadie get to him. He'd just carried on with his life as he'd wanted to lead it, on the ranch. He had loved it so much. But eventually it had taken his life.

Tears burned Jessup's eyes as he thought of all the years he'd lost with his only sibling. But having Marsh was like having Michael with him yet.

Even Darlene, Michael's widow, had mentioned that over the years that she'd helped Jessup take care of his sons. She'd also taken care of Jessup when he'd been at death's door. And he'd spent so much of his time there, leaning against it, ready to fall through if it had opened.

But it hadn't.

He'd survived, and now he had a strong new heart. Although the donation process was anonymous, Jessup was pretty sure he had his nephew's heart, that he carried a piece of Michael with him always.

He didn't want to lose his son, though. "Are you sure she's not getting to you?" Jessup asked.

Marsh grinned. "The only person I'm falling in love with…is her. She's a hoot." He patted his dad's shoulder as he walked past him. "I'm going to take a shower." He walked off, muttering, "Hearts and flowers…" And chuckled again.

She wasn't getting to Marsh, but then Marsh had a sense of humor. So Jessup didn't need to worry about him. He needed to worry about Collin. And Cash…

He was never *not* worried about Cash, though. Just as his mom had never *not* worried about Jessup.

Collin, on the other hand, had always been so focused, so intent on his goals and working hard to achieve them. Jessup had never really worried about Collin either.

He didn't have a dangerous career like Colton—a firefighter—or his older brother, Marsh—a lawman. And Jessup always knew where he was: at the hospital.

The only danger Collin was in was of working too hard and caring too much for his patients. So Jessup did worry about Collin burning himself out.

The last thing the busy cardiologist needed was his grandmother messing with his heart and his head. Hopefully she'd been honest that she was just trying to help him adopt that little girl everyone had been talking about…

But with as much as Collin worked, could he really care for a child on his own? Would he at least open himself to asking for help? But Collin had always been stubbornly persistent on taking care of himself, on handling everything on his own. Had he asked Sadie for help?

Or had she just seen that he'd needed it?

Why hadn't Jessup noticed? Why hadn't he known about Collin's desire to become a daddy to that little girl?

Jessup feared that Collin was angry at him for all the secrets he'd kept.

The door opened and Collin walked in, his steps dragging, his gaze unfocused like he was shell-shocked. "Oh, my God!" Jessup exclaimed as he rushed over to grip his son's shoulders. "Are you okay?"

Had he been in an accident? Jessup glanced

out the front window, but night had fallen so he couldn't see Collin's vehicle, if it was even there.

"Collin? Are you okay?" Jessup repeated, his heart beating fast with fear.

Collin looked at him, finally, but his dark eyes were still unfocused. "I don't know..."

"What happened? Were you in a wreck?"

Collin shook his head, and finally he focused on his dad, cupping his shoulders in his hands as well. Hands that were still pink from the burns he'd suffered during the fire. Because Jessup had gone back inside, trying to find his home health aide's young son.

Thankfully the child hadn't even been in the house. But, once again, Jessup had caused his sons to worry and suffer. With his new heart, he'd hoped to put all that behind him. But instead...

It had opened everything up about the past, about who Jessup really was and who his sons were. Sadie Haven's grandsons.

"Is this about my mother?" Jessup asked. "She was here earlier this evening looking for you." And he'd known then that was a bad sign. But she'd explained that it was about Bailey Ann.

Collin shook his head again. "No, not Sadie…"

But it was about someone. "Bailey Ann? Is she all right?" Had something happened to the child Collin cared for so much?

"She's fine for now," Collin said.

That was the way it was for heart transplants patients. They could be all right for a while, and then their bodies could reject the new organ. That was why Jessup still had his home health aide; he didn't want to put the burden of his care on his family anymore.

"Then what's wrong?" Jessup asked.

"I think I'm getting married."

Unlike his brothers, who'd adamantly insisted they would never marry, Collin hadn't said much about it. But he hadn't had to; it had been clear to everyone, especially the women he'd dated, that Collin's first priority was his calling to be a doctor.

He clearly had no interest in being a husband. But until he'd gotten attached to his little patient, he hadn't had any interest in being a father either.

So he could have changed his mind. But Jessup had a feeling that it had more than likely been changed for him…by Sadie.

CHAPTER SEVEN

COLLIN WAS FOOLISH for even considering it, but what choice did he have? He stood in the doorway to Bailey Ann's room, careful not to get too close and disturb the sleeping child. He'd showed up at the hospital early, before she'd awakened, because he'd been awake. Pretty much the entire night…

He'd tossed and turned and not just because of the uncomfortable pullout couch in the den but because his mind wouldn't shut off. He was used to that and had spent much of his life awake, worrying about his dad and his mom and his brothers and about his studies and his school and residency and fellowship…

He'd worried a lot about Bailey Ann over the past years, too. But it wasn't just thoughts of Bailey Ann that had kept him awake last night.

He'd kept thinking about Genevieve Porter.

He couldn't understand why she was so willing to make such a sacrifice for strangers. He knew all too well how easy it was to fall for Bailey Ann, but Genevieve didn't know *him* at all. She didn't know that he was not good relationship material. While he would make time for Bailey Ann, he wouldn't have any left over for a wife or even a girlfriend. But she certainly hadn't fallen for him like she had the little girl. So why offer to marry him even if she thought it would help Bailey Ann?

It was still a huge risk for her to legally tie herself to a stranger and, especially, to invite him into her home. To live with her…

She'd joked about his oath to do no harm. But he knew a lot of doctors who were first-class jerks; he'd trained under some of them and worked with other ones, like the surgeon who'd done Bailey Ann's heart transplant. He'd cared more about the prestige of doing what he did than the patient.

Collin always tried to put the patient first. That was why he was actually considering accepting Genevieve's offer, but Bailey Ann was more than a patient to him. In his heart, she was already his child. He certainly loved her like she was.

He loved her so much that he would do anything for her. Make any sacrifice…

Maybe even marriage.

Was Sadie behind this? Was that why she'd referred him to Genevieve? But Genevieve had sworn she'd never met his grandmother, and she had no reason to lie.

He was so confused. He hadn't answered Genevieve last night. He'd told her that he needed to think about it. And that was all he'd done. He'd advised her to do the same, to make sure that she was really serious about this before they took any more steps and especially before they said anything to Bailey Ann or her social worker.

He hadn't been able to stop thinking about it, to stop thinking about Genevieve. And it wasn't just because of her unorthodox suggestion on how to foster and then adopt Bailey Ann. She was smart and beautiful and successful, yet he knew nothing personal about her. They'd only known each other a day, of course, but he felt like she had walls up, that she kept stopping herself from revealing anything personal, as if she didn't really want anyone to know her. Or get close to her…

Yet she was the one who had proposed to him.

Not that theirs would be a real marriage. It was just a way to help Bailey Ann. Genevieve Porter had the house, the foster license. She had everything he needed. Everything Bailey Ann needed.

She could probably go after custody on her own if he didn't agree to this plan. Would she do that?

He couldn't foster Bailey Ann right now on his own. But Genevieve could. And as she'd warned him about the other foster family changing their mind about keeping her, custody, even as a foster, would give her an advantage with the family court judge.

He didn't know anything about her, though. Even though he'd tried to find out more…

How could he marry her? And more importantly, how could he trust her with what mattered most to him? With Bailey Ann?

WELL BEFORE DAWN, Genevieve had given up trying to sleep. And because just being in her kitchen had reminded her of the night before, of her outrageous proposal to a stranger, she'd headed into the office.

But she could see Collin Cassidy there, too, sitting across from her in that black cowboy hat like some bull-riding champion. She'd thought then of how he even had the name of a rodeo rider. But while he looked the part, he had chosen an entirely different career.

A hard one that had required years of studying and training and sacrifice. Genevieve understood that—hard work and sacrifice. And she also understood the frustration of wanting to help someone and not knowing how...

And being too late to make amends like she'd been with her sister.

She could help Bailey Ann now. They both could. But her method was extreme. And probably foolish...

Genevieve felt like a fool. What had she been thinking to propose to a stranger?

Yet he hadn't said no. He probably would, though. While he wanted to make a home for Bailey Ann, that home he'd probably envisioned hadn't included a wife he hadn't wanted.

Genevieve should have been used to that,

to being the wife that wasn't wanted. Had Bradford ever really loved her? In the beginning she'd thought so. But then she'd disappointed him…

And eventually whatever love he'd felt for her had gone away. But if there was no love to begin with, there was nothing to lose.

No way she could disappoint if there were no expectations for either of them. It would only be a legal union, not an emotional one. That was the only reason she'd proposed— because she knew she was in no danger of falling in love with Dr. Collin Cassidy, no matter how good-looking he was. She was not going to let herself fall for anyone ever again.

Like Bradford had said, she'd shut down after all their disappointments. She'd closed herself off. It was safer that way. She couldn't get hurt again if she didn't risk her heart.

Maybe she should have opened herself up some more to Collin, just enough to explain the reason she'd made that proposal. And to assure him that she had no ulterior motives.

She just wanted to help an abandoned little girl because she knew all too well how Bailey Ann felt. And because there had been other people in her life that Genevieve should have helped and hadn't.

She couldn't make it up to Jenny anymore. But she could pay it forward…

She could help out Bailey Ann.

A thought struck her. If Collin didn't think marriage was a good idea, that didn't mean Genevieve couldn't help. What if she did it on her own? It wouldn't give Bailey Ann what she wanted—Collin as a father—but maybe she would at least be able to keep her here in Willow Creek.

She checked the time, wondering if it was too early to call…

SADIE AWOKE WITH a start, then squinted against the light streaking through the blinds of her suite. A little sigh whispered out near her and she turned her head to see Feisty lying on the pillow next to her. The long-haired Chihuahua was a tiny ball of black fluff and attitude. And, at the moment, nerves. She licked Sadie's cheek, as if grateful that she was alive.

Feisty had been there the day that Sadie's heart had stopped, but the little dog had been shut outside the door, desperate to get inside the room with her. As if she'd known…

Her frantic barking was what had drawn the others. And Sadie's grandson Baker, a former army medic and paramedic, had saved her life with the help of Taye Cooper.

Feisty had saved her life, just like Sadie had saved her years ago from dying in a hot car. Her previous owners hadn't appreciated Sadie taking a crowbar to their Cadillac, but they were lucky she hadn't taken it to them for nearly killing this sweet creature.

Though not everyone knew she was sweet. She tended to bark and growl and even bite.

Feisty reminded Sadie of Lem, small but tough. Smart and loving with a heart of pure gold. They needed to go ahead and get hitched. They were too old to wait around. That was one of the reasons Sadie had wanted those hearts and flowers up all over town.

She would probably marry Lem where they'd met, where they'd gone to school together, where she'd terrorized him in city hall.

Her cell phone vibrated. And Feisty yipped. It was probably Lem calling as he did every morning.

Yes. They needed to get hitched soon, so he wouldn't have to call. So he would be here with her and Feisty.

She reached for her cell and saw it wasn't Lem's contact info on her screen. It was Jessup's. And according to her screen, she'd missed some other calls from him already.

Concern struck her that he'd called so early. He'd had to have a good reason…or an emergency. Either for him or his sons…

Her arthritic finger shook as she accepted the call. "Is everything all right?" she asked, her already deep voice gruff now with the fear rushing up on her.

"No," Jessup said. "Everything is not all right."

Sadie shot up in her bed, and Feisty yipped with concern. "What is it? Your heart?" Hers was thumping madly in her chest. She wasn't sure if that was a good thing or a bad thing, though. But wasn't it beating fast better than it not beating at all?

"Not mine," Jessup said. "You're messing with Collin's, though, aren't you?"

"What?" she asked, confused. She used to be such an early riser, but after her health scare, she needed more rest than she usually did.

"You're meddling too much," Jessup said.

"I don't know what you're talking about…" she murmured. "Bailey Ann? I want to help him adopt her." She just wasn't sure if she could.

But she hoped that someone else was able to help him.

"How?" Jessup asked. "By encouraging him to marry a stranger?"

"What? You're not making sense."

"Exactly!" Jessup exclaimed. "None of this makes sense. How do you think this scheme is going to work? He's going to be miserable."

"I don't know anything about a marriage," she insisted. "But I do know that he will be miserable if he loses Bailey Ann."

"I don't believe that you don't have anything to do with this," Jessup said. "It has your fingerprints all over it. This is one of your matchmaking schemes, probably why you cooked up this whole Valentine's Day in August thing."

Sadie nearly chuckled, but she didn't think her son would appreciate her amusement at the moment. She'd cooked up that celebration for herself, for the love she felt. But Jessup hadn't opened up his new heart to anyone, nor had he opened up his old one to anyone else since his wife had died.

He didn't understand how important love

was. Sadie did. But even if Collin had managed to get an appointment with the lawyer already, he couldn't have fallen for Genevieve Porter yet.

But she couldn't think of anyone else he might be marrying. They would have just met, so this couldn't be for love. It had to be about Bailey Ann. But she couldn't imagine her practical, no-nonsense grandson coming up with this scheme.

No. It would have been Genevieve Porter's idea. Her scheme…

And why?

What was her ulterior motive in all of this?

Had Sadie made a mistake? Had she been so blinded by her own romance that she'd been too understanding, too optimistic about other people's motives?

But now she was as worried as Jessup was. Worried that she'd made a terrible mistake…

CHAPTER EIGHT

BEFORE BAILEY ANN woke up that morning, Collin had been called down to the ER for a consult. And after that, he'd had to take his appointments in the clinic attached to the hospital. So he hadn't seen her yet that day, and it was already getting close to lunchtime. Maybe he would bring her down to the cafeteria with him. Or maybe even to the little café close to it since she was getting tired of staying in the hospital.

She could probably be out of it soon, if she had a foster home where she could get a lot of rest and supervision. That hadn't happened at the last one, and this one Mrs. Finch had found for her in Sheridan was just temporary and the family wasn't even trained yet.

The social worker had been so confident that she'd found her a safe placement last time. That one had been here in Willow Creek, but they hadn't managed her medications correctly and she'd been so sick when she'd been checked back into the hospital.

Thinking of that, of how close he'd come to losing her, he ran up the steps from the first floor clinic toward her room on the third. He was still in the stairwell when he heard her cry out, "No! No!"

She was used to needles so even if someone was taking her blood or giving her a shot, she wouldn't cry about it like he could hear her sobbing now. He ran up the last couple of steps and down the hall to the open door.

A woman was in the room with her. Not a nurse or Genevieve Porter. It was an older woman with dark hair and a weary-sounding voice. Mrs. Finch. Her back was to Collin, so she didn't see him.

And Bailey Ann had buried her face in her hands, so she didn't see him either.

"Bailey Ann, you know I've been looking for another foster family for you," Mrs. Finch was saying as if it had been a great burden, as if the child was a great burden. "So you should be happy that I've found one for you."

The little girl's shoulders shook with the sobs she tried to muffle with her hands. And Collin's heart broke.

He'd been worried about Genevieve building up her hopes yesterday. But he hadn't figured on Mrs. Finch coming to dash them all away—Bailey Ann's and his.

"I don't wanna…" Bailey Ann pulled her hands away from her face and saw him standing in the doorway. "I don't wanna leave Dr. Cass. I wanna stay with him!"

"You shouldn't want to stay in the hospital," Mrs. Finch said. "Other people, people sicker than you, need this bed and his medical attention."

Collin sucked in a breath, stunned at how insensitive the social worker was being with the child. But then she continued, "You need to go to school and make friends and live the life your new heart has enabled you to live." And he couldn't argue with that.

She'd spent more time in the hospital than out of it. As the social worker had just said, she needed to live the life her new heart had given her. And staying in the hospital was not really living, not like she should be.

Although it was still summer vacation right now, school would be starting soon. And she should be attending, making friends, learning…

"Why can't I live with Dr. Cass?" Bailey

Ann asked. She was looking at him when she posed the question, and the plaintiveness of her tone squeezed his heart.

Mrs. Finch hadn't noticed him yet, so she answered Bailey Ann instead. "He's not a foster parent," she said. "And he works so much that he wouldn't be able to take care of you—"

"He does here!" Bailey Ann interjected.

"With help," Mrs. Finch said. "He has nurses and medical assistants that are here around the clock. He can't take care of you on his own."

He wanted to call her on it, wanted to say she was lying. But she was right. He had to work; he couldn't take care of Bailey Ann on his own.

But he wouldn't necessarily have to do it alone if he accepted the proposal Genevieve had offered him last night. If she hadn't changed her mind...

He couldn't bring it up to Mrs. Finch or Bailey Ann until he knew if Genevieve was serious about it. And if she was...

He would take her up on her offer as soon as possible. He would do whatever he could to keep Bailey Ann with him. Even marry a stranger...one he found far too appealing for his peace of mind.

"THANKS FOR COMING HERE," Genevieve said as she led Sue back to her office. She'd ordered lunch in since Sue had taken a break from the hospital to meet her. She would have met her in the cafeteria, but she hadn't wanted to run into Collin.

In case he didn't accept her proposal, which looked unlikely given his reaction the night before, Genevieve needed a contingency plan in place so that she could at least keep Bailey Ann here in Willow Creek. But he might be furious to find out she was going after the little girl without him. And if anyone else figured out that Sue had called CPS on the Havens because of her, a lot more people would probably be furious with her.

Unless someone had already figured it out…

But why would Sadie Haven have given her a referral if she knew and why wouldn't she have told Collin? Maybe Genevieve was just paranoid because she felt so guilty over the problems she'd inadvertently caused her nephews.

But she couldn't worry about that right now. She was already too worried about Bailey Ann.

"I was glad you called," Sue said. "I thought you were upset with me."

"I was upset with me, not you," Genevieve said. "You were only trying to help me." It had been sweet of the nurse to try to help Genevieve, a virtual stranger. Genevieve had left Willow Creek so long ago and her parents not long after.

"Yes, well…" Sue muttered. "I should have handled everything better. I didn't realize…"

"Your intentions were good," Genevieve said. She cleared her throat. "Sue, I need your help again."

Instead of looking put upon, like the woman had every right to be, she smiled instead and released a little shaky sigh. "That's good. That's really all I wanted to do, Genevieve. Your mother and I were so close in high school."

High school was a long time ago for the nurse, but Genevieve wasn't about to point that out to her. Not when she needed her.

"I appreciate your assistance," Genevieve said. "And I'm sure Mother does, too." Though Genevieve really had no way of knowing. She hadn't spoken to her mother in months. Not since…

She sucked in a shaky breath and reminded herself of the reason she'd asked Sue to come to the office for lunch. "I hate to ask you to do anything else, but it's for a good cause." Bailey Ann had no one to help her but Collin.

Whereas her nephews had…all the Havens. CPS had assured Sue that the boys were very well loved and cared for. They didn't need Genevieve any more than anyone else ever had…except for Bailey Ann.

"I'm sure it is," Sue said. "I trust you."

Genevieve had done nothing to earn that trust. Sue didn't know her at all—unless she and Genevieve's mother had talked about her over the years. At one time, Genevieve would have cared, but she'd shut down about her mother just as she had about Bradford.

There was no sense in opening herself up again and again to more pain.

"I got my foster care license when I first moved here," Genevieve said. "And I'd like to open my house up to foster a child."

"That is a good cause," Sue said, but her brow furrowed slightly. "Are you talking about your nephews? Isn't that why you got your foster license?"

"They weren't the only reason." She'd also

had her license in DC and back there she had never considered that she might have to foster Jenny's kids. She'd never thought Jenny would die so young. "I've always wanted to foster kids who needed a good home." She needed to be needed as much as they did.

"That's wonderful," Sue said with the pride and approval Genevieve had never received from her own mother.

"I want to foster a little girl who's in the hospital right now," Genevieve expounded. "She recently had a heart transplant."

Sue gasped. "You want to foster Bailey Ann?"

Genevieve nodded. "Yes. You know about her?" Sue worked in the ER, but Genevieve supposed the hospital wasn't that big. And Bailey Ann might have been in and out of the ER a lot during her short life and her heart issues.

"Everyone at the hospital knows Bailey Ann," Sue said. "How did you find out about her? Did her social worker contact you?"

Genevieve shook her head. "No. After I got licensed here, I had asked to wait awhile before taking any children…" Because she'd needed to find out what the situation with her nephews was. If they didn't need her, would they want to know her? Would they hate her for how she'd ignored their mother all these years? Or worse, would they be like so many other people and not care at all? That was why, in addition to her own shame and regret for how she'd treated her sister for so many years, she hadn't had the guts to reach out directly to the Havens. "No. Dr. Cassidy contacted me about Bailey Ann."

"Dr. Cassidy… You know he's Sadie Haven's grandson, don't you?"

Genevieve blinked. "Collin's last name is Cassidy."

"Long lost branch of the family. He is definitely Sadie's grandson," Sue insisted.

Genevieve's mind reeled. Why had Sadie referred him to her for help with the adoption? Especially if she knew who Genevieve really was?

It was past time that Genevieve summon the courage to reach out to the Havens and find out exactly what Sadie knew about her. And what about Collin?

Did he know who she was and what she'd done?

And if so, there was no way he was ever

going to accept her proposal no matter how platonic it had been intended. Her only intent had been to help Bailey Ann, just as it had been with her nephews. She'd failed with the boys, but that didn't mean she had to give up. While they might not want a relationship with her, like so many other people hadn't, she at least owed them an explanation and an apology.

LUNCH TIME AT the ranch was so much chaos and so much fun with all the little boys running around the kitchen, trying to help Taye. Miller, Dale's seven-year-old son, had started taking cooking lessons from her first, and now the younger ones wanted to be like him.

Or at least, the brothers all did. Their new cousin, five-year-old Caleb Morris Haven, just wanted Taye's cookies. He snuck one now, and Sadie caught his gaze and wriggled her eyebrows.

He froze for a second, his hand literally in the cookie jar. But he wasn't afraid of her. He'd never been afraid of her like some kids were because she was tall and had a gruff voice and wasn't soft and cuddly like the usual grandmotherly type. And because she wasn't the usual grandmother type, she held up two fingers and mouthed the word *snicker-doodle* so he would know to steal her one of those. They were her favorite.

The chocolate chip cookies were Caleb's favorite. It was an ongoing debate between them—which cookie type was the best. He grinned and pulled out a bigger handful. He'd probably gotten her chocolate chip, figuring she would give it to him. At five, the kid was already a schemer; Sadie loved him so much. He slipped around the long, stainless-steel-topped island and over to where she sat at the end of the dining room table that was so big they could all sit around it, even as their family kept expanding.

When Jenny and Dale got married, Sadie had remodeled the old farmhouse to add a wing of bedrooms, this enormous kitchen and her suite to the main floor. Her other grandsons had teased her that it wasn't necessary to add on as much as she had because they'd been determined to remain single. But she'd been scheming even then… She'd just had no idea how it would all turn out.

Her and Lem?

That was ridiculous but it worked. They worked.

And now Collin and…

Genevieve Porter?

"You two are going to ruin your lunch!" Taye said, pointing her spatula at Caleb and Sadie. She was tall, like Sadie, with a long golden blond braid tossed over her shoulder and piercing blue eyes. She was fierce, fiercely loving and loyal and protective. She was the one—along with Sadie's youngest grandson, Baker—who was going to adopt Jenny and Dale's orphaned sons. Jenny would have loved her, just as she'd loved Sadie, because people often compared Taye to Sadie. Not that Sadie had ever been able to cook.

She popped one of the cookies into her mouth, savoring the taste of brown sugar and vanilla along with the chocolate.

"Hey!" Caleb exclaimed. "You don't like chocolate chip."

"I don't want you getting into trouble alone," she explained with a grin.

"He usually gets me in trouble with him," Ian said. Ian was five like Caleb and had welcomed the boy as his best friend when Caleb's widowed mother had first moved back to Willow Creek with her young son.

Caleb held up his small hands, which had smears of chocolate on them. "I wasn't with you in the barn the day you got knocked down. You got in that trouble on your own!"

Ian gave a little sigh and nodded. "And I got Colton in trouble, too." Colton had been with Ian in the barn that day and hadn't known yet how dangerous the horse was that Ian had been trying to show him.

Midnight was a beautiful beast, but he had caused as much trouble on the ranch as…

Sadie's cell phone vibrated in her pocket. Since lunch hadn't started yet, she pulled it out; otherwise she would have ignored her phone during a meal with the kids. But she didn't want to miss any more calls from Jessup, especially if he was still angry with her.

However, the number appearing on her screen didn't belong to either of them, but to a law firm. And it wasn't the one Sadie had always used.

It was the one she'd referred Collin to, which might have been a big mistake. Like trying to coddle Jessup all those years ago and driving him away instead. If she'd messed up with Jessup's son, she might push him away once again.

So maybe she shouldn't even take this…

Or maybe she better and do some damage control. "Hello?" she said, speaking over the babble of the kids around her.

She heard a gasp. Maybe her caller hadn't expected Sadie to answer her call or maybe she'd heard all the kids.

"This is Genevieve Porter," she introduced herself.

And Sadie sucked in a slight breath at how similar her voice sounded to Jenny's. She was glad, with Ian standing so close to her, that she hadn't put her cell on speaker. She wasn't certain how he would react to hearing someone sound so much like his mom.

But they'd grown used to Dusty being around the ranch, and as their dad's twin, he looked exactly like him.

"What can I do for you, Genevieve Porter?" Sadie asked.

"I'd like to talk to you," she said. "Is it possible to meet with you? You could come to my office or…"

"A lawyer calling *me* for an appointment? Shouldn't that be the other way around?"

"I understand I owe you for a referral."

"Collin."

"Yes. My payment is going to be an explanation, if you'll give me the chance…"

"Of course I will. And since I was in town yesterday, I'd prefer if you came out here."

"I can come to Ranch Haven?" she asked, as if she didn't believe her.

"You've always been welcome here, Genevieve," Sadie assured her. "Always."

A little quivery breath slipped out of the speaker as if the lawyer was about to cry. Tears burned Sadie's eyes too as she thought of how families hurt each other, and how sometimes they didn't get the chance to make up for their hurts.

She'd gotten lucky with Jessup. Hopefully she hadn't screwed that up with putting Collin in touch with this woman. But if Genevieve could help him…

"I have an appointment, but I can come out after that," Genevieve offered. "If that works for you…"

"Come out for dinner," Sadie offered.

"This… I'm not…" Genevieve floundered for the words. "I just…need to talk to you."

"I know. It's long overdue."

"Yes," Genevieve agreed. "It is…"

"So dinner then. You know your way here?"

"I'll find it," Genevieve said. "Thank you."

The line clicked off, leaving Sadie to wonder what the lawyer was thanking her for.

The invitation to dinner?

The chance to explain?

Or referring Collin to her?

CHAPTER NINE

COLLIN'S STOMACH HAD knotted itself so much that he was surprised he could stand up when he slid out from beneath the steering wheel of his car. He'd felt sick since he'd overheard Bailey Ann and the social worker. And while he'd tried to calm the little girl, he hadn't known what to tell her.

He couldn't make promises to her only to disappoint her as so many other people already had in her life. Because he knew that no matter how much both he and Bailey Ann wanted it, he couldn't foster the little girl on his own. And adopting her was going to be a lengthy process that would mean she would go into that foster home in Sheridan for a while.

And if their training to take care of her wasn't enough for them to do it properly, her placement with them could be a very short term, but she might not survive.

Before Mrs. Finch had left the hospital,

he'd asked why she hadn't waited a bit longer to tell Bailey Ann about the placement. "And there's no foster home here in Willow Creek where you could place her?" he'd challenged.

She'd shaken her head. "No one with experience caring for a child with Bailey Ann's special needs."

He wondered at that. Did Mrs. Finch know that Genevieve was available? Was she considered unsuitable, and would that change if he married her?

At the moment he just wanted to talk to her. So as soon as he'd been able to get away from the hospital, he'd driven over to her office. As he crossed in front of his vehicle, he focused on the building a few yards down from where he'd found the parking spot at the curb of Main Street where all those heart-shaped balloons and decorations fluttered in the faint afternoon breeze. The office looked dark inside, with no lights shining behind the blinds that were already pulled. He hoped he wasn't too late to catch her for the day.

But at least he knew where she lived.

He would knock on the office door first, just to be sure. As he started down the sidewalk toward the law practice, he noticed a familiar looking vehicle parked closer than his. That big SUV that had followed him first to the hospital before he'd followed it to her house.

Despite the SUV's tinted glass, she was visible inside, behind the wheel. Perfectly still. As if she was hoping he didn't notice her.

His stomach knotted more. She'd probably changed her mind about her offer to help him and Bailey Ann. And he couldn't blame her for rethinking it. He'd been a fool not to jump on her offer the moment she'd made it.

What other options did he have? Mrs. Finch definitely wasn't going to let him foster Bailey Ann without help.

He knocked on the side window, and she jumped and whirled toward him, making him realize that she hadn't even noticed him. Maybe she'd had her eyes closed. Meditating?

The window lowered, and she said, "I'm sorry. I didn't see you."

"You seemed a million miles away."

"Not yet," she muttered.

His stomach tightened more. "Are you leaving town?" he asked with alarm. What had happened between their dinner last night and now?

"Not forever," she said, "Or at least, I hope not."

"What's going on, Genevieve?" he asked. "Is everything all right?" He didn't really expect her to answer, though, since she'd successfully deflected all his personal questions the day before.

She peered at him, her brow furrowed slightly. Then she asked, "Why are you here?"

And he swallowed a groan of frustration. He would have pushed, would have pressed her to finally answer him, but he did have a reason for coming to see her—a really important reason.

"Bailey Ann," he said. "Her social worker told her about the move to Sheridan."

Genevieve's mouth fell open on a gasp. "Oh, no. She was upset."

It wasn't a question. She knew. From one meeting with the little girl, she knew her better than her ongoing social worker. Knowing how many cases the woman carried, Collin tried to cut her some slack. There was only so much she could do with the resources she had.

Collin hoped he had more. "Yes," he said. "I'm sorry."

"I'm saying yes," he repeated. "To your proposal, if the offer is still open…"

Despite all the Valentine decorations dangling from the streetlights around them, there was nothing romantic about the situation. In the middle of the street, talking through her car window like a cop giving her a citation.

She released a shaky sigh. "I don't know if that's going to be possible any longer…"

"Because you're going away?" he asked. Was that why she'd changed her mind?

"Right now I'm just heading out to Ranch Haven," she said.

"You've been summoned?" He should have guessed. Sadie had referred him to Genevieve, so of course they had some connection. Though Genevieve had claimed she'd never met her.

Had Genevieve lied to him? And was she actually part of one of his grandmother's schemes? Was that why she'd really proposed? And if so, then he shouldn't trust her enough to marry her even if it was in name only.

"Not so much summoned. I actually asked to meet her," Genevieve said.

"You really haven't ever met her before?" he asked with skepticism.

Genevieve shook her head. "I know *of* her. I've never met her."

"She's definitely a local legend," Collin said. "I'd known *of* her long before I met her, too."

"She's your grandmother," Genevieve said.

He nodded. "I found that out a few weeks ago."

"I just found that out today," she said. "I didn't know that yesterday…"

"When you proposed?" His head began to pound. "Is that why you're changing your mind about your offer?"

She sighed. "No. But you might…or maybe she will… I don't know what she wants…"

"But you said you're the one who asked to see her." He was so confused.

She nodded. "I don't know why she referred you to *me*. I don't know what she wants from me."

So if Sadie had cooked up a scheme, Genevieve didn't know any more about it than Collin did. And at the moment he didn't really care. He cared only about Bailey Ann.

And maybe a little bit about this woman who was so generous and caring herself…

"I can go with you to the ranch," he offered. And he reached for the door handle.

But it didn't budge. While she'd lowered the window, she hadn't unlocked the door.

"You should be there," she agreed. "But let's drive separately."

"It's a long drive," he said. "Nearly an hour. We could…"

She shook her head. "We may want to leave at different times."

"Want or need?" he wondered aloud.

She shrugged. "I don't know." Her delicate features were tense as if she was as tied up in knots as he was.

"I'm sorry," he said, compelled to apologize for his grandmother despite having no idea himself what was going on.

She shook her head. "*You* don't owe anyone an apology, Collin."

His grandmother was stubborn. While he hadn't known her long or well, he knew that about her because she was so much like his dad. "But Sadie might not—"

"She doesn't owe anyone an apology either," she said. "I do." She exhaled a shaky breath. "And I better get to it." She turned on the ignition then and raised that side window before Collin could say anything.

As she pulled away from the curb, a soft

pop rang out, and when she drove away, Collin noticed a balloon on the asphalt. It must have escaped from the light post, and her big SUV had run it over, leaving the heart shape flat and mangled on the asphalt.

Despite the warmth of the summer day, a chill raced over him. He'd been so worried about Bailey Ann this entire time, about her heart, but he hadn't realized until now that maybe he should be worrying about his own as well.

GENEVIEVE WASN'T SURE if Collin had decided to follow her or not. If he had, she'd not noticed him in her rearview mirror. She waited outside the enormous two-story farmhouse for a while, but he didn't show up. Sucking in a deep breath, she stepped out and walked up the steps to the front porch that wrapped around the house.

The house was big, and the property seemed endless with pastures and fields on both sides of the long drives and so many buildings. Ranch Haven looked more like its own town, with all of its barns and houses and even an old one-room school building.

Their parents had warned Jenny that she'd

wind up living in poverty if she married her high school sweetheart. They'd underestimated the daughter they'd disowned and the son-in-law they'd never acknowledged.

The sister Genevieve had turned her back on…

Genevieve was glad her sister had known love and happiness. She wished she'd been able to find something like this for herself. She'd never been able to make that family of her own that she'd wanted with Bradford.

Now she had nothing.

Tears stung her eyes, but she blinked them back and forced herself to ring the doorbell. She wasn't going to wait for Collin to arrive; she didn't need or expect him to be her backup, not when the Havens were his family.

But some of them were also hers.

The door creaked open and one of them stood in front of her. He looked more like Dale with the sandy blond hair and hazel eyes. "Are you a CPS lady?" he asked.

And she sucked in a breath and shook her head. "No. I'm not."

He blew out a little shaky sigh and nodded. "Okay then, you can come in."

A twinge of guilt struck her. However well-meaning Sue's call had been to CPS, she'd upset these boys. And that was the last thing Genevieve had wanted to do. Although the child left the door open, she hesitated to just walk inside unless an adult greeted her. While she hesitated, something black and furry rushed onto the porch and bounced around her, yipping and snarling.

Even the dog didn't want her there.

Maybe he thought she was a CPS lady, too.

"Feisty won't bite you," another little boy said as he stepped onto the porch and scooped up the dog, which then licked his face. "She just wants attention." He looked like the last boy, just a little bigger. Probably Bailey Ann's age…

Seven. From the note on the back of the family portrait Jenny had sent her, Genevieve knew who they all were. This was Miller. Jenny had given him her maiden name. The name she and Jenny hadn't shared. Her stepfather hadn't offered it to her, to adopt her. She'd never been good enough. And then when Jenny had gone against their wishes…

She hadn't been good enough either. But she'd given her oldest child their last name. She'd still wanted a connection with her family, which was probably why she'd kept track of Genevieve and sent her letters and that family portrait. The last one they would ever take.

Miller cradled the dog in one arm. He held a spatula in his other hand, which he used to wave her into the house. He started off down the hallway.

Genevieve stepped inside and closed the door behind her. Then she followed the child down a wide foyer that separated formal rooms toward the back of the mammoth house.

Miller spoke to her over his shoulder. "Grandma told me to bring you back to the kitchen for dinner. Taye and I are just finishing cooking."

"He's my seven-year-old sous chef," a young woman said as Genevieve stepped into the kitchen. The room was enormous, with a high ceiling, fireplace and wall of windows that overlooked a back patio. The many cabinets were stained a deep green that complimented the brick floor, backsplash and fireplace hearth and chimney. A stainless steel counter topped a long island. And on the other side of that, between the wall of patio doors, was a long table. A woman sat at the head of that table, her back to the unlit fireplace. Long, snowy white hair flowed around her gently lined face, and dark eyes studied Genevieve closely.

Genevieve couldn't meet her gaze, mostly because her attention was drawn to the toddler the woman bounced on her knee as he squealed and called to his great-grandma, "Horsey! Faster, horsey! Faster!"

Sadie obliged, bouncing him harder and higher, and he erupted with giggles. Tears glistened in the older woman's eyes for a moment.

And Genevieve remembered...

Sue had told her what the boys had gone through. The oldest one, Miller, had had to have surgery on his broken leg and physical therapy afterward to walk again. Ian, the middle one, had had a concussion that had affected his short-term memory, and he'd kept asking where his parents were, only to be told over and over about their deaths. And the toddler, who'd once babbled and giggled endlessly, had stopped talking except for when he woke up screaming from nightmares.

Genevieve wasn't sure where Sue had gotten the information, but Willow Creek, though bigger than she remembered, was still a small town. And everyone knew and talked about the Havens.

"I never get sick of hearing that," a man's deep voice drawled. He'd come up behind the woman at the counter and wrapped his arms around her.

She leaned back against him and smiled up at him with so much love, the same love he reflected back at her and then at the giggling toddler. Miller leaned against them both, as if confident they would hold him.

The man looked like Collin, tall and broad, with dark hair. His eyes were lighter, and he was younger. This was the one who wanted to adopt her orphaned nephews.

Ian had come back to her and now he tugged on the sleeve of her suit jacket. "Who are you?" he asked with curiosity.

She opened her mouth, but she wasn't sure what to call herself. And Sadie answered for her. "This is Genevieve Porter."

The kids didn't react to her name. Neither Baker nor the woman, Taye Cooper, reacted. They didn't know who she was then. But someone behind her let out a soft gasp, and she turned to find Old Man Lemmon standing behind her with Collin at his side. He knew who she was, but clearly he didn't know what she was doing there. Beneath the white strands of hair, his forehead furrowed in confusion.

"Genevieve is my guest for dinner," Sadie said as if she'd sensed everyone's unspoken question.

But she hadn't given them the real answer. Was she waiting for Genevieve to do that? To reveal who she was and explain herself?

She didn't even know where to start.

As if Sadie sensed that, she waved her over. "Come sit by me…"

The woman was as intimidating and compelling as Genevieve had been told. Despite every instinct in her body warning her to turn and run, she started toward that table.

But as if he didn't think she would find it on her own, a hand caught hers. A small hand. And Ian smiled up at her encouragingly. "Sit by me," he said.

"Are you a firefighter?" Baker asked with a chuckle.

Clearly, in her suit and heels, she wasn't dressed like a firefighter.

"He usually only wants firefighters to sit beside him," the former firefighter explained. According to Sue, Baker Haven had resigned from that position to take over Dale's job as ranch foreman.

He also wanted to take over Dale's position as father to these boys. Boys that Genevieve had also wanted...

"WHAT IN THE Sam Hill is that woman up to now?" Lem muttered.

"Which woman are you talking about?"

Lem glanced up at the man standing next to him in the entrance to the kitchen. Tall and broad and a little older than Michael's sons, it was one of the Cassidys. Lem wasn't adept at telling them apart yet.

"Either of them," the older man said. "Sadie's usually scheming. And that lawyer can't be trusted..."

The man's throat moved as if he was struggling to swallow something down. Then he rasped out the question, "She can't? Then why did Grandma tell me to contact her for help with Bailey Ann?"

Lem swallowed a groan, knowing that he'd screwed up. It wasn't Colton standing next to him but his twin, the cardiologist. He should have known that; Collin wasn't wearing the hat. But he wasn't wearing a white jacket or scrubs either like Lem's granddaughter Livvy usually wore.

"You'll have to have ask Sadie about that," Lem murmured. He was going to be in trouble for running his mouth. He needed to get his fiancée to the altar fast, before she changed her mind about marrying him.

CHAPTER TEN

WHY WOULD SADIE refer him to a lawyer who couldn't be trusted? It made no sense, but Collin couldn't get close enough to Sadie during dinner to ask her. He didn't get close enough to Genevieve to ask her either because the little Haven boys had gathered around her, Miller on one side of her and Ian on the other with his friend Caleb next to him. And the toddler, little Jake, had taken a seat on her lap. He leaned back and peered up at her, as if fascinated with her as she talked to his brothers.

She was beautiful, but it was something else seeing her with these kids. They were even more drawn to her than Bailey Ann had been, and she and the little girl had instantly bonded the day before.

This was even deeper than that…

He sat across from them, in one of the chairs in the middle of that long table, too far from Sadie to question her. So all he could do was mutter to himself, "What is it about her?"

"It's her voice."

He glanced at Katie, Jake Haven's red-haired wife. "What?"

"You've noticed how they've taken to her," Katie said, "even more so than they took to Colton."

"And you think it's her voice?" Collin asked. While Genevieve did have a sweet-sounding tone, he wasn't sure kids would make much notice of that.

Katie nodded. "She sounds exactly like their mom."

Collin felt a twinge of pain for what those kids had endured, for the tragic loss of both their parents. "Did Jenny have any family?" he asked.

Katie shook her head. "Not that she talked about. They disowned her when she married Dale out of high school."

They watched the kids and Genevieve for a while. Then Katie sighed. "Jenny was a sweetheart. She and Dale were my first accounting clients when I moved back to Willow Creek and opened my business. But they'd both taken accounting courses and really didn't need my help. They were just being supportive and kind."

"This town is certainly welcoming," he agreed. He'd found a place here. He wondered if Genevieve was finding her place, too. And he wondered why Lem thought she couldn't be trusted.

"They don't look anything alike, mind you," Katie mused, as she stared across the table at the blond-haired woman. "She looks more like Emily than Jenny…"

Emily was the schoolteacher whom Sadie had hired to come out to the ranch to home-school the older boys and be the nanny to little Jake. She was now engaged to Ben, the mayor. Collin had heard that she'd been the one to propose, like Genevieve had proposed to him.

But he and Genevieve were strangers while Emily and Ben were clearly in love. They sat farther down the table, leaning against each other. Jake was on the other side of Katie, his arm wrapped loosely around the back of her chair. And Baker and Taye were sitting close together, too, on the other side of Collin. Somehow he'd gotten sandwiched between two of the three happy Haven couples.

There was a fourth couple that had been married the longest and would soon be ex-

panding the family with a set of twins. Dusty
and his wife were actually at Collin's family
ranch. He'd been in the process of buying it
when the house caught fire. Fortunately the
barns and other outbuildings had survived,
but they were in need of repairs, something
Dusty had apparently started early to get his
bronco horse out of the barn here at Ranch
Haven.

The bronco had been responsible for Ian
taking a trip to the ER with Collin. But he
looked fine now as he stared with fascination
at Genevieve.

Katie reached around Collin to tap Taye's
shoulder. She sat on the other side of him.
"And I thought you were the kid whisperer,"
Katie said to the cook.

"That was Emily."

"Was, when she first got here," Katie agreed.
"But you took over."

Taye sighed. "Took me a while, though. It
wasn't like it is with Genevieve."

"She sounds like Jenny," Katie said. "Doesn't
she?"

Taye sucked in a breath, and her eyes widened. "Could it be…?"

"What?" Collin asked. "Could what be?"

"Is Genevieve Jenny's sister?"

"Jenny had a sister?" Collin was the one who asked the question since he hadn't grown up in Willow Creek. Had Genevieve?

"I think she did," Katie said. "Wasn't there a much older sister? She'd left town when Jake and I got to high school. I think she even had a different last name..."

The color suddenly drained from Taye's face, and she jumped up so fast that her chair would have fallen over if Baker didn't catch it. "Boys, want to help me with dessert?" she asked. And she clapped her hands together and forced a bright smile, but it didn't reach her eyes.

"What's going on?" Baker whispered to her. Clearly he'd noticed her reaction, too.

"Ask your grandmother," Taye whispered as she headed toward the kitchen.

"You're going to love this dessert," Miller told Genevieve as he scrambled up from the bench.

"Do you really set the bananas on fire?" Ian asked with awe. He and Caleb swung their legs over the bench and chased after Miller.

And even the little guy crawled off Genevieve's lap to toddle off behind the older boys.

Genevieve stared after them all with such an expression of longing and awe.

Could she be Jenny's sister? The boys' aunt? No one seemed to know her here, and that kind of secret-keeping concerned him.

He thought again of Lem's comment that she couldn't be trusted. What did the deputy mayor and Taye and Katie know about this woman? About Jenny's sister? Was she the one who'd called CPS? Was she the one who'd made trouble for the family? For Collin's family?

If that was the case, then Collin would be a fool to think she would help him. For a moment last night, during dinner at her house, he'd begun to hope that there might be a way for him to keep Bailey Ann in Willow Creek with him. But now he felt it all slipping away—Bailey Ann and his hope.

EVERYBODY WAS STARING at her, making Genevieve feel like she was having that nightmare—the one where she was arguing in court while naked. But this time, when she woke up, she was actually naked and vulnerable. The nightmare wasn't just a dream but her reality.

"Why's everyone so quiet?" Ian asked with naive directness.

He was a sweetheart. They all were. But then they were Jenny's kids, so of course they were. Jenny had been a sweetheart. Genevieve had overheard the red-haired woman saying that to Collin.

The red-haired woman... Katie Haven. She'd met them all before dinner. There'd been introductions around the table. But all Sadie had said was her name, not who she was.

Clearly they'd figured it out anyway.

But nobody probably wanted to address it in front of the little boys. Maybe the Havens didn't want the kids to know that she was their aunt.

She leaned closer to Sadie and asked, "Can I speak with you alone?"

Sadie nodded. "I think that would be wise."

"Grandma..." Baker began, his deep voice full of anger and confusion.

She shook her head. "It's not... It's fine... I'll explain later."

"I want to hear it now," Collin said.

"Can he join us?" Sadie asked Genevieve.

She nodded. That was why she'd wanted him to follow her out here. It was time to come clean about everything, including her role in the CPS scare with the boys.

She only hoped they would believe that she had never intended for Sue to call CPS. Genevieve had just asked the woman to find out what she could about them, to keep her apprised of what was going on with them. But from the way they were all staring at her, with such suspicion, Genevieve didn't know if they would believe her.

Looking for a sympathetic face, she focused on Old Man Lemmon—Lem, she reminded herself. Everyone here called him Lem. She wondered if he remembered her from Christmases so many years ago. He'd been the Santa on whose lap she'd sat.

He frowned at her, and she was reminded that he wasn't Santa. There were no fairy tales, no happily-ever-afters, at least not for Genevieve. As she followed Sadie down the hall, with Collin behind her, she felt as if she was heading to court. But instead of defending someone else, she had to defend herself. Not that she had much of a defense.

Sadie opened a door and led them into a sitting room with two easy chairs and a television. The older woman settled into one of the chairs and pointed Genevieve toward the other. Was this the witness chair, and Sadie's the bench?

Collin shut the door and leaned back against it, as if blocking everyone else out. To protect her? Or to keep her from escaping?

He was the one who asked the first question. "So are you Jenny's sister?"

"Yes."

He sucked in a breath. "That's the first personal question you've actually answered."

"It's not something I'm proud of," Genevieve said.

"You're not proud of Jenny?" Sadie asked, her deep voice sharp with outrage.

"No! I'm not proud of myself," Genevieve said. "I'm not proud that I dropped out of her life when our parents disowned her. She and I were never really close..." She winced at the sound of her own voice, of her excuse. "But that was my fault, not hers."

"You're older than she was," Sadie said, as if giving her an excuse.

"A little over six years," Genevieve confirmed. Jenny would have been thirty this year. Genevieve was thirty-six, probably a few years older than Collin was.

"And you pushed yourself in school, graduating early, so you were gone from Willow Creek even before Jake got to high school," Sadie continued.

"How do you know so much?" Genevieve asked with wonder. Was Sue right about the woman?

"Your sister idolized you," Sadie said. "She talked about how smart and beautiful you are."

Tears rushed to Genevieve's eyes so quickly that she couldn't blink them away before one trailed down her cheek. She wiped it off with a shaking hand. "She was the beautiful one," Genevieve insisted. "The smart one." The child her parents had really wanted, not the unplanned one that Genevieve had been for her mother. The embarrassment...

"Jenny was beautiful," Sadie agreed. "Inside and out. She was just an angel, and now she is..." Tears trailed down the older woman's face now.

And Genevieve found herself reaching across the space between them to squeeze her hand. "Thank you," she said.

Sadie blinked furiously and asked, "For what?"

"For loving her like she deserved to be loved," Genevieve said. While her life had been cut too short, at least she'd had that: unconditional love.

"Nobody loved her more than Dale did," Sadie said with a wistful smile. "They were so close, so committed and so beautiful together. And they made three beautiful children."

Yes, even though it had been short, Jenny's life had been full. She felt a deep ache. Just as she'd resented Jenny for being the child her mother really wanted and not the mistake, she had probably been jealous of Jenny's happiness, too, because Genevieve had never been as happy.

That resentment was the real reason Genevieve hadn't kept in touch with her. The shame overwhelmed her now, and she began to shake. None of it had been her younger sister's fault.

Sadie turned her hand over and squeezed Genevieve's. "Why didn't you contact me when you moved back to town?" she asked.

That shame overwhelmed Genevieve. "I didn't find out that Jenny died until two months after their funerals." Bradford's new wife had finally and almost gleefully passed on the letter that had been sent to Genevieve's old address. "I'd missed the funerals. I'd missed so much of my sister's life. I came here because I wanted to get to know the boys. To be available to care for them if they needed that."

The room was silent, both Collin and Sadie listening intently. It was finally time to own up to what she'd done. "The CPS investigation… It was my fault."

"You called CPS on them?" Collin asked, his dark eyes hard as he stared at her.

"She didn't call," Sadie said.

Sue was right. The Haven matriarch did know everything. Somehow she'd figured out who the anonymous caller was.

"No, I didn't call. But it was my fault," Genevieve said. "I'd reached out to the person who'd called—"

"To start trouble?" Collin interrupted.

She shook her head. "I just wanted to know how the boys were doing. If they were healthy and healed and safe." She blinked back tears. "I'm so sorry. I certainly didn't mean to cause them any harm. I can see just by watching them with the family how loved they are. That's all I could ever want for them."

"But why didn't you let any of us know who you are?" Sadie asked.

"I didn't know what Jenny had told them about me. She'd had every reason to hate her family for how she was treated."

"Jenny couldn't hate anyone," Sadie said. "Not with that big heart of hers. But she was like me with Jessup, she stopped talking about what was too painful for her."

"So they don't know about me?" Genevieve said. She'd already guessed as much when the little boy hadn't recognized her when he opened the door. She hadn't sent Jenny family pictures because she'd had no family to take pictures of. And because of her law career with a high-profile firm, she hadn't even maintained a social media presence. And truthfully, she just always preferred to keep her private life private.

Sadie shook her head. "No. But we can tell them—"

Genevieve shook her head. "No. Let Taye and Baker decide that. I need to apologize to them, too." Another time; she felt more than naked now. She felt raw, like her skin had been peeled away. She turned her focus to Collin. "I need to apologize to you, too.

When you told me Sadie had referred you, I should have explained right away how she might have known about me. But you didn't say she was your grandma…"

"Still…" Collin began, but he said nothing more. He just moved away from the door, walking farther into the room.

And as he did, Genevieve had a sudden, overwhelming desire to run. She jumped up from the chair and rushed out of the room. Then she ran down the hall and out the door as if someone was chasing her.

But nobody was. Not even that fluffy, feisty little dog. The only thing that chased Genevieve out of Ranch Haven was her own guilt.

SADIE STARED OUT the open door with shock. She hadn't realized the girl would run. And she was too old to chase after her. She left that for Collin to do, but instead he dropped heavily into the chair that Genevieve had so abruptly vacated. "Aren't you going to go after her?" she asked.

"Why?" he asked.

"Aren't you engaged? Your dad called me this morning yelling that you were going to marry a stranger and that it was my fault."

"This *is* your fault," Collin said. "You set me up. You used me as a pawn in one of your schemes."

The man was too smart for her to deny it, so she just nodded. "Yes."

Her affirmation seemed to drain the anger from him and he chuckled. "I was warned…"

"Who?"

"Pretty much everybody who's ever met or heard of you warned me," he said.

"You're exaggerating." It surprised her that he was capable. He always seemed so literal.

"Not much," he said. "You used me to find out more about her, about the threat to the little boys."

"She's no threat." Sadie knew that for certain now. Genevieve's tears had been real and ripped from her. She was suffering so much guilt and regret that Sadie's old heart ached for her. "And I really do believe she could help you get Bailey Ann."

He snorted. "By marrying me? Did you two cook that scheme up together?"

"I hadn't met her until today," Sadie said. And now she regretted that she hadn't reached out sooner—that she hadn't made sure that Jenny's family knew about her death so they would have the chance to attend the funeral, to see the boys and know for themselves that they were okay.

But in the beginning, in those first few months, they hadn't been okay. They'd all been struggling. Baker and Taye had helped the boys, though. They were doing so much better now.

"So you don't really know anything about her then," Collin said.

She knew more than he realized—more than she'd remembered until recently when she'd had Ben check out the lawyer who'd called about the boys, and then she had realized who that lawyer really was. She knew that Jenny wasn't the first daughter her family had disowned; Genevieve had pretty much been the first. And it was clear to see she'd suffered for it and she was still suffering.

"I don't think it's a good idea to get involved with her," Collin said.

"Why not?"

"She obviously has a lot going on—a lot of pain and guilt and whatever—and I don't want to add to her stress or hurt her."

"What about you?" Sadie asked. She figured he was worried about getting hurt, too.

He sighed. "After how she conducted herself when she first got to town, how she didn't reach out directly to you or to the boys, how could I trust her?"

"Is Bailey Ann worth the risk?"

CHAPTER ELEVEN

COLLIN HAD ONLY had a few moments alone with Sadie in her suite before a bunch of his family had rushed in. They might have stormed in sooner if not for the smoke detector he'd heard pealing out along with smoke from the kitchen.

He had no intention of staying for dessert. So he snuck out past everyone firing questions at Sadie and slipped down the hall and out the door. Genevieve's massive SUV was gone. And he felt a flash of concern that she was driving, as upset as she was. Would she be able to see through her tears?

Worried that she might have gone off the road, he drove slowly along the route she would take home. And his heart hammered heavily with dread that he might find her the way Baker had found her sister and his brother, their small SUV twisted and turned over in the ditch after it had skidded off the icy road. He couldn't imagine how Baker had felt. Although he was a paramedic, he hadn't had his rig with him or backup. He'd struggled to keep his family alive while he'd waited for help to arrive.

Collin had felt somewhat like that the last time he'd treated Bailey Ann, when she'd showed up at the hospital so weak and sick. And before that…when they'd waited for a heart for her…

She was his family. And he was hers…

The only family she had. He had to find some way to make that legal. And for that, he needed a lawyer he could trust.

Collin didn't think he could trust Genevieve. He had so much trouble trusting people. His own father had lied to him all his life.

Sometimes he felt like there was even more his dad hadn't shared with him. But he couldn't confront his dad like he wanted to; he wouldn't do anything that might risk his health. Although apparently he already had.

He'd told Dad last night that he might be getting married, and that had upset him enough to call and yell at his mother. Even though Collin hadn't told him who had introduced him to his bride, Dad had somehow known that it was his mother.

Probably because Sadie Haven was so notorious for her meddling. Collin hadn't been exaggerating when he'd told her that a lot of people had warned him about her. His own dad had and his cousins and most of the people he worked with at the hospital.

Sadie has a way of making people do things she wants.

Sadie gets what she wants.

But Collin wondered about that. Yes, she had a way of making things happen, but she'd endured so much loss, too. His dad had been missing from her life for years. Her younger son had died. Then her husband and now her grandson and granddaughter-in-law.

Jenny. That made him think of Genevieve again. Apparently the sisters hadn't seen each other in years. Remembering Genevieve's tears and the misery in her voice, he focused again on the road, making sure that her vehicle hadn't veered off it. But there was no sign of the big SUV, not even in her driveway when he turned into it. Hopefully it was parked in the garage where she'd parked the night before.

Or maybe she'd just kept driving. When he'd talked to her outside her office, she'd made some cryptic comments, as though she might not stick around town. Had she thought Sadie would drive her out?

Or had she thought it would just be too hard for her to stay once everyone knew she was Jenny's sister?

She'd been so upset when she'd talked to Sadie, so apologetic, so broken...

He studied her house, the sprawling ranch with the brick and stone facade. The many windows shone no light. Was she inside? And if she was inside, why was she sitting in the dark?

His heart beat a little faster with concern for her. Needing to know where she was and if she was okay was more important right now than even expressing his anger with her for not being honest with him, as so many other people hadn't been honest with him.

How could he hold a stranger accountable when he had yet to hold his family accountable?

He shut off his car and stepped out, onto her driveway. Instead of following the sidewalk to the front door, he knocked on that side one she'd opened for him yesterday. There was no bell to push, so he knocked again, harder, hoping she would hear it.

If she was in the house…

But was her SUV parked in the three-stall garage, or had she just kept driving—right out of Willow Creek?

He wouldn't blame her if she had.

She had no family here now but her nephews. And who knew if Baker and Taye would even let her see them again…if they believed she'd encouraged that person to call CPS on them?

He could understand if they refused because they wanted to protect children who'd already suffered too much. That was why he wanted Bailey Ann. To protect her.

And because he loved her…

But he might have already lost her. Mrs. Finch was clearly not going to give him a chance to foster if he was on his own. But Bailey Ann wasn't the only reason he was worried about Genevieve leaving. For some reason he just hated the thought of her being so alone…and heartbroken. And he wanted to make sure she was all right.

He knocked one more time, his knuckles chafing a bit from the force of it. And finally the door rattled and opened. She stood before him, her face red and puffy from tears. But her chin was up, her body tense, as if she was bracing herself for an attack.

He stepped inside the house and closed the door. Then he wrapped his arms around her and pulled her trembling body against his. And he held her as she cried.

GENEVIEVE LINGERED IN the half bath off the mudroom as long as she could justify doing, before Collin probably started to worry that she'd slipped out the side door and run away again.

She was too embarrassed to face him. But more than that, after sobbing all over his shirt, she was also unsettled. She'd gone from crying in his arms to…

Feeling something she hadn't felt in a long while. Aware…

Of his warmth, of his long, deceptively muscular body, and of his gentleness and his empathy.

She hadn't felt so cared for, so protected, so seen in…maybe ever. And that was scarier than showing up at Ranch Haven to confront the intimidating Sadie March Haven. Genevieve's intense fear was because she couldn't give her heart to anyone, ever again. It just hurt too much when things ended.

And for her, they always seemed to end. It was more important that she focus on her job, on helping people she could help, on people who needed her help. Her nephews didn't need her; they had the entire Haven family.

And Collin didn't really need her either. But for a moment, while she'd clung to his long, lean body as he'd held her, she'd needed him. And she couldn't let herself feel that way again. Everyone she'd ever needed had wound up rejecting her. It was safer to shut down.

She leaned over the pedestal sink to splash a little more water on her face, trying to bring down the swelling and redness.

Not that she cared what she looked like; her looks had never gotten her the kind of attention and respect that she'd craved. So she'd learned to stop craving it.

She dried off her face with the hand towel, drew in a deep breath and opened the door. She could hear movement in the kitchen. Doors opening. A mug clinking. The whistle of the teakettle she kept on the six-burner gas range. Bemused, she stepped into the kitchen.

Collin didn't notice because he was behind a cupboard door, rooting inside the cabinet.

"What are you doing?" she asked.

He leaned back, closed the door and held up a tin. "I assumed you're a tea drinker."

He was holding one of her herbal collections while the teakettle continued to whistle. She shut off the burner and confirmed, "Yes, I am. If I don't have my cup of chamomile before bed, I can't shut off my mind."

"I thought I was the only one who couldn't do that," he said. "My brothers can go right to sleep, but I just lie there, thinking…" He shook his head a little and focused on her again, staring intently at her. "And speaking of thinking…"

She braced herself, waiting for the anger she'd expected when she'd opened the door to him.

"That you need chamomile tea to sleep is the first personal thing you've freely admitted to me," he said.

Something about him compelled her to tease him, like she had the night before. He just seemed so serious despite Bailey Ann thinking he was funny with his dad jokes. "Remember, I'm not charging you." She attempted a smile. "So everything I've said has been free."

"When will you start charging me?" he asked.

She narrowed her eyes to study his face now. His was not red and puffy; his was perfect. The man really was unreasonably good-looking. "What do you mean?" she asked. "I thought you came here to yell at me, not for legal advice."

"You thought I was going to yell and yet you opened the door anyway?" he asked.

"I already ran away once." And she regretted how she'd left the ranch, without even saying good-bye to her nephews. What if she never got to see them again?

And they'd been so sweet to her. Had they been drawn to her because she sounded like Jenny? It had almost hurt to hear that she and Jenny had shared the same voice. It was the only thing they'd had in common. They'd been so different, much more than six years and different fathers separating them.

Pride and resentment had also held Genevieve back from developing a real relationship with her sister. And now she would never have the chance.

Tears began to pool in her eyes again, and before she could blink them back, Collin touched her shoulder. "Hey," he murmured.

His touch, and that sympathy in his deep

voice, jolted her. She shook her head. "I'm fine."

"Don't lie to me," Collin said, and he looked pained. "Please, don't lie to me."

"I didn't lie to you," she said.

"A lie of omission is still a lie to me," he said. "My dad never telling us that we're really Havens, that he's Sadie Haven's kid, that we had an uncle and cousins and grandparents…" His voice trailed off, gruff with what sounded like tears of his own. Or maybe it was just frustration.

She reached out to comfort him now and closed her arms around him. And he tensed within her embrace. She dropped her arms, and he stepped back.

"I just want openness and honesty from now on," he said. "No more lies, secrets… whatever…"

"I want to help Bailey Ann," she said. "That's the truth."

"Why?"

She released a shaky sigh then and forced back down the sobs that threatened to escape with it. "It's for selfish reasons," she admitted. "But that doesn't mean I can't do some good. I want to help that little girl because I didn't help Jenny."

"She died because of that crash," he said. "Baker was first on the scene, and there was nothing he could do. There's nothing you could have done either."

"I'm not talking about when she died," she said. "I'm talking about when our parents cut her off—when she chose to marry Dale. I could have stepped in, tried to change things, but I didn't. I was so caught up in my own life. In college and law school…and she kept reaching out but I never responded. Once I left here, I never looked back."

"What could you have done?" he asked. "Could you have gotten your parents to change their minds?"

She snorted. "No. Jenny's dad was my stepdad. He barely acknowledged me. And Mother never listened. But *I* could have been there for her. And I wasn't. I failed Jenny."

He studied her intently.

"That's why you came to Willow Creek. Why you bought this house and got your foster license here," he said. "You wanted the boys."

"I wanted to be ready," she corrected. "I

didn't know what the situation was, just that my sister and her husband were dead. That's why I started asking around and preparing…" She released a shaky sigh. "And I should have just gone straight to the ranch and explained myself. That I thought her kids had been orphaned, and I know how hard it can be to get kids out of the foster care system. I thought if I had the job and the house and the license, I could take them if they needed me." And in some way she'd wanted them to need her; she'd wanted to be needed. "That's why I had…a friend of my mother's…check on them for me…"

"Nurse Sue?" he asked.

Maybe he was a bit like his grandmother. All-knowing…

"I should have just reached out myself," she said. "But I didn't know how the Havens felt about me, about my family, if they hated me for how we treated Jenny. And I couldn't face that because…"

"You hated yourself," he said.

He was definitely a lot like his grandmother.

She cleared her throat. "Collin, you have to believe me. I had no idea how loved they are. I didn't want to make trouble."

He nodded, still studying her. Did he believe her? "You had a foster license in DC, you said," he pointed out. "Why?"

She sighed. "That was for other reasons. Old reasons that don't matter anymore. It has nothing to do with Jenny. Or the situation you and Bailey Ann are in. But if I can help you two… I want to be there for Bailey Ann. I know it won't make it up to Jenny, but maybe I'll feel like less of the horrible person I feel like I am now."

"So much so that you asked me to marry you," he reminded her.

And heat rushed to her face. "That was for Bailey Ann."

"I know. And that's why I showed up at your office this afternoon. I want to accept your proposal," he said.

She sucked in a breath, shocked that he would still consider it. "Even now?"

"As long as I know all there is to know about you," he said. "I can't handle any more surprises."

"But this won't be a real marriage." She needed to make that clear, for her sake more than his. She didn't expect him to fall for her. And she couldn't fall for him.

He nodded. "I know this is for Bailey Ann. But since she's going to be around you, I have to know that I can trust you with her."

After what had happened with the little girl's previous foster family, she understood. "Okay. You are going to have to help me with her medical stuff," she warned him. "And as for me…" She sighed. "I graduated high school early, intent on getting into college and law school, on becoming someone that my parents would be proud of, and I met my husband in law school. He came from a wealthy, prominent family that was all about carrying on their blue blood heritage. Of course we waited to start a family, making sure we did the travel, established our careers, bought our big house and joined all the country clubs. Maybe we waited too long."

"You're only in your thirties," he said.

She shrugged. "I struggled to conceive… even with IVF. Every round failed. Except for…" Her voice cracked, the pain still fresh despite the few years that had passed. "A couple of times I got pregnant but miscarried."

"I'm sorry," he said. "That's why you got the foster license."

"I know there are a lot of kids out there

who need homes." And she had needed a child. "I wanted to foster and adopt. My ex-husband wanted to carry on his lineage. After the IVF failed with us, he didn't even want to try using a surrogate. Now he has a new wife and toddler and another on the way."

A big, loving family in their old house. He'd kept that. He'd kept everything of the life they'd built together but her. Just like her parents had done with Jenny, he had easily replaced her with someone better, with some-one who'd given him what he'd wanted.

At least he'd given Genevieve a generous cash settlement for her half of that old life. And that settlement had helped her set up here in Willow Creek.

She released a shaky, self-deprecating chuckle. "Was that more than you wanted to know?" she asked.

He nodded.

And she tensed.

"Because now I want to hurt your ex," he said. "And I'm not usually a violent man."

"I wanted to hurt him, too," she admitted. But she'd realized that she couldn't hurt some-one who didn't care about her.

That was why she couldn't let herself care

about anyone, especially not her next husband. Because that was the only way she could protect herself from getting hurt again.

LEM DIDN'T LIKE it when Sadie got upset. The last big upset she'd had was over Jessup, and her heart had literally stopped. He hadn't been there for her then. But he was here now, sitting beside her in her suite as the conversations finally wrapped up with her family. Once he would have felt like he was intruding, but now her family was going to be his, too.

Baker and Taye were the last to leave Sadie's suite, closing the door behind them. She'd assured them that Genevieve was not a threat to their plan to adopt the boys, but Lem wasn't as convinced as she was.

He waited until the door closed to ask, "Are you sure you can trust her?"

"Oh, yes," Sadie with that certainty and assurance that used to infuriate him. Her confidence that she always knew what she was doing had made him defensive, had made him feel as if he didn't know what he was doing.

Now it reassured him because of all the times she'd been proven right. But this time...

"You don't know her," he pointed out. "You don't know anything about her."

"She's Jenny's sister."

"Her *sister*," he said, and he reached across their chairs to stroke the back of her hand. "She's not Jenny." He knew how much she'd loved her first granddaughter-in-law. How much she missed her. Jenny Miller Haven had been a very special young woman.

"She reminds me of her, though," Sadie said.

"Her voice," he agreed. He'd noticed it, too. "But just because she sounds like her, doesn't mean that they have anything else in common. From what I remember, they weren't even raised together. Genevieve's grandparents raised her while their daughter finished high school and college."

"Exactly," Sadie said. "That's how I know I'm right about her."

He couldn't follow her line of reasoning, but maybe that was because his head was beginning to pound. Probably from the smoke in the air—the bananas Foster hadn't gone off as planned. Fortunately Taye had had a kiddie version of the treat that hadn't caught fire.

"Good thing she was gone," Baker had bitterly remarked to him. "Or she might report us again."

"I would still be careful," Lem advised Sadie now.

Her cell vibrated. He wasn't surprised. Maybe the Cassidys who hadn't been present had heard about who she'd referred Collin to... The enemy.

"Hello, Collin," she greeted her caller. As she listened to him, a grin spread across her face, crinkling the skin around her dark eyes. "That's great news," she said. "Don't worry about the logistics. Ben and I will help you with those." She disconnected the call and turned toward Lem to announce, "Collin and Genevieve are getting married."

And he nearly choked on his saliva. Feisty, sleeping on his lap, growled softly, probably annoyed at being startled. "Are you serious?" he asked.

She nodded.

"This is the fastest one of your match making schemes has worked yet," he said.

But her grin slid away and she sighed. "It hasn't worked."

"But they're getting married," he said.

"But they're not in love."

And he knew that was really what Sadie wanted for her grandkids: love. The kind of love she and Jake had shared. The kind of love she and Lem shared now.

He reached over and touched her hand again. "It took us a while to get there," he said. "But we did."

"Eighty years," she said with a slight chuckle.

"Hopefully they're not as stubborn as we are," he said.

She sighed again. "I don't know. He's my grandson. And Genevieve's been through a lot. She may not be open to love again."

"She was good with her nephews," Lem said.

The little boys hadn't taken to her like they had just because of her voice. She had been very sweet with them and had given them her undivided attention.

"Loving kids is easier than loving a significant other," Sadie said. "Kids don't hurt us like a lover can."

That was true.

It had taken a lot of courage on his part to open up his heart again after losing Mary. But part of his heart had probably always belonged to Sadie March.

CHAPTER TWELVE

A COUPLE OF days had passed since that night at Ranch Haven, and Collin had been waiting for the proverbial other shoe to drop. That night, he'd called Sadie and told her about his impending nuptials, and she'd mentioned getting Ben onboard. Though he didn't know for sure why just the mayor...

He'd expected her to also let everyone else know. And he'd expected his dad and brothers and even Darlene, who'd helped raise them after their mom died, to talk to him about it. To try to talk him out of marrying a stranger...

But he'd heard nothing about it. Either Sadie hadn't told them or she had and had somehow convinced them that he was doing the right thing. He wasn't as sure about that.

He wasn't even sure if it would work. But he parked his car outside Genevieve's office for the meeting she had called, the meeting to find out if their getting married would even make a difference in his quest to foster and adopt Bailey Ann.

He'd arrived early, hoping to spend some extra time talking to her. He hadn't seen her since that night. He hadn't even talked to her on the phone; she'd just texted him about the meeting today.

She must have been watching for him because she met him at the door.

"Good. You're here," she said, and she reached out and tugged on his sleeve, pulling him along behind her to her office.

The white-haired receptionist didn't glance up as they passed her desk. Either she was preoccupied or totally uninterested.

"I'm glad you wore your white coat. That will look better to the social worker."

"Mrs. Finch sees me in this all the time," he reminded her. That was the meeting she'd set up, with the social worker.

"Yes, but you wearing the coat is a visual reminder for her that you have the medical expertise to deal with Bailey Ann's heart condition."

"She knows that."

"But she still hasn't considered you for adopting or even fostering her."

"Because I don't have a house of my own or the day care provider with medical care experience."

"I do."

"You do?" he asked with surprise. "I mean. I know about the house." And it was an impressive house with four bedrooms and three and a half baths on the main level with a big backyard. "But you have medical day care?"

"I have Nurse Sue."

He groaned. "She's the one who called CPS."

"Yes, but as well as being an ER nurse, she's also been a neonatal and pediatric nurse, and she's agreed to help us," Genevieve confirmed.

"Why?"

"She was a friend of my mom's," she said. "And for some reason, she wants to think she still is."

"But she isn't?"

"My mom doesn't have friends," Genevieve said. "She only has my stepdad."

Collin couldn't say much. As Colton had pointed out, he was probably his only friend. Collin had always been too busy with studying and work to sustain any relationships—friendship or romantic.

"Maybe the apple doesn't fall far from the tree," she said, "because I didn't make time for any friendships of my own. I didn't even make time for my sister." Her slender shoulders drooped beneath the heavy weight of guilt she seemed so determined to keep carrying.

"I never met Jenny," he said. "But from what I've heard about her, she was a very sweet person."

Genevieve blinked furiously, as if fighting back tears. "She was."

"Then I don't think she would want you to keep beating yourself up about the past."

Genevieve heaved a heavy sigh as she dropped into the chair behind her desk. "No, she wouldn't."

Instead of taking a seat in one of those leather chairs in front of her desk, Collin sat on the edge of the mahogany on the corner closest to her. Since holding her those couple of times a few nights ago, he was so drawn to her. He wanted to be close to her and touch her again and see if he reacted the way he had that night, with that little zip of awareness that had felt like electricity zapping him back to life. He hadn't realized he'd been dead to the world, so very focused on everything but himself.

"So stop," he said, but he wasn't talking just to her about her guilt but to himself about this attraction. He couldn't afford the distraction now. No. Bailey Ann couldn't afford it; she couldn't be separated from him, for her sake as much as his. She didn't want to go to Sheridan any more than he wanted to let her go.

Genevieve nodded so emphatically that a lock of hair fell across her face. Without thinking, he reached out and brushed it off her cheek. She was so beautiful. But she looked exhausted, too, with dark circles beneath her eyes.

"Are you sure you want to do this?" he asked.

"Stop beating myself up about the past?" she asked.

His lips twitched into a slight smile at her weak attempt at humor. "I meant marry me."

"I already asked you," she said, and she was smiling, too.

His heart did a little fluttery thing it had

never done before. Maybe the stress was getting to him. "But are you sure?"

She glanced at the delicate gold wristwatch she wore. "We'll know in just a few minutes if it will make a difference to Mrs. Finch."

If it didn't, there was no reason for them to marry. Genevieve had been smart to request this meeting first.

This was all about Bailey Ann. Usually Collin wouldn't have had to remind himself of that, but…with his grandmother's penchant for matchmaking he was a little uneasy.

"How do we convince her that this makes a difference?" Collin asked. "Do we act like the engagement is real and we're madly in love?" And why did the prospect of pretending to adore her have that little fluttery thing going on with his heart again? If that kept up, he might need an EKG. Find out if it was an actual arrhythmia. Since Sadie had one, maybe it ran in the family…

Or maybe it was just stress, the same stress that must have been keeping Genevieve awake at night.

"I thought you were a doctor, not a thespian," she teased him. "A cardiologist, at that.

You know how the heart works. So how do you pretend that you've given yours to me?"

He pressed his hand against his chest. "I would act like it beats faster and harder every time I'm near you…" But he wouldn't necessarily be acting.

She snorted. "I don't think you're that good an actor, Dr. Cassidy, so we should probably just stick with our motto of being open and honest."

"With each other," he clarified. "I think it would be wiser to make Mrs. Finch think that we're actually marrying for the right reasons."

She snorted again. "What are those?"

He held up his hands then. "I don't know…" But he would have assumed love. "You're the one who was married before."

She sighed. "Yes, but I think I married him for the wrong reason," she said. "No. He married me for the wrong reason."

"So what is the right reason?" he asked.

"Bailey Ann."

He knew why she was doing it, that she was somehow hoping that helping Bailey Ann would alleviate some of the guilt she felt over her sister, brother-in-law and nephews. That helping Bailey Ann might somehow make up for how she felt she'd failed her family. "I appreciate your sacrifice."

"Marrying a handsome, successful doctor is not a sacrifice," Genevieve said with a flirty grin.

And his heart definitely had an arrhythmia, skipping at least one beat before hurrying up the ones that followed like an uncoordinated kid trying to play hopscotch. He sucked in a breath, leaning toward her, drawn to her beauty. Her eyes fluttered closed as she leaned in, too. He felt the imminent kiss, hanging in the air between them, and—

A throat cleared behind him, startling him. Mrs. Finch. He realized Genevieve must have noticed her and had been acting for her benefit.

But he had a little flicker of concern over how easily she'd fooled him into thinking that she was really flirting, that she was really attracted to him. He would have to keep reminding himself that she was only doing this for Bailey Ann and for her sister.

FOR ONCE, Hilda had actually shown one of Genevieve's appointments back to her office. Of course she hadn't bothered announcing it, but fortunately Genevieve's ears were sharp and she'd heard them approaching.

Collin, on the other hand, had clearly been taken by surprise, nearly falling off the desk as he whirled toward the doorway. He seemed guilty, like they'd been caught doing something they shouldn't have been. But if they really were engaged, they should flirt. And more…

He'd been about to kiss her.

Had she wanted him to?

Her stomach tightened with nerves and frustration as she realized she had. She'd really wanted that kiss. She should have been glad that they'd been interrupted before that had happened, before she let herself start thinking this engagement was real. That the marriage, if they went through with it, would be real.

"Mrs. Finch is here," Hilda said, and she was smiling, which was probably the first time she had smiled at Genevieve. Despite the couple of months Genevieve had been with the law practice, the receptionist hadn't warmed up to her.

"Thank you, Hilda," Genevieve said with a smile of her own as she stood up. "And thank you for finding time to meet with us, Mrs. Finch. I'm sure you're very busy."

Hilda hesitated a moment before turning to walk out. But she closed the door behind herself so it wasn't as if she'd been nosy about the meeting. It was almost as if she'd known what it was about...

Had Sadie spoken to her? Genevieve knew Collin had called his grandmother and confirmed their plan; he'd been with her, in her kitchen, when he'd called Ranch Haven.

Genevieve needed to call there herself, not for Sadie, but for Baker and Taye, to apologize and assure them herself that she didn't intend to fight the adoption.

"I am quite busy, as Dr. Cassidy knows," Mrs. Finch replied. "So I don't know why he's engaged a lawyer to talk to me, but I assume it's about Bailey Ann."

"It is," Collin said.

"But I'm not here as a lawyer," Genevieve added. "Collin isn't a client. He's my fiancé."

Mrs. Finch's brow furrowed. "You didn't mention that when you asked me about fostering Bailey Ann."

"I didn't want to speak for Genevieve," he said.

And that was probably quite open and honest of him. A smile twitched her lips. "Collin wanted to make sure that I was onboard for a child with special needs. I'm already a certified foster parent."

"I'm aware," Mrs. Finch said. She must have checked out Genevieve after she'd called her to meet. "But you haven't accepted any placements yet. We can't authorize your first one being a child with complex medical needs. You'd need more experience first."

Genevieve had expected this. "I'm marrying someone who knows everything about Bailey Ann's medical history and her current condition as well as her future needs," she pointed out, and she stepped closer to Collin.

He slid his arm around her waist, showing a united front. A unit. A couple.

She didn't know if she'd ever really felt like half of a whole before. Her life and Bradford's had been so separate, so different.

"You're both busy professionals," Mrs. Finch said. "So who will be with Bailey Ann when you're working?"

"I have hired a nurse who will be with Bailey Ann when Collin and I are both at work." She was going to insist that Sue accept payment. "But I have a very flexible schedule and can do most of my work from home."

Mrs. Finch continued to study them with skepticism. "When will you be married and cohabitating?"

"As soon as we can get the license," Collin answered.

"This all seems very sudden," the social worker remarked. "How long have you been engaged?" And her dark eyes narrowed as she stared at Genevieve's bare hands.

Collin tensed and glanced down at Genevieve.

"The engagement is recent," she answered honestly. "But our history is long. My sister was married to his cousin. Jenny and Dale Haven."

The older woman gasped and shook her head. "I'm so sorry. Of course everyone in town knows about that tragedy." She glanced at Collin then. "I didn't realize you're related to the Havens."

He nodded. "Sadie is my grandmother." And instead of sounding exasperated, he actually sounded a bit proud.

Genevieve glanced up at him with a smile. "I'm sure your grandmother would be happy to talk to Mrs. Finch as well." Why not use the old woman's intimidating reputation?

Mrs. Finch shook her head. "I need to check

with my supervisor and see if this is something he would even consider since we've already found a suitable placement for her."

It was clear that she didn't want to consider it, consider them. Collin must have picked up on that as well because his shoulders sagged as if with defeat while Genevieve bristled with indignation.

"That placement is only temporary," Genevieve reminded her. "We're moving up our wedding date, so that we can provide a safe and secure and permanent home for Bailey Ann."

Mrs. Finch narrowed her dark eyes, clearly suspicious of their relationship.

"We can also petition the court for immediate custody of Bailey Ann," Genevieve said. "I don't believe any family court judge would choose to put this vulnerable child into a home with strangers over a home with the one constant she's had in her life. Collin. If you ask Bailey Ann, I'm sure she'll tell you what she'd prefer."

"I'll do that," Mrs. Finch said. "We will also arrange for an inspection of your house, and we'll need your marriage license on file."

"That won't be a problem," Genevieve said. "As Collin already told you, we're getting married as soon as possible."

Before Collin could confirm, his beeper rang out. "I'm on call," he said. "I need to get back to the hospital." He sounded reluctant.

"Go ahead, dear," she said. "I think I can handle the rest of the meeting." And she rose up on tiptoe to press her mouth against his cheek in a soft kiss. He had a little bit of stubble, which tickled and made her lips tingle. Or maybe that was just the contact with him…

Collin glanced down at her once, his eyes dark and soulful as his arm tightened around her. Then he released her, almost as reluctantly as he'd sounded about heading back to the hospital.

"You go," she assured him. "I'm sure you're needed."

Bailey Ann needed them both. They had to pull this off for her.

But with the way Mrs. Finch studied them, with all that skepticism, Genevieve wasn't sure if they had fooled her or they should have even tried.

It was too late to back out now.

COLTON DIDN'T KNOW what was going on with his twin, just that Dad was worried about him. He knew that Collin was stressed over Bailey Ann, so that was probably it. And Colton didn't want to add to his stress but he also needed to share what he knew or at least suspected about Cash. And so, even though his double duty shift as a Willow Creek firefighter and paramedic had ended, he came back to the hospital. It was the one place he knew he could always find Collin. And usually the woman Colton loved, Dr. Livvy Lemmon, too.

It was because of her that he was here; he'd made a promise to her that he would stop shouldering the weight of this secret on his own. That he would share it with someone besides her; while she was happy he'd told her, she was also worried about him and didn't think he should try to figure out what to do without input from someone else. He couldn't tell Marsh or his dad.

He wasn't sure Collin was the best option either. The man was usually so black-and-white, so by the book. But if their dad was right, and Collin was considering marrying a woman he'd just met in order to foster Bailey Ann, then he was capable of stepping into a gray area.

Colton hoped Dad was wrong about that.

But the minute Colton stepped into his

office, Collin dropped his cell phone and grinned. "I was just going to call you."

He sounded upbeat, but there was no spark in his dark eyes. His hands, still pink from his burns, shook a little as he clicked off the cell and dropped it back onto his desk. He was standing, too, instead of sitting in the chair behind it…like he was all nervous energy.

That was sometimes how Collin was— always working so hard, never shutting off his mind or his drive. But there was something else to it tonight…something that had Colton, for once, feeling what his twin was feeling. That nervous energy gripped him, and he reached into his pocket for the lighter, wrapping his hand around it.

Then, almost impulsively, he pulled it out and dropped it onto Collin's desk, next to his cell phone. Collin stared down at it, and all the color drained from his face. His hand shook even more as he reached for and picked up the smoke-stained pewter lighter. With the finger of his other hand, he traced the letters. The two *C*s that had been engraved in the metal so many years ago.

He'd been there with Colton, standing in their oldest brother's doorway, watching him pack his duffel bag to leave. They'd both seen him toss that lighter into the bag. "Where did you get this?"

"In the ashes of our family home," Colton replied.

And Collin sucked in a breath. "Cash was there? You think…" He swallowed hard as if he was choking on the accusation.

An accusation Colton didn't want to make either. He shrugged. "I don't know. And I don't know what to do with it."

"Tell Marsh," Collin urged him, and he dropped the lighter as if it had burned him. "Give it to him."

"He'll have to make it part of the record. And my boss—my former boss—already ruled the fire was probably just a result of the house needing major updating and repairs…" Repairs they hadn't been able to afford because of all of Dad's medical bills. "But the insurance adjuster is still investigating."

"And you're worried Dad might get blamed for this? It's even more of a reason to give that lighter to Marsh."

"He can't investigate the fire anyhow. He's no longer working for Moss Valley, and we're his family. If someone else gets involved, Dad will find out."

Collin sucked in a breath and dropped heavily into his chair. "Oh…"

"I'm not the doctor but I don't think that would be good for him—to worry about Cash any more than he already does."

Collin nodded. "You're right."

"So what do we do?" Colton asked the question that had haunted him for weeks.

"I don't know," Collin said.

And now Colton dropped into one of the chairs in front of Collin's desk. He was used to his smart twin having all the answers.

"I almost wish you hadn't told me," Collin murmured.

"You wanted to know what's been bothering me, and you guessed it had to do with Cash," Colton reminded him. He pointed at the lighter. "That's it."

"That's why you've been looking for Cash, bothering Becca…"

Colton nodded. "Yup. Were you calling me about that or…"

Collin shook his head. "I was calling to ask you to be my best man."

Colton released a shaky sigh and leaned back

in his chair. "So you're really going to do it? You're going to marry a stranger?"

"She's not a stranger anymore."

"Do you love her?" Colton asked. Because he knew how quickly someone could fall. He'd fallen that quickly for Livvy Lemmon, quicker than he'd even realized.

Collin shook his head. "It's not about love. It's about Bailey Ann."

"Of course it is," Colton said. "Everything you do is for someone else."

"What?"

"You became a doctor because you were trying to save our parents. When Mom was gone and Dad's heart started failing, you switched from renal failure to cardiology. *Everything* you do is for someone else. When are you going to start doing something just for you, Collin?"

"This is," his twin vehemently insisted. "I want Bailey Ann. I don't want to lose her."

That much was true. Colton could see that his brother loved that little girl. He loved her so much that he was willing to sacrifice his own happiness for her. And Colton had a horrible feeling that was exactly what he was doing, that this marriage of convenience was not going to make him happy at all.

CHAPTER THIRTEEN

COLLIN FELT LIKE he'd signed Bailey Ann out of the hospital to play hooky from school. But school wasn't starting for a couple more weeks yet, and medically she was doing so well now. The outing was going to be good for her.

Because, as he'd told his twin, Bailey Ann was his whole reason for doing what he was doing today: getting married. At the ranch…

Sadie had insisted on hosting their wedding at Ranch Haven. He knew she enjoyed getting all of her family out here, but he suspected she also wanted Genevieve here. To prove to her that her nephews were happy and healthy? To make sure that she wouldn't try to take them away from Baker and Taye? From the ranch?

She'd obtained her foster license and bought the house and vehicle specifically for those boys. For the sister she felt she'd abandoned. But now that she knew they were happy and loved, she had no intention of jeopardizing that for them. He believed that; he hoped the rest of his family did as well.

And he hoped that they appreciated what she was doing for him as much as he did. After parking on that circular drive, right in front of the steps leading up to the wraparound porch, he glanced across his console at Bailey Ann.

Her dark eyes were wide with shock. "It's sooooo big," she murmured in awe.

"Yes, it is," he said. Much bigger and nicer than the house where he and his brothers had grown up. He still struggled with his dad's decision to keep their Haven heritage secret. But he also understood how sick his dad had been and how he hadn't wanted his mother to suffer with him like she had when he'd been growing up. Worse yet, he hadn't wanted to reconnect with her just as he was dying.

And there'd been so many years when it had looked like he wouldn't make it…

That panic struck Collin's heart as it always did when he thought of how it had been growing up like that, with that constant fear and uncertainty. He didn't want that for Bailey Ann. He wanted to make sure she was safe and secure with him as her dad instead of just her doctor.

"You ready?" he asked her. Because he was…except for one thing…

He and Genevieve had gotten the marriage license a few days ago, but they'd both been so busy that they hadn't really had time to talk. He hadn't had time to tell her about what Colton had shared with him about that lighter and the possibility that Cash might have had something to do with the fire that had destroyed his family home. And they'd promised to always be open and honest with each other…

But when they'd applied for the marriage license, he'd been more focused on their marriage and on making sure she drew up a prenuptial agreement protecting her assets. Making sure that she felt safe with their agreement.

Colton's truck was here, despite his misgivings about this situation, and so was Genevieve's SUV. She'd bought a dress for Bailey Ann and had texted him to bring the little girl to Sadie's suite when they arrived. The seven-year-old was the reason for the marriage, so of course they wanted her to be their flower girl.

"I'm ready for the wedding," she said with a big smile. "For you to marry Genevieve and become my mommy and daddy."

His stomach flipped a little with concern. "Remember that Genevieve is just helping us out because we're friends. And she wants to make sure that you are taken care of the best way possible." That was how he'd explained it to her. That he had to marry Genevieve so that Mrs. Finch would let Bailey Ann stay with them.

"I know," she said. The little girl smiled at him with that look Sadie sometimes had, like she knew something no one else did.

"Let's go inside and find Genevieve," he said.

Bailey Ann quickly unclasped the belt from her booster seat and reached for the car door handle. She wasn't able to open the door on her own, though. It was too heavy for her, or she was still a little weak from her last ordeal.

He rushed around the front of his car and helped her out. When he would have picked her up, she shook her head. "I'm too old to carry," she said. She glanced shyly up the steps of the porch where three boys stood, all of them in jeans, Western shirts and white cowboy hats.

Caleb, the most outgoing of them, greeted her first. "Hi! Who are you?"

"I'm Bailey Ann," she said, and she hurried up the steps, panting just a bit from the exertion as she joined them on the porch.

"I'm Caleb, this is Ian—my best friend and cousin—and this is Miller."

Miller was seven, like Bailey Ann, so Collin had hoped they would bond. Bailey Ann needed friends her own age, but Miller just gave her a cool nod. Collin knew the kid had been struggling since his parents died, but he was doing better now. Though he'd had no problem with Genevieve, it might take him a little longer to warm up to another new relative.

Or at least Collin hoped Bailey Ann would become a new relative—that he would foster her with Genevieve and then he would be able to file for adoption of her, too.

The screen door flew open and a pudgy little boy toddled out onto the porch. He held up his hands to Bailey Ann as if he wanted her to pick him up.

"Hi, little one," she said, gushing with excitement, and she reached out as if she intended to pick him up.

Worried that the child was too heavy for her, Collin picked him up instead. Little Jake, as if to steady himself, reached for his tie.

"Watch out. He'll choke you," Ben warned as he joined them on the porch. "Trust me."

Collin wasn't sure he should; Ben seemed as much their grandmother's partner in crime as Lem Lemmon did, maybe more so. Although sometimes that was handy to have on your side. "You helped push our marriage license through," Collin said. "Thank you."

Ben shook his head. "Grandma thinks I have more power than I do." He was the mayor. "There was no reason to push it. We had plenty of time since she insisted on this big shindig at the ranch. You okay with that?"

Collin glanced down at Bailey Ann, who was smiling up at the little boy and making faces at him. She looked so happy. "Yes."

"What about your bride?" Ben asked. "She seemed a little nervous when she showed up a few minutes ago."

"That might not have anything to do with the wedding," Collin reminded him. She might still be worried about her place in the family; or, like him, she might be wondering if they were doing all of this for nothing, if Mrs. Finch refused to give them a chance. Maybe that was the reason for Bailey Ann's knowing look—because Genevieve had talked to her, too, about how they were already like family because her sister had been married to Collin's cousin. And that the wedding was just going to make it official so they could become her foster family. They'd wanted to be honest with her but not build up her hopes too much in case Mrs. Finch didn't approve them for the long term.

Ben reached out for Little Jake. "I'll take him. You take the flower girl to get ready."

"You're a flower girl?" Caleb asked.

Bailey Ann eagerly nodded.

"She's the reason we picked the flowers from the garden this morning," Miller reminded his younger relatives.

"It was fun ripping the petals off them!" Caleb exclaimed.

Bailey Ann's dark eyes widened with surprise. "Did you hurt them?"

Miller snorted. "Flowers don't feel anything."

"They're alive," the little girl pointed out.

Miller's hat slid lower as his forehead wrinkled with confusion.

Chuckling now, Collin took her hand and led her into the house. "We need to see Genevieve," he told her, and they knocked on the door.

"If that's Collin, you can't come in." That was Darlene's voice drifting through the door. "It's bad luck for the groom to see the bride before the wedding." She sounded almost desperate about it. Had she seen her husband before the wedding?

Darlene was Collin's aunt, though her identity had been another of the secrets he'd learned later in his life. He and his brothers had believed she was their mother's best friend. After his mother died, Darlene had lived with his family, helping care for them and their father. It turned out she'd been married to Jessup's brother, the one who had died in a ranch accident. Darlene had blamed herself for his death and decided to make amends to Sadie for costing her a son. So she'd set out to find the long lost Jessup and bring him home. But when she'd seen how sick Jessup was, she'd stayed and helped them instead, under the incorrect assumption that her own family hated her.

They hadn't. But Collin didn't know what he and his family would have done without her. He and Marsh probably wouldn't have been able to go off to college, for one thing.

"Darlene," he called back to her. "It's okay. I have Bailey Ann—"

The door opened but only enough to show Darlene, whose slight body still managed to block most of the room from his view. "Hi," she said to the little girl. "I'm so happy to meet you. I'm Aunt Darlene."

She was so much more than an aunt to him. "Or you can call her Grandma, like the boys do," Collin said. "She helped raise me and my brothers, so she's like my mom."

Tears filled Darlene's hazel eyes as she turned to him with surprise. Had she never realized how he felt about her? How they all felt about her?

He felt a pang of regret for not saying that sooner. For not thanking her more for all that she'd done for them. "She's a very special lady," Collin said.

Darlene stepped out into the hall. "Go inside, sweetheart. Miss Genevieve bought a beautiful dress for you." The little girl squeezed through the opening before Darlene pulled the door shut behind her. Then she hugged Collin.

He hugged her back tightly. "Thank you so much, Darlene. I don't think any of us would have survived without you."

She smiled but shook her head. "You're all so strong and smart. You didn't need me as much as I needed you."

That made him think of Genevieve. He knew she was doing this for him and Bailey Ann as a way to let go of her guilt over her sister. Darlene's story wasn't so different, and look how well that had turned out.

"I love you," Darlene told him. "But I'm not letting you in there to see her before this wedding."

"But I just need to talk to her for a moment. There's something I have to tell her."

"The wedding is starting soon," Darlene said. "It's going to have to wait."

With all the people around, it probably wasn't the best time to share such a major secret. Someone else might overhear—someone like Marsh, who would feel compelled to do something about it.

Then he heard Bailey Ann squealing with excitement from inside the suite. She was what was important right now. She was the only reason he probably ever would have agreed to get married. He'd never been able to make a relationship last beyond a few dates. He didn't have the time to give a girlfriend the attention she deserved; he certainly didn't have enough to give a wife.

But this wasn't a real relationship. It was just a marriage of convenience.

"THIS ISN'T REAL," Genevieve wanted to say. But she kept the words inside for Bailey Ann's sake. Not just because she was in the suite with her now, but because she knew Mrs. Finch would probably interview their family and friends about their union in order to make sure that their home would be secure for Bailey Ann.

People didn't necessarily have to marry for love, though. She doubted Bradford had really married her for love, or he wouldn't have divorced her when she'd been unable to give him the child he'd wanted. She would have been enough for him if he'd really loved her.

Although there certainly was love present. Collin and Bailey Ann loved each other, and Genevieve was already falling for her, too.

The girl twirled around in the dress Genevieve had bought. "Thank you for helping me pick that out," she told Becca Calder. She'd run into the Realtor in the boutique where she'd been trying to figure out Bailey Ann's size. "And thank you for coming here with me today."

Worried that everyone at the ranch might be hostile toward her, she'd wanted at least one friendly face with her. She and Becca had hung out a few times since she'd helped Genevieve find her house. The Realtor had a ranch and had even taught Genevieve how to ride.

"I wish your daughter could have come as well," Genevieve said. Bailey Ann needed friends her own age; she seemed so alone at the hospital. She was thrilled that Mrs. Finch had given her permission for Bailey Ann to join them today.

"She's…with a friend today," Becca said.

Rumor had it that her husband had divorced her before her daughter Hope was born. Genevieve had no idea what their custody arrangement was or if they even had one. Would Collin share custody with her if they were allowed to adopt Bailey Ann?

"But we'll get them together soon. How about you? Are you ready for this?"

No. And she had a feeling that Collin might have been having doubts, too. Was that why he'd wanted to talk to her? To call it off?

But he wouldn't have let Bailey Ann in the room, wouldn't have let her get dressed, only to disappoint her. He loved the little girl too much to call off this wedding.

The suite was filled with women. Ones she'd met like Jake's wife, Katie. There was Emily, who was the schoolteacher engaged to the mayor, and Taye. It was Taye that she approached after Becca. The tall woman had a smear of frosting on her cheek. The other women had been gushing over all the food she'd prepared, including some pastries sitting on a tray in the suite.

"Thank you so much for all you've done," Genevieve told her.

"Miller helped with the cooking and baking," Taye replied with a small smile.

"I'm really sorry," Genevieve said.

"That he cooked?" Taye asked with a slight laugh. "He's getting better than I am. And Juliet, Melanie's mom, is a great cook, too. Everyone pitched in to help."

"I'm not talking about the food," Genevieve said. "Though I am grateful for that as well. I'm also grateful for how you've taken care of the boys. It's very clear how much all of you love them and how much they love all of you. And I'm very sorry that I did something that scared you into thinking that love was in danger."

"*You* didn't," Taye said, and her smile reached her dark blue eyes now, warming them. "Sadie told us exactly what happened."

Genevieve smiled, too, as she followed Taye's glance across the sitting room to the older woman who'd squatted down to Bailey Ann's eye level to talk to the little girl. "Sadie probably knows more than I do about that."

Taye chuckled. "Sadie knows more than everybody does about everything."

"I still feel responsible."

"Yeah, for a lot of things that you shouldn't," Taye said. "I am marrying a man who does that. But he's working on it. You need to work on it, too, on letting go of the past and focusing on the present and future."

She wasn't sure of either right now. What if Collin had wanted to talk to her because he was having doubts? Was she going to be left at the altar?

She really didn't know him well enough to know if he would back out once he'd given his word. She definitely didn't know him well enough to marry him, if she were marrying for love.

But again she reminded herself that he wouldn't disappoint Bailey Ann. The little girl twirled again and reached up to touch the wreath of flowers Sadie had so painstakingly bobby-pinned into her dark curls. This was some amazing family Collin had. That Bailey Ann would have. Genevieve felt that pang of envy she used to feel for her sister. She'd wanted a family like this.

But she had to remind herself again that this marriage wasn't real. This family wasn't hers, and she would have to find a way, again, to deal with the disappointment and loneliness once Collin got custody and they ended their marriage of convenience.

LEM SHOULD HAVE been used to Sadie involving him in her schemes. This time he'd been tapped into service as the celebrant, the one actually performing the wedding. He'd done it before, several times, over his career as mayor and now deputy mayor of Willow Creek.

But he couldn't remember a groom and best man ever looking as grim as the twins standing on his left, out on the patio behind the kitchen. With the additional wings that had been added to the house, the patio was almost like a courtyard, with twinkle lights dangling between the wings. One side was open to a field of wildflowers behind it. It really was a beautiful place to get married.

He was surprised this was the first of the Haven weddings that had happened here. Jake and Katie had gotten married in the church in town. Dusty and Melanie had married in some chapel in Vegas before Melanie had even come to Ranch Haven. She'd come as Miller's physical therapist, though, not the rodeo rider's runaway bride. No one but Sadie had known they'd married. And Ben and Emily, while engaged, weren't getting married until her winter break. Then it would be too cold to get married in the courtyard. Maybe they'd get married in city hall.

Taye and Baker should get married here, but Sadie was afraid that would have Taye taking on too much of the work herself, as she had for today.

Where did Sadie want to get married? She hadn't told him yet, just that it wouldn't be at a tattoo parlor. He'd suggested it because he wanted them each to have their rings tattooed on. She liked the idea, but the artist would have to come to them. Where? Here? Was that why Sadie had had the wedding at the ranch? So that he would see how beautiful it would be?

She opened a patio door from the kitchen and made a gesture. The ceremony could begin. Marsh and Jessup started some recorded music that played out of the speakers mounted to the outside of the house. And Lem knew he should be turning to watch for the bride, but he couldn't take his eyes off Sadie.

She didn't often wear a dress. The few times he'd seen her in one, it had been black, for funerals. Today she wore a long pale blue dress that swirled around her boots as she walked to a seat at the front.

He wondered if he should ask her if she wanted to do it today. Get hitched here and now.

But he didn't have the tattoo artist yet. And

this was Collin's day, despite how grim he looked about it.

Was he going to go through with it?

A little girl bounded through the patio doors, giggling as she tossed flowers everywhere. She skipped down the aisle toward Collin, and the grimness left his face. He smiled brightly at the little girl who stopped to throw her arms around his waist and hug him. Then she drew back and whirled around to take a seat next to Sadie.

The music changed, and they all turned toward the back.

Genevieve Porter appeared. She wore a simple cream-colored dress, and her blond hair was caught up with some pins and flowers. She looked nothing like sweet Jenny, but she was very beautiful. Did that beauty go as deep as Jenny's had?

Was that why she'd agreed to this marriage? For this little girl?

Or was Sadie wrong about her? He worried this was all a terrible mistake.

CHAPTER FOURTEEN

COLLIN HAD BEEN struggling with the burden of that secret Colton had given him to carry as well. He hadn't wanted to marry Genevieve without telling her. But then he'd seen Marsh and Jessup on the patio, and he knew he couldn't say anything where they might overhear it.

Then Bailey Ann had come bounding down the aisle like an exuberant puppy with so much love and joy…

And that love and joy had filled him. He couldn't lose her, not to Sheridan and definitely not to a worse fate than that. The fate she might suffer if the foster family didn't follow her medical orders exactly.

When she closed her arms around him to hug him, he knew that while he might not be doing the right thing, at least he was doing it for the right reason: her.

She pulled away from him to sit with Sadie,

like they were already the best of friends. Or granddaughter and great-grandmother...

With this marriage, Bailey Ann was getting more than just him. She was getting an entire family. He hoped Mrs. Finch would see that.

The music changed and everyone turned toward the open French doors. Genevieve stepped out onto the patio, and the sunshine caught and shimmered in her pale blond hair.

"She looks like an angel," Bailey Ann murmured in awe.

She was certainly beautiful. One of the most beautiful women he'd ever seen. But she also looked so vulnerable. Maybe it was his family and being here at the ranch intensifying all that guilt she carried over her sister that had her looking fragile.

Because he'd seen her strength; she'd shown it when she'd dealt with Mrs. Finch. She was strong and smart, but she didn't look as confident as she should have been.

Maybe that was his fault. He was the one gaining so much from this marriage of convenience. She might be doing it to ease her anguish over her sister, but that wasn't exactly convenient for her. Maybe she'd changed her mind.

After that first step onto the patio, she hadn't

moved. She just stood there, staring down the short aisle at him. He braced himself, expecting her to turn around and run back inside, to run away like she had the last time she'd been at the ranch.

But her slender shoulders squared, and her chin came up and she took a step forward. She looked so alone, walking herself down the aisle. She'd had no one to give her away, but somehow that was fitting. She was her own woman and this marriage had been her idea.

The wedding, of course, had been all Sadie, but he and Genevieve hadn't argued with her about it. They needed as much evidence as possible to show CPS that their marriage was real.

Genevieve might seem fragile just now, but she was strong. Probably because she had never had anyone else she could rely on. So Collin met her halfway down the aisle and he walked those last few steps with her to the front.

While he had Colton standing up with him, she had no one on her side until Bailey Ann popped out of her seat and ran up next to her. She grabbed the small bouquet of wildflowers that Collin hadn't even noticed his bride was holding. "I'm the flower girl," she told Genevieve.

And Genevieve smiled at her. "Thank you."

"I wanna be fower grr…" Little Jake said, and everyone laughed.

Bailey Ann walked from the front to where Little Jake sat on Baker's lap in the middle row. And she gave the toddler a handful of petals from her basket. He clutched them in his pudgy fingers and grinned at her. And Bailey Ann grinned back, happiness radiating from her. She was loving this: the ranch, the ceremony but most of all the family.

Collin looked down at his bride and saw that she was watching the little girl, too, and she was smiling as much as the kids were. That palpitation struck his heart again, that strange flutter, and then a flood of warmth. He was definitely going to need to give himself an EKG.

Genevieve turned and saw him staring at her, and the smile left her face as it tensed. As she tensed…as if bracing herself… For what?

For marriage?

For him?

"Shall we begin?" Lem asked, and he stared at both of them as if making sure that they wanted to do this. As if he didn't think that they did…

Collin nodded.

Then Genevieve nodded, too, and some of that tension eased from her. Or maybe that was because Bailey Ann was back at her side, holding her hand again.

"All right then," Lem said. "Let's get these two married…"

His voice faded to a buzzing in Collin's ears. He couldn't focus on the words; he just had to focus on the intent. He couldn't pledge his love and commitment to Genevieve, not when he hardly knew her. This wasn't a love match. They shouldn't have had this wedding at the ranch. They should have just made a quick trip before the judge, just the two of them.

Colton nudged him, and the buzzing receded so that Collin could hear his name being called. He turned toward Lem. "Do you?" the older man asked, as if he was repeating the question.

He didn't need the whole question. He knew what Lem was asking, what was expected. He focused then on Bailey Ann, who peered around Genevieve to smile at him. And then he looked at his bride, whose smile was more uncertain, but who was here for him. For him and Bailey Ann.

Perhaps the choice of wedding venue had been a mistake, but the marriage? He was ready to go ahead with that. He nodded, then cleared his throat and said, "I do."

Lem turned toward Genevieve. "Do you take this man for your husband?"

There were no promises of love and cherishing. At least, not in her vows. Collin couldn't be certain what he'd pledged. But she nodded, like he did, and rasped out the two words as if she was choking on them. "I do…"

"I now pronounce you husband and wife," Lem finished.

Bailey Ann stepped forward and tugged on Lem's jacket. "You gotta tell them to kiss."

The little minx knew they were just friends. He'd made that clear to her but, once again, she reminded him of Sadie.

Lem glanced down at her and smiled. "You heard her," he said. "Collin, you may kiss your bride…"

He couldn't refuse, not without insulting Genevieve and disappointing Bailey Ann. So he leaned forward and brushed his lips across her cheek.

"Not like that," Bailey Ann said. "You're married now. You gotta kiss her on the lips."

Collin narrowed his eyes and studied the face of the child he wanted to officially make his daughter. "What do you know about kissing, young lady?"

"That's what it shows on the daytime soaps I watch with the nurse aides," she replied.

He looked to Genevieve for her consent and she gave him a sweet smile and nodded.

And Collin lowered his head again. This time instead of brushing his lips across her cheek, he brushed them across her mouth. Or at least that was what he intended to do, but that buzzing was back, not just in his ears but inside his body. It seemed to move through him like an electrical current, like he'd been shocked.

And he was…

And he found himself lingering over her mouth, kissing her longer than he'd intended. And he found himself wishing he never had to stop.

GENEVIEVE HADN'T KNOWN what to expect on her second wedding day, especially once she'd agreed to let Sadie host it at the ranch. The only thing she'd known for certain was that it would be uncomfortable.

For her.

Probably for Collin.

With the way he'd been acting since showing up at the ranch, wanting to talk to her before the ceremony, zoning out during the vows…

She'd feared he was going to back out. But then he'd said "I do." And she'd been compelled to say the same despite the sudden rush of nerves that had attacked her.

And this kiss…

Even the first brush of his mouth across her cheek had startled her, had started this tingling feeling…but now with his mouth on hers, kissing her deeply, she felt a rush of something more than nerves.

Then Bailey Ann tugged on her hand, pulling her back from him. "You're going to need to breathe," she warned them.

And everybody laughed.

Then Bailey Ann stepped between them. After looping her basket—with Genevieve's bouquet inside—over her arm, she grasped both their hands and tugged them down the aisle toward the open French doors. "Now it's time for cake."

"Yay, cake!" Katie's little boy, Caleb, exclaimed.

"You gotta see it," Miller said as he rushed out of his seat and followed them down the short aisle and into the kitchen. "I helped Taye decorate it." He took Genevieve's other hand, tugged her away from Bailey Ann and led her toward the kitchen counter where the cake had been set up with cupcakes and cookies around the base of it.

For as quickly as the ceremony had been thrown together, Genevieve had not expected all the flowers and decorations and food. And this beautiful three-tiered cake with buttercream icing and flowers in as many colors as the field of them out back.

"It's beautiful," she praised Miller. "Like something you'd see on the cover of a bridal magazine."

"Taye did most of it," he said bashfully. "She can do anything." There was such awe in his voice, such love for this woman who would be his mom now that Jenny was gone.

Tears stung Genevieve's eyes over the loss of her sister and over what she had lost. More than her life, she'd lost her children.

"Are you my aunt?" Miller asked suddenly, and his face flushed. "People are saying that."

Genevieve nodded. "Yes, I am. I am your mom's older sister. I've been gone from Willow Creek for a long time—longer than I lived in it. That why I was never around like I want to be now. That's also why I didn't know about the accident."

"It's okay," Miller said. "It was really bad then, but it's better now."

"You're amazing," she said. She'd been so broken after her divorce and all the other disappointments that had come before and after it. But he'd endured so much more than she had, and he was so young.

He smiled and shrugged. "Like I said, Taye did most of the work."

Taye came up behind him and slid her arm around his shoulder. "I couldn't do it without you. He's like my right arm now. He helped with the potato salad and the chicken salad, too."

"I can't wait to try it all," Genevieve said. But with the way her stomach was churning, she wasn't certain she would be able to eat.

She'd been nervous about coming back out to the ranch, about the wedding, about the marriage of convenience, but those nerves were nothing compared to how she felt about that kiss. She wasn't just nervous anymore; she was afraid. She did not want to start feeling again.

She'd shut down even before her divorce, and she wanted to stay that way, to not open herself up to a significant other. She didn't want to make herself vulnerable to love again only to be rejected when her husband realized she wasn't what he wanted. And Collin didn't really want her anyway. She was just a means for him to foster and adopt the little girl he loved.

She drew in a deep breath, reminding herself of that, of the real reason for this wedding, for this marriage...

Bailey Ann.

Who squeezed in between her and Miller now. The little boy jumped back as if afraid he was going to get cooties. "It's such a pretty cake," Bailey Ann said, oblivious. "Now you and Dr. Cass have to hold hands and cut it and then feed each other a piece..."

"I didn't realize there are so many weddings on soap operas," Genevieve mused.

Taye chuckled. "Oh, there are. When I worked

at the diner in town, the owner always had her *shows* running on a TV in the kitchen. I have to admit I got a little addicted, too. Not like Caleb to my chocolate chip cookies, but…"

"Those cookies?" Bailey Ann asked, pointing to the ones arranged around the bottom tier of the cake.

"We should eat lunch first," Genevieve suggested. She needed something more solid in her stomach before she started in on the sugary treats.

"No, cut the cake!" Caleb called out from behind her. Then he began to chant, "Cut the cake! Cut the cake!"

And Ian joined in. Bailey Ann cast a furtive glance at Miller, then she quietly added in her voice. "Cut the cake."

Miller glanced back at her, then he added his to the chant, his just a little deeper than the younger boys.

Little Jake just yelled, "Cake! Cake!" And he finally released the handful of flower petals Bailey Ann had given them. He threw them up in the air, and since Baker held him, he was already up quite high. They rained down on Genevieve and Bailey Ann, Miller and Taye and the cake.

Somebody touched Genevieve's hair, plucking a petal from it. Not somebody. Collin. She instinctively knew it was him because her heart beat faster and her breathing deepened.

She turned to find him standing behind her. Close.

"I guess we better cut the cake, Mrs. Cassidy," he said. "Before we have a mutiny on our hands."

Taye smiled and handed over a cake knife. "Sorry," she said. "I could say that it's not usually chaos like this around here, but I would be lying." But she was beaming with love.

Genevieve didn't know how well her sister had known Taye Cooper, but she knew that she would have loved her and she would have approved of a woman like this, so nurturing and patient and sweet, as the mother for her children now that she could no longer be.

Collin leaned close to her and whispered, "I'm sorry."

She had no idea what he was apologizing for...

The chaos?

Calling her Mrs. Cassidy?

Or that kiss?

"Thank you, Grandma," Colton said as he leaned over and kissed her cheek.

He was wearing the black cowboy hat, but even without it, she would have known which twin he was. And he was not the one who'd just gotten married, although she wished he would do it soon.

He and Livvy Lemmon were so in love and so well suited to each other. But they weren't the only couple who needed to hurry up and get married.

She glanced around for Lem. But he was so short and her family was so big that she couldn't see him over or around all of her grandsons. Knowing him and loving him for it, Sadie guessed Lem was probably crouched down and entertaining her great-grandchildren. Children were so drawn to him. Not just children. She was, too…even when she'd thought she hated him.

She focused on Colton now, reaching up to pat his cheek. These Cassidy grandsons were as big or bigger than her Haven ones. "What are you thanking me for?" she asked. "I didn't think you actually approved of your brother getting married."

But he still had served as his best man,

standing beside him, offering support or maybe urging him to run while he could. But while he'd seemed a bit distracted during Lem's service, Collin hadn't run. And when he'd kissed his bride…

It had seemed real for both of them.

Sadie had hoped that this would work out for them both and especially for Bailey Ann.

"I'm thanking you for helping me look for Cash like you promised," he said.

He'd asked her a couple of weeks ago with a strange urgency. What Colton had been carrying alone had something to do with his missing brother. Sadie understood that all too well, given all those years she'd been missing her oldest son while she'd kept the burden of that from her grandsons, choosing to focus on them instead.

But she'd never stopped searching for Jessup.

"I haven't done much yet to find him," she reluctantly admitted. She'd been distracted with her own engagement and then with Collin's.

Colton pointed across the room to his dad. No. Not to his dad but to the dark-haired woman standing next to him. "I thought that's why you invited Becca."

"No, she's Genevieve's guest." And the local Realtor. Sadie hadn't bought or sold anything recently, so she hadn't used the young woman's services.

Colton glanced at his new sister-in-law with interest. She was feeding her husband a slice of cake, but when his lips touched her fingers, she jerked back and nearly dropped it. There was definitely something there.

Something that neither of them, from the shocked look on Collin's face, considered all that convenient.

Sadie smiled.

"Becca was my brother Cash's best friend since they were little kids," Colton said. "If anyone knows where he is, she does."

Sadie already had an inkling of her own, especially after she'd learned about Cash's scholarship to a veterinarian program. But before she could focus on Cash, she had to make sure that Collin would be okay. That both he and Genevieve would be okay. No. More than okay. Happy.

CHAPTER FIFTEEN

COLLIN HAD LOST Genevieve for a while at the ranch when Miller had whisked her into the house. And during the party in the kitchen, after feeding him a piece of cake, she'd disappeared for a while. And now, even though she sat next to him, she seemed a million miles away instead of just a few cushions of the large sectional couch in her family room.

Bailey Ann sat between them, still wearing the flower girl dress that she wanted to wear forever, watching TV through half-closed eyes. An animated movie played, music humming from the surround sound speakers.

She was in awe of Genevieve's house. So was he, really. But it wasn't just the house. Genevieve had made popcorn with the popcorn maker in the corner of the family room. And with real butter drizzled over it, it tasted just like it did in the movie theater. Her TV was nearly the size of a movie screen, too.

She'd really gone all out for the nephews she thought she might need to shelter.

While Collin agreed with Baker and Taye adopting them and being their primary guardians, he hoped they would allow the boys to visit their newfound aunt. With the way they'd all taken to her, it would not be upsetting to them at all.

But he could tell it was upsetting for Genevieve when she saw them. Even though she smiled and laughed with them, there was such sadness in her beautiful eyes. Maybe that was why she was so quiet now.

Or maybe she was totally regretting what they'd just done even though it had been her suggestion. "Will it really work?" he wondered aloud.

And she jumped as if he'd startled her. Had she forgotten he was there?

She glanced at Bailey Ann whose eyes had completely closed now. Pieces of popcorn were stuck to her dress along with a few wayward flower petals. She smiled at the little girl. "It has to. She's so happy."

When they'd left the ranch, it had been midafternoon. Genevieve had suggested they come back here to rest for a while after the excitement of the day. Bailey Ann had been far more excited than they'd been and far more exhausted.

"Mrs. Finch authorized us having her for the day," he said. "But do you think she will extend that?"

"I'll work hard to make sure that she does," Genevieve said. "She had so much fun."

"Maybe too much," Collin admitted with concern. She'd gotten really tired at the ranch. And while she'd enjoyed the movie and popcorn, she'd barely been able to keep her eyes open. He needed to wake her up for one more dose of the drugs he'd brought along with them.

Genevieve's teeth nipped into her bottom lip as she stared down at her. "Is she all right?"

"Just tired." He touched her shoulder and the little girl grumbled in her sleep.

Genevieve smiled. "Hey, sweetheart, we need to hang up your dress so you can wear it again." She glanced at Collin. "Maybe soon, with all the engagements in your family."

"And she's the only girl," Collin said.

"She was already special without that distinction."

"All the kids are special."

"Yes, they are," she said with such raw longing in her voice that tears glistened in her eyes.

Sympathy flooded him. "Are you okay?" he asked. "Was today too much for you?"

She opened her mouth, as if about to speak, but Bailey Ann jerked awake and stared up at them. Her dark eyes were wide as if she was shocked to find herself with them both. "Did today really happen?" she asked. "Am I out of the hospital?"

"Yes, you are," Collin said. "And to keep you that way, we need to get your meds and get you to bed."

Genevieve jumped up from the couch and rushed off before he and Bailey Ann could move. "I'll get everything ready," she said over her shoulder, her voice drifting in as she hurried down the hall.

Was she just trying to help?

Or was she wanting to escape?

Once they got Bailey Ann settled, he would try again to get her to talk, to make sure she was okay and to share with her what he should have before they'd gotten married. No more secrets, they'd promised each other. That should have been part of their vows. Maybe it had been; he'd been so distracted that he hadn't been able to hear them.

And like Bailey Ann, he was not entirely sure anything had really happened. Was the little girl out of the hospital with him and his…wife?

He was married.

Or had it all just been a dream? It might as well have been because it wasn't real. And it couldn't be. They couldn't get their emotions involved and risk hurting each other or worse yet, hurting Bailey Ann.

"SWEET DREAMS," Genevieve whispered as she leaned over the race car bed and kissed Bailey Ann's forehead. The little girl was already back to sleep after her meds and her bath. A slight smile curved her lips.

"She looks like she's already having them," Collin remarked.

"Yes, she does," Genevieve agreed. Because the bed was so low to the ground, she'd had to kneel next to it to reach the little girl. Collin offered her his hand to help her up.

That feeling moved through her again— like a shiver but full of warmth and vitality instead of cold. She wanted to tug out of his light grasp and run away from him and from it. But she knew they had to talk about the plan with fostering Bailey Ann, how they could convince Mrs. Finch to let her stay for more than a day and a night. How they could keep her forever…

But then Genevieve realized she wouldn't have forever with her. She was just a means to an end, Collin's way to foster and adopt. But once he adopted the little girl, he wouldn't need Genevieve anymore. Bailey Ann wouldn't need her either. She'd only wanted a dad: Collin.

But of course, Genevieve had known that was what she was getting into when she'd made the offer. That was the only reason she'd made it, because it wouldn't be long term. Since her parents had already signed away their rights and there was no one to contest the adoption, it could happen in six months with approval from CPS and a family court judge. Six months…

Surely that wouldn't be long enough for emotions to get involved. She would be safe, invulnerable.

But she didn't feel that way now. And she didn't like it. Flustered and upset with herself, Genevieve turned away, which had his hands falling away from her shoulders. Then she slipped quietly into the hall.

He was right with her every step, his long legs keeping up with her. She didn't want to go to her bedroom yet, didn't want him walking her to the door and talking to her there.

And she knew he wanted to talk even before he said, "Can you give me a few minutes, Genevieve?"

She nodded and turned back toward the family room. "I should redo that room for her," she said.

"She picked it out of all the bedrooms you showed her," he said. "She loves it."

She'd decorated the three children's rooms with her nephews in mind. One bedroom theme with race cars, one with superheroes and the third with a cowboy theme. But little girls could like all those things, too. Still...

"You don't think I should change it to something more girlie?" She gestured at the animated cartoon playing on the television. "Like princess-y or something?"

"I don't think you need to change anything," he said. "I take it you decorated them for your nephews?"

She nodded.

"How are you feeling now, getting to know them, seeing them with the Havens?" he asked. She drew in a deep breath.

"I'm happy that they're doing well. That they're loved so much. But I have to admit that I'm also a little disappointed that they don't need me. I know that sounds incredibly selfish, but we agreed that being open and honest is the best policy."

He flinched now.

And she realized why he'd wanted to talk to her before the wedding. "I take it you haven't been…" A twinge of disappointment passed through her chest. She didn't know why she'd expected him to uphold their deal, though. She didn't even really know him.

And now she was married to him.

"Had you changed your mind?" she asked. "Did you decide not to marry me but went through with it anyways?"

He shook his head so vehemently that it tousled his dark hair. She wanted to reach up and smooth it back into place because Collin was always so put together, so calm and steady. He was exactly what a little girl, one who'd gone through all the medical and familial upheaval that Bailey Ann had endured, needed in a father.

Not that Genevieve had any experiences with fathers. She'd never met her biological one. Her mother said he left Willow Creek for college and never looked back. And her stepfather had made it clear that Jenny was his, but she was not. And even Bradford hadn't become a father until after he divorced her.

"No, this has nothing to do with you," he said. "I wanted to talk to you about my family."

"I know they're not exactly thrilled about your sudden marriage," she said. They'd all been so kind to her, but she sensed they were also cautious. They probably thought she was pretty desperate to propose to a stranger or that she was flaky.

Collin grinned. "They certainly never expected me to be the first one to get married," he said.

"Why not?"

"I decided long ago to never get married." He chuckled. "Guess that's a strange thing to tell my wife."

"I'm not really your wife," she reminded him.

"Legally you are."

"Not romantically, though." At least not for him. She was starting to feel all these things she'd vowed to never feel again. Attraction…

He shrugged. "It doesn't matter. I didn't intend to get married for any reason. I'm too busy with work and my family to have any time to see a girlfriend, let alone a wife."

"But you want to adopt a little girl," she reminded him.

"I will make time for her," he said. "And now that my dad is doing better, after his heart transplant, I don't feel the same urgency to work as hard as I once did."

She nodded. "I get that. I used to love being a lawyer. I did a lot of things in DC. I worked with big corporations. Politicians. I even considered running for office myself but when I couldn't have a child, it all seemed so empty." Like this house had until tonight, until she and Collin and Bailey Ann had sat on the big couch and watched the big TV. Then it had finally felt like a home.

"So…since you're my lawyer, does that mean you have to keep my secrets?"

She tensed and studied his face. "I didn't think you had any secrets."

"I didn't until Colton decided to share his

...n me," he said, then uttered a groan of frustration.

"Oh, that's different then," she said. "If your twin asked you to keep something secret, I don't expect you to tell me that. I just wanted us to be open and honest about things that mattered to each other and to Bailey Ann."

He clenched his jaw so tightly that a muscle twitched in his cheek. Whatever this secret was, it was troubling him.

"Is that what's had you so distracted today?" she asked. She'd been so certain that he'd changed his mind.

He nodded. "I just… It's big…and I know it's not a secret I should be keeping…or Colton should be either but I don't know what to do with it…"

She drew in a deep breath then. She'd intended for this marriage to just be temporary and impersonal with the focus on fostering a little girl who needed someone in her life she could count on. But now…

Now this was beginning to feel like a real marriage. Not necessarily the marriage she'd had, but one in which the couple talked and shared their thoughts and feelings.

Or maybe this was just real friendship. Genevieve hadn't had many of those either. Just the superficial friendships she'd made at work and in the social circle she'd married into when she'd married Bradford. None of those people had reached out to her during her divorce or after her move, though, so they hadn't been real friends.

"Share it with me," she said. "And yes, it will stay confidential like all those legal agreements I drew up."

His lips curved into a slight smile then. "Should I have read those documents more closely that you had me sign?"

"You had me draw them up," she reminded him. And his insisting on a prenup to protect her assets had cemented for her that she was doing the right thing in helping him and Bailey Ann.

"Yes, but I can read medical journals, not legal jargon."

"Do I need to be concerned about legal ramifications with this secret?" she asked. His twin seemed as honorable a man as Collin was. She couldn't believe he had shared something with him that would have Collin this concerned.

"I'm not worried about me," he said. "Although maybe I should be since we're already under heavy scrutiny from Mrs. Finch."

"She has Bailey Ann's best interests at heart," Genevieve said, reminding herself as much as him.

He nodded and sighed. "I know. I just wish she could see that I'm in Bailey Ann's best interest."

"We'll make sure of that," she assured him. "And now that you've stalled, have you changed your mind about sharing?"

"I told you about my brother Cash, right? The one who ran away seventeen years ago?"

She nodded. "Becca's friend. Yes."

"I think he's back."

"You've seen him?"

"No, but Colton found a lighter that we both saw Cash take with him when he left."

"Okay. Where did Colton find the lighter?"

"In the ashes of my family home..." He stared down at his hands, at the skin that was still pink and new from the healing burns.

She gasped. "You think he started the fire? Is that why you're so upset?"

"We don't know what to think. Cash was so mad when he left, but that was so long ago.

Plus, he had such an affinity for the ranch. If he knew Dad was selling it, he could have started it on fire out of spite…"

"Or there could be an innocent explanation—like he could have toured the ranch with a strange Realtor, or maybe with Becca, and dropped the lighter then," she said. "That it had nothing to do with starting the fire."

Collin expelled a heavy breath and nodded. "That makes sense. That makes so much sense." Then he reached out and hugged her. "Thank you. Thank you for making me feel better."

But with that hug, he'd made her feel worse because he'd made her feel, again, entirely too much. Blinking against the sudden rush of tears, Genevieve pulled back and forced a smile. "Call your brother," she said. "I'm going to head to bed. It's been a long day."

He nodded.

She hesitated before leaving him, though. "Do you need any help setting yourself up in a guest room? I can show you where the extra linens and towels are."

He smiled. "No. I already put my overnight bag in the superhero room."

"Of course you did…"

"Bailey Ann picked it out for me," he insisted, but his grin had widened as if he was as excited about sleeping there as Bailey Ann had been about her room. "Of course, the bed in there isn't nearly as cool as the one she has."

"You would have hung off the end of the race car," she pointed out. He was so tall. So handsome…

And now he was her husband. But he wouldn't be sharing her bed. So she hurried off down the hall toward her room and away from temptation.

"You did what?" Colton asked his twin. Then he lowered his voice and glanced around the mostly empty hospital lobby. He was waiting for Livvy's shift to end so they could spend some time together before she needed to go back to her grandfather's house and crash.

He definitely hadn't been expecting a call from Collin on his wedding night, but then he was aware that this wasn't a real marriage. So why had he told Genevieve about Cash and that dang lighter?

"She's a lawyer," Collin said. "And she's my wife."

Colton snorted. "She's a stranger. One who's

already proved she can't be trusted. I still think you're making a mistake."

"I didn't call you about my marriage," Collin reminded him. "I called you about Cash."

Colton listened to his twin's theory about their oldest brother. No. Not Collin's theory. It was Genevieve's and sounded a lot like an excuse a lawyer would give in a courtroom for reasonable doubt.

The problem was that Colton doubted the theory more. "You think he came back to look at the ranch to buy?"

"Maybe he came over with Becca," Collin suggested, "when she was showing it to another client. Or…maybe there's some reasonable explanation for the lighter turning up that has nothing to do with the fire. Maybe he even gave it to Becca. They were close, remember?"

Collin was right about that, and as Colton had told his grandmother, if anyone knew where Cash was, it was Becca. Maybe he needed to show her the lighter and make her see how serious this was—especially if the insurance investigator deemed the fire an arson.

"This is your wedding night," Colton reminded him. "Your honeymoon. Shouldn't you be enjoying it?"

"I did...with popcorn and a Disney movie," Collin said. "Bailey Ann is so happy."

"What about you?" Colton asked. He knew how his brother always put himself last, and never more so than now when he'd married a stranger so that he could foster a little girl.

And he worried that if Collin kept sacrificing his happiness for others, he would never know true love and happiness for himself.

CHAPTER SIXTEEN

COLLIN DIDN'T KNOW how she'd managed, but somehow Genevieve had talked Mrs. Finch into letting them keep Bailey Ann on a trial basis. He'd heard her argument. Her house was close to the hospital. A registered nurse watched her whenever Collin wasn't home. And most of all, it was what Bailey Ann wanted. And then she'd put Bailey Ann on the call to confirm all of that and to plead.

He wasn't sure which of them had won over the social worker, but for the moment, Bailey Ann was allowed to stay with him and Genevieve.

His mind flashed forward to a day sometime in the future when he had adopted Bailey Ann. At that point, he and Genevieve could go their separate ways. He'd never be able to thank her enough for what she'd done for him and the little girl.

He worried, though, that Bailey Ann wouldn't

be eager to leave. She was already attached to his faux wife, and she would probably plead with him one day to leave her here with Genevieve, like she'd pleaded with Mrs. Finch.

And then he would be alone again even if he was with his family. He had never felt as seen with them as he felt with Bailey Ann and even with Genevieve. She watched him, listened to him, comforted him like she had on their wedding night.

Surely she had to be right about Cash. He hadn't started that fire. But then she hadn't been there that day he'd run away, so many years ago; she hadn't seen how angry he'd been then. If she had, she might have considered it like Colton was.

Might have worried about it like Collin did when he let himself worry about something other than keeping Bailey Ann. She was doing so well. She was so happy.

He'd never seen her as happy as she'd been since the wedding. Even when he'd left to go to the hospital, she hadn't been upset. Probably because Genevieve had stayed home with her and Nurse Sue. It seemed the older woman had fallen for the little girl, too. Her sometimes icy demeanor had completely melted away with the child. And with Genevieve…

Sue had a great affection for his wife, which was probably why she'd gone overboard in her reaction to Ian getting hurt. She'd wanted Genevieve to get the boys because it was clear how much Genevieve needed children.

Genevieve was so attentive and sweet with Bailey Ann. He wondered at her ex-husband. Why hadn't the man encouraged and supported her in fostering children? Why had he only wanted a child with their DNA? DNA didn't matter to kids; only love mattered. And Genevieve had so much of it to give.

She seemed completely unaware of how wonderful she was, though. And at the moment, she was completely uncomfortable. "I know you have to go to work," she said, as if convincing herself as much as him. "But can you go in a little later…after Sue finds a replacement for herself?"

Sue had gotten sick, and she rightfully didn't want to put Bailey Ann's health at risk. The little girl was stronger now, but her immune system was being suppressed so that it wouldn't reject her heart. It wouldn't be able to reject a bug either.

He was actually a little nervous that Sue might have already exposed her, and maybe that was why Genevieve was so on edge as well. He went over the medicine schedule with her again even though it was written down as well next to the automatic pill dispenser he'd set up for them. "You won't be able to forget," he said. "The alarm on this thing won't shut off until you take out the pills. You've got this."

Genevieve's teeth nipped into her bottom lip but she nodded. "Okay..."

"What's wrong?" he asked.

"I've taken parenting classes, but my time around kids has been limited," she said, and then lowered her voice to a whisper and continued, "and I've never been alone with one with a health condition."

"Bailey Ann is doing well," he reminded her.

"But what if she picked up Sue's bug?"

"She's fine," he insisted. "I checked her temperature and ears and nose. She's clear." And he prayed that she stayed that way.

Genevieve released a shaky breath and nodded. "Okay, that's good, and Sue said she would send someone over."

"You'll be fine," he said. Then he glanced at his watch. Thankfully her house was close to the hospital, just as she'd told Mrs. Finch. But still. "I'm going to be late…"

"Go," she urged him. "Like you said, we'll be fine." Then she glanced around nervously. "Where is she?"

"Right here!" the little girl said as she popped into the kitchen with them. "Are you going to work, Dr. Cass? Or can I call you Daddy now?"

Warmth flooded his chest. He wanted that so badly. But what if it didn't happen? He'd warned Bailey Ann about getting her hopes up, but his were up, too. And he didn't know what he would do if this all didn't work out.

"You and Genevieve are my foster parents now," she pointed out. "Can't I call you Mom and Dad?"

"Mrs. Finch only approved us on a trial basis," he reminded Bailey Ann and himself. After all the setbacks over the years with his father's health and even with Bailey Ann's, Collin had learned long ago not to get his hopes up too high. Not to expect too much…

"What's a trial?"

"You've been in them before," he reminded her. "Like when we tried drugs for just a certain amount of time to see if they would work. And then if they didn't we stopped them. That was a trial basis. To see if it worked, then deciding whether to continue or stop."

"But this is going to work," Bailey Ann insisted, her voice rising a bit as if she was on the verge of tears.

Genevieve hunched down and slid her arm around the little girl's shoulders. "It's not up to us to decide if it's working or not, though," she cautioned the child. "It's up to Mrs. Finch and her supervisor and eventually it'll be up to a judge."

Because this lawyer he was married to would take it to court if she couldn't convince the social worker and her boss. She was strong and determined, and he was so very happy she was on their side. He smiled at her. "Okay, ladies, I have to go to work or my patients will get mad at me."

"Not me," Bailey Ann said with a smile. She hugged his legs. And he leaned over and kissed the top of her head. "Kiss Mommy, too," she said.

"What?" Genevieve rasped out the word just as she'd rasped out her wedding vow, like she was choking. Her blue eyes glistened, too.

"I'm going to call you Mommy and Dr. Cass Daddy," the little girl declared with defiance. "And if Mrs. Finch says I can't, I'll do what she does to me. I won't listen."

Collin had to bite the inside of his cheek to keep the smile off his face. He didn't want to encourage her mutiny. "We need to be respectful of Mrs. Finch," he said. "She's just trying to help you."

"Then she'll let me stay here forever!" Bailey Ann said.

And longing tugged at Collin, not just for this special child but for what she wanted. Everything. The family...

He'd set her up for disappointment no matter if Mrs. Finch okayed her staying here or not. Because they couldn't stay forever, and he should have made that clearer to her from the beginning. He had told her that Genevieve was just a friend helping them out for a few months.

"Kiss Mommy," she urged again.

His beeper went off. He was already late. He didn't have time to explain to Bailey Ann what the situation really was. So he just brushed his lips across Genevieve's cheek.

"That's not like you did at the wedding," Bailey Ann said.

He smiled now and shook his head. "I don't have time. I'm late," he said. "I'll see you both later."

And he rushed out despite the guilt plaguing him. He didn't feel bad leaving Genevieve alone with Bailey Ann. He felt bad that he was letting the little girl believe that this was real and that it could last.

But maybe she knew better than anyone that nothing was guaranteed to last forever. Not family. Not love. Sometimes not even a heart.

FOREVER. THAT WAS how long it felt like Collin had been gone when it had probably only been minutes. Forever was what Bailey Ann wanted, not just with Collin but with Genevieve as well. And Genevieve wanted that, too.

But they had both tried, separately, to make it clear to the little girl that they were just friends. That they had gotten married for her to stay here, but that it wasn't permanent. Just like the social worker had said and Collin had repeated to Bailey Ann, this was just on a trial basis.

They hadn't wanted the little girl to believe

that their marriage was a genuine love match. But clearly she'd begun to think that.

Maybe that was okay, though, because if the social worker questioned Bailey Ann about their relationship, the little girl would tell Mrs. Finch that it was real and not just for her.

But it was just for her.

And Genevieve needed to remind herself of that, too. That this wasn't forever. She just wanted to help Bailey Ann and Collin find their happiness because she knew how hard that was. She hadn't found her own. And even though Jenny had with Dale, that hadn't lasted.

So no one was guaranteed forever. She needed to make sure that Bailey Ann made it through today. This was the first time she'd been left alone with the child, and unfortunately Sue hadn't been able to find a replacement.

Genevieve had just taken Sue's call about it, and when she clicked off her cell and sat it on the counter, her hand shook slightly.

Bailey Ann reached across and clasped her fingers and squeezed. Sometimes it was so hard to believe she was only seven; she was so mature, as if she had an old soul.

Or maybe an old heart…

And again, Genevieve couldn't help but wonder…

Was it Jenny's?

"It's okay, Mommy," Bailey Ann said.

Longing squeezed Genevieve's heart. She'd wanted for so long for someone to call her that, but knowing that it wouldn't last was so bittersweet. And she was beginning to realize that everything about this marriage of convenience was inconvenient for her.

Especially these feelings…

And not just the attachment she was forming toward Bailey Ann and vice versa…

The attraction she felt for her husband was especially annoying. She'd shut down those type of feelings long ago; she wasn't supposed to have them anymore.

But whenever he touched her, like he had with his lips just brushing across her cheek, or sometimes when he even looked at her a little too long, she felt a zip of something moving through her. Almost like an electrical charge…

And she hated it. She hated feeling so alive and aware again. Because it scared her…

Like she was scared now.

Bailey Ann was so empathetic that she must have felt it, too. "You don't have to worry," she said.

Genevieve smiled and sighed. If only she could make herself believe that…

But she was getting so used to having a husband and a daughter.

What she'd always wanted…

But she wouldn't have them forever. And when she lost them she would be devastated, more so than she had when her marriage to Bradford had ended.

She would only have this husband and daughter until Collin could adopt Bailey Ann. Technically they would probably have to adopt her together and then she would award him full custody when they got divorced.

Maybe he would give her visitation, like they were a real married couple. Maybe he would see that it would be good for Bailey Ann to have Genevieve continue being part of her life. Or maybe, once his fake marriage was over with his fake wife, he would find a woman he really loved and wanted to marry. And this new woman would become Bailey Ann's mother just as Bradford had found a new wife and a real mother to his children.

Genevieve had only signed on to get Collin ready to foster and adopt. And that was all he wanted from her. That and to keep Bailey Ann alive.

She glanced at that mechanical pill dispenser that sat on the counter next to her cell phone. What if the batteries had run down? Shouldn't there be some kind of green light for her to know it was working? If the batteries weren't working, would she be able to open it?

The machine was designed for people with dementia who either took their pills too often or forgot to take them at all. It was intended to keep them from overdosing or underdosing. It was perfect for kids, too, but only if it was working. And if Genevieve was close enough to hear it.

"I don't know if I should trust this thing…" she murmured with a worried glance at it. She always struggled with trust…but somehow she'd won the trust of this little girl who was so sweet and straightforward.

"Trust me," Bailey Ann said. "Dr. Ca— Daddy has told so many people how I'm supposed to take these pills that I remember how." And she recited the names, doses and times as if she was reading from the paper that Collin had written out that lay on the counter next to the pill dispenser. Just in case…

He didn't entirely trust it either then. He might not trust anything or anyone either as well.

"That's impressive," Genevieve said. "It's like you read it off this sheet."

Bailey Ann shrugged. "I heard him say it so many times I think I hear it in my sleep sometimes. It won't be like that last foster family."

"That is what I was worrying about," Genevieve admitted. "I don't want you to get sick again because of me."

"I won't," Bailey Ann said. "I'll take my meds when you give them to me."

Genevieve tensed. "What…"

Bailey Ann's face flushed, and her shoulders sagged a bit. "Nothing…"

Genevieve could have dropped it. She sensed that she probably *should* drop it. But she was compelled to prod like Bailey Ann was a hostile witness on the stand. And they only got hostile when there was something they didn't want to admit. "What are you talking about?"

Bailey Ann shook her head. "Nothing."

"Dr. Cass—Daddy and I made a promise to always be open and honest with each other," Genevieve said. With each other. Not Mrs. Finch. "You need to be the same with us. Open and honest."

Bailey Ann looked up and studied her face for a long moment. "'Kay…"

"No secrets between us," Genevieve prodded again.

Bailey Ann smiled and then sighed, like Genevieve had earlier. "'Kay," she said again. "I didn't take all the pills Mrs. Morely gave me."

"Okay. Who's Mrs. Morely?"

"My last foster mom. I could call her Marcy, but I didn't want to." Her breath hitched a bit, and tears pooled in her eyes. "I didn't want to be there. I told Mrs. Finch that but she wouldn't listen."

"I'm sorry," Genevieve told her. "I know that it's frustrating when someone won't listen to you." She'd felt that way so often, with mother and stepfather, her grandparents and most of all Bradford. She hadn't chosen the other people in her life, but she'd chosen him. So that was her fault.

And it was also her fault that she'd turned away from the one person who would have listened to her: Jenny. She blinked and focused on the little girl. "So tell me. I'm listening. What happened because you were frustrated?"

"I didn't take my pills like I was supposed to. I just pretended to when Mrs. Morely gave them to me."

Genevieve's heart was beating too fast. According to Collin, the child had nearly died because she hadn't been getting her antirejection meds. She cleared her throat and asked, "Why did you do that?"

Had she wanted to hurt herself? Dread rose up in her. She'd read so many books on parenting, preparing herself to be a foster mother. But reading about it…and actually trying to handle a situation like this…

"I wanted to go back to Dr. Ca—to Daddy. I wanted to be with him. And I knew if I got sick again, I would get to see him more."

Tears stung Genevieve's eyes now, hard. The little girl loved him so much that she'd sacrificed her health to be with him again.

But he loved her so much that that would have been the last thing he'd wanted. Unless…

"Did Dr. Ca—did Daddy know you did that?" Genevieve hoped not because then that would have meant he'd lied to her; he'd lied after promising to be open and honest with her.

Bailey Ann's face flushed bright pink and she shook her head. And now tears filled her eyes, too. "Do you have to tell him?"

Of course she had to. She wasn't sure if she could wait until his shift ended at the hospital. But then the doorbell rang, saving her from having to answer Bailey Ann at the moment. Maybe Sue had found someone after all— someone who could watch the little girl while Genevieve ran up to the hospital.

But when she opened the door, it wasn't a health professional standing on the step. Not even someone trying to sell something like replacement windows or magazine subscriptions.

She probably would have preferred that at the moment. No. It was Jessup and Sadie. Her new, temporary father-in-law and grandmother-in-law.

Grandmother-in-law… It struck her that Sadie had been Jenny's grandmother-in-law, too. Despite all the distance between them, here was one simple thing they shared.

"Ah… Collin isn't here," she told her visitors. Because she doubted that they were here to see her. But maybe Bailey Ann…

She rushed up behind Genevieve and shyly said, "Hi." And then, "Mommy, the machine is buzzing."

Genevieve's ears were, too. And she rushed off toward the kitchen, leaving the little girl to invite her grandfather and great-grandmother inside the house. She wanted to make sure the child got the medication she needed. But she suspected the little girl needed more help than that…

JESSUP SHOT A glance at his mother. So much for how wonderful she insisted his new daughter-in-law was.

She'd rushed off, leaving them standing on the front stoop until the little girl had stepped forward. She took one of his hands and one of Sadie's, like she had Collin and Genevieve's the day of the wedding at the ranch, and just as she had then, she tugged them toward the kitchen. He chuckled. She really was something.

He understood why his son had fallen so hard…for the little girl. Collin hadn't fallen for the woman; he'd only married her for Bailey Ann, so that he could foster and hopefully adopt her, too.

He knew his mother was hoping that this would become a love match, like all the matches she had made for Michael's sons and for Colton. But Colton was nothing like his twin. He was easygoing and relaxed while Collin was always so serious and focused, like Genevieve Porter.

They were probably the only two people who would consider a loveless marriage a convenience. Jessup wanted more for Collin than that.

"I'm sorry," Genevieve said when they stepped into her big kitchen.

"This is my first day without Nurse Sue to help me with Bailey Ann's medications," she said, her teeth nipping at her bottom lip. "I just want to make sure I get them right."

Bailey Ann released their hands to rush to her. "Mommy, don't worry. Remember I know…" She trailed off and glanced nervously at them. She took the capsule from Genevieve's palm with one hand and picked up a glass of water from the counter with the other.

Jessup felt a twinge of sympathy in his new

heart. He was struck by this strange thing he shared with the little girl, the gift of someone else's heart to save their lives. He glanced at his new daughter-in-law. "Those capsules have a nasty aftertaste," he said. "Do you have an orange or applesauce?"

She nodded and rushed toward her commercial-sized fridge. She pulled out both and put them on the counter.

He reached for and peeled the mandarin orange for the little girl.

She'd cocked her head and studied his face. "How do you know how yucky they taste?"

He tugged on the top of his shirt, pulling it down far enough to show the top of his scar.

And she gasped. "You have a new heart, too?"

"The best heart," Sadie said.

"My heart is good, too," Bailey Ann said.

"I'm sure it is," Sadie agreed.

"Sometimes I wonder…" Genevieve began, but she trailed off with a wistful sigh.

"You think…?" Sadie asked, silently communicating with this woman who was essentially a stranger to them.

But his mother was like that. She could bond easily with people she'd just met despite how intimidating she could be. Or maybe it was because she was so intimidating; the only people who truly impressed her were the ones who could speak easily to her.

It seemed like her new granddaughter-in-law didn't even have to speak and they understood each other.

But then, Genevieve was Jenny's sister. Of course there was a bond already there between her and Sadie.

Between bites of orange, Bailey Ann asked him about his medications and his surgeries and how many times he'd been in and out of the hospital. It was like they were old war buddies. But he was nearly sixty and she was just seven. She shouldn't have been through everything that she'd gone through.

And he wasn't sure how much more she would be able to handle.

She was already calling this woman, Genevieve, Mommy. But Collin had no intention of staying married to this stranger; he'd just intended to be with her until he adopted Bailey Ann. But what happened then?

Had any of them considered that?

CHAPTER SEVENTEEN

COLLIN FELT LIKE a coward over how he'd rushed off, leaving Genevieve to deal with all of Bailey Ann's expectations on her own. As if she hadn't been nervous enough about being solely responsible for her medical care…

Seeing his brother walking around the ER, all decked out in his firefighter gear, just served to remind him that Colton was the hero. His twin was the one who rushed into burning buildings all the time. Collin had done that only once, and it wasn't something he was likely to repeat.

Especially after the lecture Colton had given him over it, over the risks of going into that situation without the proper equipment. Colton was wearing it now, and so was the other firefighter he was helping into one of the ER bays. "You don't have to worry. The best doctors work in this ER."

Collin knew his twin was talking about

Livvy. Not him. He was just finishing up the notes for the consultation he'd been paged for—a young woman having a heart attack. Fortunately it hadn't been that. She was a mom with young kids and she was also a daughter with aging parents. With all her obligations and stress, she'd been having a panic attack. Understandably...

He felt a little panicky himself, and he knew that Genevieve did, too. So he wasn't surprised that he got a text from her: We need to talk tonight somewhere that Bailey Ann can't hear us.

This wasn't just about Bailey Ann's medications; this was about the little girl's expectations. The same thing that worried Collin. They definitely needed to talk about how to handle her calling them Daddy and Mommy and her belief that this arrangement was going to last forever despite how much they'd both warned her that it wouldn't.

Once he adopted her—if he even could—his marriage would be over. That was the deal. Genevieve hadn't wanted to get married again, and she'd only done this when she saw a child in need.

That was fine. He didn't need this marriage to have a happily-ever-after, but part of him actually wished it was possible for him to stay married to this amazing woman who was so selfless and generous and beautiful. Maybe that was all that Bailey Ann was doing, wishing, and maybe she figured if she wished hard enough, her wish would come true.

If only such a thing was actually possible...

But his wish for his mom to stay alive hadn't come true. Or his wish for his oldest brother to come home...

Or had it?

He had to focus on Bailey Ann. He had nearly lost her once when that foster family hadn't administered her meds correctly. And with heart transplants, there was always a risk of complications, of another failure...

He didn't want to take away Bailey Ann's hopes and dreams for a future, though, even one that included both him and Genevieve. But he couldn't hold Genevieve to a marriage she'd only agreed to until he could adopt Bailey Ann. No matter how much he might want that himself. Too many people had already discounted Genevieve's wants and needs. She deserved more.

His head throbbed, and he reached up to rub his temple. "Bad consult?" Colton asked.

Collin shook his head. "No. Not the one I'm here for." The one he needed to have with Genevieve probably would be. He gestured toward the curtain. "How's your coworker?"

"Some smoke inhalation. Best doctor in Willow Creek is working on him, though." He grinned. "No offense."

Collin chuckled. "None taken. Livvy is good."

"Yes, she is," Colton said with a dopey grin. The man was hopelessly in love.

Collin had once pitied, and mercilessly teased, his twin over how hard he'd fallen for Livvy, but now a twinge of envy struck him. He ignored it to rib his brother again. "I only question her judgment when it comes to you..."

Instead of being offended, Colton nodded. "I know. She could do better."

Collin shook his head. "No. You've both done well."

"How about you?" Colton asked. "How's your marriage going?"

"It's only been a few days," he reminded his twin. But he had three days of memories, not just of the wedding at the ranch but of watching movies and eating popcorn with

Bailey Ann and Genevieve. And the board games they'd played and the walk they'd taken into town, where Bailey Ann had delighted in all the Valentine decorations, insisting that they were for them. Because they'd just gotten married…

Despite all the times they'd told her they were just friends, she thought their marriage was real and this was going to last. Knots clutched his stomach that he hadn't handled all of this better.

Colton pitched his voice low and leaned closer to ask, "That bad?"

For his brother to ask that, he must have already been grimacing, but with the acrid smoke from Colton's uniform burning his sinuses, Collin grimaced again. It reminded him of the fire, of nearly losing his dad again.

"No. It's not bad," he said, all the memories of the past few days tumbling through his mind. "It's almost too good."

Colton pushed back his fire hat as if he needed to see him better, because now he was staring intently at him. "Too good? You falling in love with your wife, Collin?"

He felt that jolt he felt whenever he touched her or even sometimes just thought of her.

"I meant with Bailey Ann," Collin demurred. "It would just be hard if this doesn't work out how it's meant to…" Or if it did and she was still unhappy when he and Genevieve divorced.

"Just on Bailey Ann?" Colton asked.

"No. I want her to be happy and healthy."

"What about Genevieve?" Colton asked.

"She wants her to be happy and healthy, too. She was so worried about being alone with her today and not giving her the medications correctly." He glanced down at his phone. But her text wasn't about the medications; he knew that. It was about the little girl's expectations.

"That's not what I meant," Colton said.

He glanced up at his brother. "What?"

"I was wondering if you want Genevieve to be happy and healthy."

"Of course," he said. She'd been happy the past few days, happier than she'd been that first time they'd gone to the ranch together and she'd fled in tears. "I hope she's feeling less guilty about Jenny and the boys." But even if she was, he had a feeling that she'd replaced the guilt over them for guilt over Bailey Ann. Would she consider giving their marriage a real chance? Or had she been too hurt to ever risk her heart again, especially on someone like him who'd never had a real relationship before? "Do you and Livvy have plans tonight?"

Colton shrugged. "Our shifts don't always line up, so we usually play it by ear. But we *are* both supposed to be off this evening."

"Do you mind watching Bailey Ann for a bit? Genevieve and I need to talk without her being able to overhear us."

"So you're not trying to set up a double date with us?" Colton asked as if he was teasing, but there was concern and sympathy in his dark eyes.

"Genevieve and I need to talk about Bailey Ann's feelings if this doesn't work out," he admitted. "If we can't continue to foster her…"

"Do you ever worry about yourself?" Colton asked.

The question startled Collin. "What? Why?"

"This whole marriage of convenience thing…" He shook his head. "I can't imagine not marrying for love."

"That's because you're in love," he pointed

out. Something he'd never been. "And I did marry for love."

Colton's eyes widened with shock. "That fast?"

"I'm talking about love for Bailey Ann."

"I know why you did it," Colton said. "I just wish that you would do something for you and not just for everyone else."

"Not this again."

"Your career, this marriage…" Colton sighed. "I worry about you, and I'm sorry I dumped that whole Cash thing on you, too."

"I'm glad you did," Collin said. "No more secrets."

"You're saying we should tell everyone else?"

"I don't know what there is to tell," Collin said. "It could have been nothing, just like Genevieve said. Becca had the lighter or Cash toured the house. We don't know that it was anything more than that. And until we know what it was, it doesn't make sense to say any more about it."

Colton grinned. "So you're kind of selective with this whole secret thing?"

Collin sighed and smiled. "Yeah, I guess…" Because he and Genevieve were lying to Mrs.

Finch, or at least not being completely honest. And Collin couldn't help but wonder whether he was being completely honest with himself...

Because he wanted to go out with Genevieve and not just to talk about Bailey Ann.

"Will you babysit for a while?" Collin asked.

Colton nodded. "Of course. Since meeting our little Haven cousins and Bailey Ann, I've realized I like kids a lot more than I thought."

Collin grinned. "They have that effect on you." And he remembered the effect they'd had on Genevieve. She wanted a child so badly.

And Collin wanted her to be happy. But he was worried that they were all headed for disappointment and heartbreak.

BAILEY ANN HAD insisted on helping Genevieve pick out a pretty dress and heels for her *date* with *Daddy*. That was what Bailey Ann had called it. But that wasn't what it was at all.

Genevieve knew this, whatever *it* was, wasn't going to last. She just wanted to make sure that Bailey Ann did, that she fully understood how dangerous what she'd done with her medication had been. But first Genevieve had to talk to Collin about it. Alone.

She'd probably been so distracted during Sadie and Jessup's visit that they thought her unwelcoming since they hadn't stayed long. Or maybe they just figured she was in over her head in caring for a child with the medical needs that Bailey Ann had.

And she was…

Because she didn't want to upset the little girl, she played dress-up for a date with her husband. She and Bradford had done date nights, but usually at the country club where he'd left her sitting alone while he just had to say something to someone for a minute that had turned into far longer.

This wasn't a date. This was a meeting between two people who had an arrangement. She needed to remember, especially when she heard the creak of a door opening, and her pulse quickened in anticipation.

No. Anxiety. She wasn't sure how to tell Collin what Bailey Ann had told her.

"Perfume," Bailey Ann said. "You need to smell as pretty as you look." She picked up one of the bottles from the vanity table in Genevieve's bathroom and spritzed it, liberally, on her. So liberally that they both sneezed and Genevieve's eyes began to water.

She wiped off what had hit her cheek, but unless she washed her hair, she couldn't get rid of all of it. The doorbell rang now, leaving her no time to shower unless she wanted to keep Collin's family waiting and Collin. She'd waited long enough to tell him what she'd learned that morning.

Bailey Ann ran out of the room, maybe to escape the fumes, maybe to greet their guests. But then Genevieve heard, "Daddy! Daddy! You're home! Mommy looks so pretty. Wait till you see her! And she smells pretty, too!" She sneezed.

And Genevieve smiled as she walked down the hall and joined them in the kitchen. "I smell a little too pretty," Genevieve said. "I think Bailey Ann could get a job as a mall perfume tester."

She'd hoped everyone would laugh. But Collin just stared at her, as did his twin and the woman who'd come with them. "I'm sorry," she said. And she held out her hand. "I'm Genevieve."

"Livvy," the petite woman replied. "I'm

sorry I missed your wedding. I was on call at the hospital."

Right, Colton's fiancée was an ER doctor, and if Genevieve recalled correctly, she was also Lem's granddaughter.

Genevieve flinched, remembering the trouble the CPS call had caused. Livvy had been the doctor who had checked out little Ian. "I'm sorry," she said. "I never intended for Sue…"

"I know. She explained it, and she apologized," Livvy said.

"Doesn't Mommy look pretty?" Bailey Ann prodded Collin.

"Yes, she does," Collin said, his voice a little gruff.

"She insisted that I dress up," Genevieve said, making it clear that the dress—*blue, like your eyes*—and the heels hadn't been her idea. "Like the ladies on the soaps do when they go out."

"Where are the flowers, Daddy?" Bailey Ann asked.

"Yes," Colton said, his mouth curving into a grin. "Where are the flowers?"

Livvy bumped his shoulder. "Stop teasing your brother. And you need to pick up our dinner." She smiled at Bailey Ann. "We ordered pizza."

"Pizza!" Bailey Ann exclaimed, clapping her hands together.

"She's not going to miss us at all," Collin remarked. But he was grinning.

He had no idea how much she'd missed him.

Bailey Ann hugged Collin's waist. "I will, but you and Mommy need a date." She released him to hug Genevieve next. Then she pulled back and said, "You can go now. And get her some flowers, too."

Collin pointed at the medication dispenser and the note and said to Livvy, "You don't need me to explain any of that to you."

She shook her head. "No. Colton and I can handle this one…unless she challenges me to a game of checkers. Then I'm in trouble."

"Mommy has all kinds of games," Bailey Ann said. "And movies, too. And she even gave me some polish for my nails." She held up her fingers with the bubblegum pink polish on them. "Can I do your nails?"

"I've been wanting a spa day," Livvy said with a chuckle.

"Make sure you do Uncle Colton's when he

gets back," Collin said. "He wouldn't want to be left out."

Everyone was so happy and upbeat that Genevieve's stomach churned with dread. But she had to tell Collin. "We should go," she murmured to him.

Bailey Ann waved at them before taking Livvy's hand to tug her off down the hall.

"Yes, let's go," Collin said, and he sounded as if he was bracing himself, as if he knew that she wasn't as happy and upbeat as everyone else. "My car's in the drive—"

"Let's walk," she said. She needed the fresh air, especially with the strength of the perfume burning her eyes.

"In those heels?" Collin asked, his gaze sliding down her legs to her shoes. And his eyes seemed to get a little dark, his face a little tenser.

"I lived in the city for years," she said. "I'm used to walking in heels."

Unlike Bailey Ann who'd nearly wiped out. But she was only seven. That was why she hadn't understood how serious what she'd done was.

They walked out through the mudroom and outside. They only had to walk a block before heart-shaped balloons and decorations and pink and white and red flowers sprang up all around them.

"I feel like I'm walking through a kid's Valentine's party," Collin remarked as he glanced around them. Then he looked at her. "So, what's up?"

"I'm sorry," she said. "I didn't know how to explain to Bailey Ann that this was not a date. I don't know how to explain anything to her." Not the way he would need to.

"None of that is your responsibility," he said. "I'm sorry I had to leave this morning without talking to her about her expectations."

None of that is your responsibility...

She should have been relieved. But instead those words just reminded her that all Collin really wanted was to adopt Bailey Ann. If he could have done that without marrying her, he definitely would have.

But she'd known that from the beginning. They were strangers, after all. Maybe Bailey Ann wasn't the only one who'd started having unrealistic expectations...

COLTON HAD HOPED the date night with his wife was a good sign for his twin, that maybe Collin and Genevieve had more in common than Bailey Ann. Especially with the way Collin had looked at her when she'd appeared in the kitchen, looking more like a model than a lawyer.

Collin had seemed to lose his voice entirely when he saw her. And he must have stayed just as hypnotized, since he hadn't noticed Colton drive past them as they'd walked along the sidewalk to town and he'd driven back with the pizza. But when they returned to her house not long after they'd left, he had a sick feeling in his stomach. They both looked so grim.

And Bailey Ann was so happy.

He'd figured this marriage was a mistake for so many reasons, but Colton really wished he'd been wrong. For all their sakes...

CHAPTER EIGHTEEN

ONCE GENEVIEVE HAD told him what Bailey Ann had confessed to her that morning, Collin felt too sick to eat. And she must have sensed it as well because she'd suggested they cut the evening short.

Very short and just skip dinner altogether.

He doubted she would have been able to eat either; she'd looked as sick as he felt when she'd shared Bailey Ann's secret with him.

How hadn't he known?

How hadn't he guessed?

The foster family had sworn that they'd correctly administered her meds, but he'd been convinced that they were lying to cover up their negligence.

But instead the negligence was his. He should have known. Should have made it clear to Bailey Ann how serious her condition was. He had to do that now, and he hadn't wanted to wait another moment. So he got rid of Colton and Livvy quickly, promising that he would explain later.

Colton had been reluctant to leave but Livvy had tugged him out the door with her. "He'll tell you later," she said. She knew Collin well enough to know that he would keep his promise.

Once the door closed behind Colton and Livvy, he turned toward the little girl. "We need to talk, Miss Bailey Ann."

Her shoulders slumped and she sighed. Then she shot a slightly resentful glance at Genevieve. "You told him…"

"I had to," Genevieve said. "He's your doctor. He needs to know how you really wound up in the hospital last time."

Collin's empty stomach flipped with the memory of how sick she'd been. And he'd been so angry at those foster parents…

"And we've promised now to always be open and honest," Genevieve said. "It's not nice to keep secrets from people we love."

Tears sprang to Bailey Ann's eyes and trailed down her cheeks. "I'm sorry," she said, her voice shaky. "I just missed you so much when Mrs. Finch sent me to live with the Morelys. I didn't want to be there. I wanted to be with you!" She threw her arms around Collin's waist, holding tightly to him.

"I missed you, too," he said, patting her head. While Bailey Ann was sweet, he was also beginning to see that she was used to getting her way and as stubborn as every Haven or Cassidy he knew. She was a bit of a mini Sadie. God help them.

He unhooked her arms from around his waist and lifted her up into his arms. So that she had to face him. The tears were real. They were making her face red and her lips were quivering with sobs. His heart ached, and he wanted to just hug her and let it go. But it was too important.

Any other child he might have coddled. But he had to be straight with Bailey Ann. Her life depended on it. "I would have missed you even more and forever if your body rejected that new heart because you weren't taking your medicine. You have to remember how long it was before we found one that would work for you." He braced himself, knowing that he had to be blunt with her. "Somebody died for you to get that heart, Bailey Ann. And you were in a line with a lot of other people waiting for it. If you don't take care of it, it's not fair to the person who died, and it's not fair to the other people who could have taken it."

She began to shake now, the sobs wracking her. "I'm sorry, Daddy. I'm so sorry…"

Regret and guilt gripped him. He hadn't known how else to get his point across and ensure that, no matter what happened, she would never pull something like that again.

"Your life depends on doing everything right, Bailey Ann," he said, even as he realized all the things he'd done wrong, too. "And your life is all that matters. Even more than I want to be your daddy, I want you to be alive. So, if for some reason we can't be a family…or stay a family… I want you to promise me that you will take care of yourself and that heart."

She nodded, then—in a quivery voice— she said, "I promise."

He clutched her close against his chest, feeling her heart beat against him. But he wasn't reassured as he'd been in the past when he'd felt that beat after her heart replacement. Now he was scared that she might not keep that promise, that she might do what she'd done before when things hadn't worked out how she'd wanted them.

She might stop taking her medication. Then she would lose more than him and this make-shift family they'd formed; she would lose her life.

THE TEARS AND emotions must have exhausted Bailey Ann, who'd fallen asleep in Collin's arms. While he'd carried her to her room and tucked her into her race car bed, Genevieve had tried to grapple with all the emotions pummeling her. She felt raw and exposed when he stumbled back into the kitchen.

He looked as exhausted as the child he'd just carried to bed. Genevieve knew that she should encourage him to go to bed himself, in that superhero bedroom that had never seemed as fitting as it did now after he'd had to have such a difficult conversation with the little girl who adored him. So much that she'd risked her life to be with him again.

But she could tell that what had exhausted him most wasn't the conversation but the guilt. His shoulders bowed with it. She understood that guilt all too well. "I'm sorry," she said.

He shook his head, and his throat moved as if he was struggling to swallow. Then he cleared his throat and said, "Don't be. None of this is your fault. And I'm glad you told me."

"Are you?" she asked. Sometimes ignorance was better. When she hadn't known that Jenny was dead, she hadn't missed her as much. When she hadn't known how unhappy Bradford was with her, she'd thought they'd had a chance of making their marriage work.

But then she sighed with the acknowledgment that it was better to know the truth, even if it hurt, because then you could figure out how to go forward. If you could go forward...

She hoped to find a way to do that with Bailey Ann. "She's mad at me for telling you," she said. The look of betrayal the little girl had shot her had hurt. But she would have hurt more if she hadn't said anything to Collin and something happened to the child.

"You did the right thing," he said, offering her assurances when he looked like he needed them more. "I had to know. I made such a mess of things."

She shook her head. "No. You didn't. Trust me. I know how to make a mess of things. This isn't it."

"But she could have died." His body shuddered with revulsion at the thought. "And I had no idea."

"Who would suspect that she would do something like that?" She'd been so shocked when Bailey Ann had made the confession.

"Mrs. Finch," he said. "She was certain that that foster family wouldn't have messed up. I just thought she was covering up her own negligence over trusting the Morelys with Bailey Ann's care."

"We need to tell her," Genevieve said.

He groaned.

"It's not fair to that family," she pointed out. "And it's not fair to the children who might not have been placed with them because of what happened. There is such a need for foster families everywhere. It would be a shame if what happened with Bailey Ann meant CPS didn't place other kids with that family."

He groaned again, louder, and closed his eyes. "Oh, God, I told Mrs. Finch that she shouldn't leave kids with them that had medical needs." He rubbed his hand over his face. "I could have ruined someone else's family, someone else's health, all because I hadn't known what had really happened. And I'd assumed the worst, just like I did with Cash until you'd pointed out that it could have been innocent."

She sighed. "I don't know that it is. I just presented another possibility."

"Just like when you proposed," he murmured. "I thought I was going to lose Bailey Ann and then you presented another possibility..." His throat moved again, and his voice was gruff when he continued, "But I still might lose her."

"We'll explain to Mrs. Finch that she's so young she didn't understand what she was doing."

Collin groaned again. "I think she understood exactly what she was doing."

"She didn't know it would hurt the Morelys or other children who might have been taken from them or placed with them," Genevieve said. "And they should have made certain she took the medication. That was covered in foster parenting classes—to make sure kids take their meds."

"I should have made it clear to her how important they are," he said.

"She knows that now," Genevieve said. "She has a good heart. She just wants that heart to be with you."

His shoulders were still slumped, his face taut with stress. She stepped closer to him and touched his tightly clenched jaw. "Stop beating yourself up," she said.

"Why?" he asked. "You do it to yourself all the time over your sister."

"And it doesn't do any good," she pointed out. She didn't feel any less guilty about not staying in contact with Jenny and not getting to know Dale and the boys.

Without thinking, she stepped closer to him. "Would a hug help?" she asked.

A strange look passed over him, and then he wrapped his arms around her.

She felt that current move through her again, heating and unsettling her. But instead of pushing him away, she wrapped her arms around him, too, and hugged him back. "Do you feel better?" she asked.

He sighed. "Yes."

Then he touched her jaw and tipped her face up to his. "A kiss might help even more…"

Despite the heavy evening, she found herself smiling at that, and rising up on tiptoe as he lowered his head. Their lips met. Caressed. Held. The kiss deepened.

She felt so much…but she wasn't sure if it

was better or worse. Because she had a feeling she was making a horrible mistake...that she was starting to fall in love with her husband.

BECCA CALDER WAS a single mother with a thriving career. She was one of those people who did it all, did it well and mostly did it alone...except for some help from her parents.

Sadie didn't know the young woman well, but she was impressed with her. And she now understood that Becca was probably the key to finding Cash.

Sadie sat in the Realtor office's reception area, across from Becca's mother, Phyllis. Phyllis covered the front desk for her.

Becca came in a moment later. Competent and beautiful, she had not a hair out of place or a wrinkle in her summer suit as she swept into her office, despite her long day.

She glanced at Sadie, who sat in the reception area waiting for her, and tensed.

Sadie smiled. Becca knew why she was there.

"Colton sent you." It wasn't a question. She knew.

Sadie stood up and smiled wider at her. "I like you."

"I'm not sure if that's a good thing or not," Becca said, but she was smiling, too.

Phyllis sucked in a breath, probably worried that Sadie would judge her for her daughter's manners. Sadie laughed instead. She always respected other strong women. And a woman had to be strong to take on a Haven.

Like Genevieve Porter. She was stronger than she thought she was, stronger than Jessup thought she was. He'd been worried after their visit today. Something had definitely been bothering Genevieve, but she hadn't asked them for help. Sadie knew she had Collin to lean on.

They had each other now and given some of the things the little girl had said to her and Jessup, they were going to need each other.

"I need your help," Sadie told Becca.

"You looking to sell the ranch?" Becca asked.

And Sadie laughed hard. "I really like you."

"Will you if I don't do what you want me to?" Becca asked.

Her mother gasped again, her head swiveling back and forth between them as if she was watching a tennis match. Instead of being embarrassed, the woman should be proud. She'd raised a strong daughter.

"What do you think I want you to do?" Sadie asked.

"We both know it's not to list the ranch or find you a house, so you must be here looking for the same thing Colton has been…"

"Cash," Sadie confirmed. "I'm looking for Cash. It's time for him to come back to his family."

CHAPTER NINETEEN

COLLIN HAD A bad feeling about the upcoming meeting with Mrs. Finch. He and Genevieve had called her and informed her about what had happened with the Morelys, not wanting them to be denied a child who needed them because of what Bailey Ann had done.

The social worker had been concerned about them, too. But she'd been even more concerned about Bailey Ann. She needed to talk to her supervisor and a child psychologist and then she would meet with them again. When she'd texted Genevieve the meeting time, she hadn't said what she'd decided.

They had to wait another day to find out, and since he'd had the day off, he'd decided they needed an outing. Or maybe he'd just needed to get out of that beautiful house of Genevieve's.

He probably needed to get away from her, too. After he'd been so foolish and kissed her a few nights ago, he'd found his thoughts occupied by her. It didn't help that Bailey Ann insisted that Daddy needed to kiss Mommy whenever one of them left the house either.

But in front of Bailey Ann, he didn't kiss Genevieve like he had that night. Like he'd never wanted to stop kissing her. If the little girl hadn't cried out with fear from her bedroom, scared because of a nightmare, he wasn't sure if he would have stopped.

Confused about his feelings for Genevieve and on edge about the meeting the following day, Collin had proposed a trip to the ranch. Bailey Ann had wanted to wear her flower girl dress, but Collin had insisted that nobody was getting married that day.

Knowing Sadie, though, he couldn't be sure. She might have manipulated another one of his brothers or cousins into marriage. He hadn't seen Marsh in a while.

But that wasn't exactly an accident. He wasn't sure he could see him and not tell him about Cash and that dang lighter. And Marsh, being a lawman, probably wouldn't think of the innocent reason that Genevieve had. Collin couldn't deal with that now. He was most concerned with Bailey Ann.

And she was concerned with him, staring

at him with suspicion. "You really know how to ride a horse?" she asked as he carried her into the big barn. After Ian had gotten hurt there, he was determined to make sure she stayed safe for as long as he could.

"I grew up on a ranch," he told her.

"What about you?" she peered over his shoulder at Genevieve who walked behind them. "Do you know how to ride horses, Mommy?"

If she'd been upset with Genevieve over telling him what she'd done with her medications, she wasn't upset with her any longer. Or maybe she was just desperately trying to hang on to her happiness because she sensed the same thing he did…

That something was going to go terribly wrong. Maybe it already had.

From one of the stalls came a horrible sound, more than a whinny. It was a kind of frenzied screech, and hooves kicked against the wood. This was why he'd carried Bailey Ann and maybe why Genevieve walked behind them. They'd heard about that bronco. The one that had inadvertently injured Ian.

As well as hiring some "horse whisperer" to work with the animal, Dusty had intended to move him to the barn that was still standing at the Cassidy Ranch, but it had needed repairs, not from the fire but from all the years the ranch had been neglected. He felt a pang of the guilt he always felt when he thought of the ranch. But Dad's health and medical bills had been and were still more important.

"I didn't grow up on a ranch," Genevieve answered Bailey Ann, collecting herself after the bronco's awful whinny. "But I've ridden horses before. Just a few weeks ago I went for a ride at Miss Becca's ranch."

Collin turned to her. "Becca has a ranch?"

She nodded. "Yes, with a really beautiful barn and some horses." The bronco kicked that stall door as it reared up inside it, and she flinched and added, "Some very gentle horses."

"We have gentle horses, too," a little blond-haired boy said as he ran into the barn. He clutched a bunch of carrots in one hand and a small plastic bag in the other. Caleb. He was the blondest of the boys.

Ian and Miller followed him in; they both had sandy hair. And Miller still had a slight limp to his gait.

Bailey Ann wriggled down from Collin's arms as if embarrassed that he'd been carrying her. He caught her shoulders before she could follow the others to the stall where the horse thrashed around inside.

"You shouldn't go near him," Genevieve warned before he could, her voice cracking with fear.

"None of them are allowed without an adult with them," Baker called out, his voice loud with authority as he trotted in behind them with Little Jake propped on his hip. While he was the youngest of his brothers and his cousins, Baker had chosen to take on the most responsibility by adopting his late brother's and Genevieve's sister's kids.

"I know! I know!" all the boys called back to him.

Baker glanced at Genevieve, as if checking to see if she believed him. He still didn't entirely trust her.

Collin did. He wasn't sure why after so many other people he cared about had lied to him. But for some reason he did.

Maybe because she'd been so quick to share with him what Bailey Ann had confessed to her. Part of him wished she hadn't told him because now he blamed himself— and they also had to meet with Mrs. Finch.

"And we do indeed have gentle horses,"

Baker assured Genevieve. "Nobody rides Midnight but Dusty."

"Did he really win him in a bet?" Collin asked, wondering about this new branch of his family that he was still getting to know.

"Yes!" Caleb exclaimed. "The owner bet Dusty that he couldn't ride him eight seconds, and Dusty stayed on even longer than that. He thinks Midnight let him do it, though, because he wanted to be with us. He's my best friend."

"I'm your best friend!" Ian indignantly declared.

"You're my best human friend," Caleb assured him. "Midnight is my best animal friend."

"What about Feisty?" Ian asked.

"She's Miller's best animal friend."

"She's Grandma's dog," Miller said as if embarrassed that the little dog had been dubbed his friend. His face was a bit flushed, too, and he looked away from Bailey Ann who'd come up next to him.

"Who's your best friend?" she asked him.

He shrugged. "Uncle Baker."

Baker made a sound in his throat, and those

pale brown eyes of his glistened a bit in the shadows of the big barn.

"Or Miss Taye," Miller said with a slight grin, as if he was teasing his uncle.

"They're grown-ups!" Caleb snorted.

"Grown-ups can be your best friends!" Bailey Ann hotly defended Miller. Then she added, "Dr. Cass was my best friend before he was my dad. And Miss Genevieve, too, before she was my mom. She listens to me." She glanced at Genevieve and sighed. "Sometimes too much."

Collin nearly laughed, but he held it together...until his gaze met Genevieve's. She could have been upset with the comment, over what could happen tomorrow when they met with Mrs. Finch. But there was amusement twinkling in her blue eyes.

Bailey Ann was as cute as she was maddening. He loved her so much, even though he realized now that she'd been playing him a bit. All the time she'd spent in and out of hospitals had made her somewhat precocious. Or maybe she was just a lot like a Haven—stubborn and intent on getting what she wanted.

Miller actually looked right at her then and

he nodded. "Yeah, grown-ups can be your best friends." But he wasn't talking to Caleb. He was agreeing with her.

Collin smiled. Both of these kids could use a best friend their own age. And they understood each other from the harrowing experiences they'd lived through, better than even the grown-ups in their lives probably did.

"Do you know how to ride a horse?" Miller asked her.

Bailey Ann looked away from him now and shook her head, embarrassed. But then she touched her chest. "I couldn't. I had a bad heart my whole life. I just got a new one a little while ago."

Maybe someone had told the kids about her already because none of them seemed all that surprised. In fact Miller just nodded. "I haven't been able to ride for a while because of this." He touched his leg. "It was messed up really bad. But it's better now, so I'm just starting back up. I'm a little rusty."

Collin stepped back to whisper to Genevieve. "I think we lost our best friend."

She had pressed a hand against her heart, and she nodded now. "I think we did."

He was joking, but after tomorrow's meeting, would they lose her for real?

GENEVIEVE'S HEART FELT like it was breaking for so many reasons. Maybe just because it was too full of love. For the kids…

Just the kids…

She wasn't falling for Collin. At the moment, clutching the saddle horn and the reins, she was just trying not to fall off the horse. Bailey Ann rode in front of Collin, and Genevieve felt a flash of envy for the little girl. But then she knew it wouldn't have been smart for Genevieve to sit that close to Collin. She would have been so on edge that the horse would have felt her nerves.

The one with him and Bailey Ann on it was plodding calmly along; the one with her on it had stopped moving entirely.

"You're pulling so hard on the reins that Peanut Butter thinks you want her to stop," Baker pointed out. They were now heading back to the barn, along the route he'd already taken them around the ranch. He was at the rear with Little Jake now instead of the front.

Heat flushed her face. She should have known that; Becca had given her a quick riding lesson that day. She knew how to ride, but she was so distracted over that meeting tomorrow with Mrs. Finch. Not to mention Collin. That kiss they'd shared kept replaying through her mind, keeping her awake, making her want something she had no business wanting anymore. Love.

Though she didn't want to open herself up to that pain and disappointment again, it didn't matter what she wanted at this point; she had a feeling that it was coming anyway.

She eased her grip on the reins a bit to urge the horse to move again, but Baker reached out and caught her reins, holding them up.

"I've been wanting to talk to you alone," he said.

She glanced at Little Jake, who was riding in front of him. But Little Jake's eyes were closed, his body slumped. The movement of the horse must have rocked the toddler to sleep.

She braced herself, expecting Baker to blast her over the ordeal with CPS. While Taye had forgiven her, Baker might not be as compelled to do that. He was obviously very protective of their nephews. "I'm sorry," she said. "I really never meant to cause any trouble for them. I only wanted to make sure they were okay."

"They weren't…for a while," Baker admitted. "Neither was I."

She remembered what Collin had told her. Baker had been first on the scene of that horrific accident. She shuddered, thinking of what he must have seen, how hard it must have been to treat his family. No wonder he'd quit being a firefighter and paramedic and had become the ranch foreman, which was what Dale had been.

"I'm sorry," she said again, her voice cracking with sympathy for them all.

"Don't be," he said. "I believe you had their best interests at heart."

"But I don't know them—not like you do," she said. "I can see how much you and Taye love them."

Baker cuddled Little Jake closer. The toddler had the dark hair and eyes of his uncles. And his mother. Jenny had had dark hair and eyes; she'd been so beautiful.

"We all love them, but…" His voice got so gruff he had to clear his throat. "I really believe that it's best for them to have one set of guardians instead of all their uncles and aunts trying to raise them."

Realizing he was telling her to butt out, she flinched. "I understand…" And she really did. She could see how Bailey Ann had played that foster family to get what she'd wanted: Collin. Kids with divorced parents often took advantage of the situation and played them off against one another. If so many people tried to act as their parents, the kids were going to be confused by the rules and lack of rules.

"I want *everyone* to be involved in their lives," he said. "But as uncles and *aunts*."

Wait. She drew in a shaky breath. He *wasn't* telling her to butt out; he was inviting her in. "I want that, too," she said. "That's all I wanted."

He pushed back his hat and arched a dark eyebrow. "Really? Colton told me about your house…"

Heat flushed her face and it wasn't just from the sun beating down on them. "I wanted to be prepared in case they needed someone to take them." She reached out now and touched his arm. "But I realize you and Taye are all they need."

"I didn't believe that in the beginning,"

Baker said, and his topaz eyes glistened a bit. "Miller hated me."

"But he said you're his best friend…"

"We came a long way," Baker said, "with the help of a child psychologist and Taye. We're going to get married soon. As soon as Sadie and I can figure out where we can set it up without Taye doing all the work."

"Like she did for my wedding."

"Miller really does help her, and Dusty's mother-in-law, Juliet, does, too. But I don't want her to even have to think about anything but us."

"I'll do whatever I can to help."

"Help us adopt the boys."

"Sadie has a lawyer working—"

"We want you," he said.

She smiled. "I can't fight it if I'm facilitating it?"

His mouth curved into a slight grin. "That might have been part of it. But we've also seen what you're doing for Collin and Bailey Ann. The sacrifice you're making for them."

Sacrifice…

It didn't feel like that now, with both of them living with her. But when they weren't…

Her stomach dropped at the thought of it,

of going back to that empty house, that empty existence.

She shouldn't have waited for Bradford to come around to the idea of fostering. She should have just done it on her own. And she could have when she'd moved to Willow Creek, but she'd been using her nephews as an excuse to wait.

But she hadn't even sought them out. She'd been so scared of being hurt and disappointed again. Of feeling again...

Bradford had been right about one thing; she had shut down during their marriage.

"We don't know yet how that's going to work out with Bailey Ann," she said. She and Collin hadn't told anyone else what had happened yet but Mrs. Finch. She was tempted to tell Baker because she was so worried.

But he had enough on his plate right now.

"If you're too busy..." he said, giving her an out.

She shook her head. "No. I'll never be too busy for you and for them. I'll get right to work on it."

"Good," he said. "Grandma's lawyer is nice and all but he's probably older than she is and has a tendency to nod off during appointments."

She laughed. "I know who you mean. He has nodded off on me a time or two. I was hoping it was just a brilliant strategy on his part."

Baker laughed, too.

"Mommy!" Bailey Ann called out.

Genevieve and her horse both jumped a bit, the horse's hooves pawing at the ground. Baker reached out to steady her as Collin came up alongside her.

"Sorry," Collin said, apologizing to her. "We came back to make sure you were doing okay." He glanced at his cousin, as if worried that he'd been giving her a hard time.

Bailey Ann looked worried, too. The child was so empathetic that she'd probably picked up on their fears over that meeting with Mrs. Finch, that they might take her away from them. They'd wanted to reassure her that it wouldn't happen. But they just didn't know…

If they lost her, Genevieve wouldn't just lose Bailey Ann; she would lose Collin, too, because the little girl was the only reason he'd married her.

LEM WATCHED SADIE watching her family as they all crowded around the island in the big kitchen at Ranch Haven. Just back from a long horse ride around part of the extensive property, the kids were *starving* for cookies of course. He'd managed to sneak a couple himself before they'd burst back into the house.

The cookies were good, especially the snickerdoodles. The taste of nutmeg and cinnamon lingered on his tongue. But the look on Sadie's face was what gave him the most pleasure. Happiness and love.

She loved all her family so very much. Then she glanced over at him, and that look stayed on her face. She loved him, too.

He was a lucky man. He kept thinking that he needed to marry her as soon as possible, but with her family—their family—still a bit unsettled, he wasn't sure if now was the time to push her. He knew she'd met with that pretty Realtor, trying to get information out of her about Cash.

And that she was concerned about Collin and Genevieve, too. And, most of all, that sweet little girl…

They all seemed so happy, like Sadie's plan was working. Of course she'd denied that she'd had a plan when she'd referred Collin to the lawyer, to Jenny's sister, but Sadie didn't ever *not* have a plan.

He needed her to tell him what the plan was for their wedding. Since the tattoo parlor was out, did she want to get married here? On the ranch?

Or did it hold too many memories of Big Jake for her? She'd remodeled and built on to it so much since Jake had passed that it wasn't the same place they'd shared.

It was a place Lem felt comfortable sharing with her now.

Despite being old and set in their ways, they'd managed to adjust to suit each other.

He loved her so very much.

She looked away from him to where Collin and Genevieve stood at the counter with Bailey Ann. Her brow furrowed, and he followed her gaze to see what had concerned her.

They looked so happy, but there was also something a little off. As if they were trying too hard to look happy for the little girl...

Something was wrong.

He had no doubt that Sadie would find out what and would come up with some way to try to fix it. But she'd learned the hard way, the same way he had through the loss of ones they'd loved, that some things were beyond even their control.

CHAPTER TWENTY

YESTERDAY HAD BEEN a fun day. Maybe too fun because it had been hard for Collin and Genevieve to get Bailey Ann settled and asleep that night. Or maybe, despite their efforts to get their minds off the meeting with Mrs. Finch, she'd felt their anxiety.

Their fear...

And from the grim look on Mrs. Finch's face, it was obvious they'd had every reason to be fearful. She'd just come out of Bailey Ann's bedroom where she'd insisted on having a private conversation with the little girl while he and Genevieve had paced around the island in the kitchen.

"Can I get you anything, Mrs. Finch?" Genevieve asked. "Coffee? Tea?"

He didn't know if she was being a gracious host, or if she just wanted to put off whatever bad news Mrs. Finch was about to give them. And from the look on her face, he doubted it was anything else.

Even Genevieve, who seemed to work hard to find the positive in a situation, didn't seem as if she'd found one now. Not like she had with Cash's lighter. And Sadie's lawyer. He'd overheard the conversation she'd had with his cousin, how she'd considered Sadie's lawyer was deliberately using a strategy instead of accidentally falling asleep. Genevieve Porter was so many things. The smart and savvy lawyer. The woman who carried such guilt over her sister and nephews. The generous optimist...

"I am very disappointed," Mrs. Finch said. "I had hoped this would work out."

"It will," Genevieve insisted.

Mrs. Finch shook her head. "I was concerned that there was an unnatural attachment between Dr. Cassidy and his young patient, and this proves it."

Collin sucked in a breath. "What are you saying?"

"That's why I was hesitant to place her with you and why I considered it might be better to move her to Sheridan."

"Collin and Bailey Ann are like father and daughter," Genevieve said. "And they should be father and daughter."

"Not if it puts her health at risk."

THE DOC'S INSTANT FAMILY

"*Not* being with him put her at risk," Genevieve said in his defense.

But was that accurate? He could almost understand what Mrs. Finch was thinking.

"That was because she wasn't taking medication so that she could see her doctor again," Mrs. Finch. "That's why it's an unhealthy attachment for her—when she would put her life in jeopardy like that."

Collin's knees shook a bit, and he had to lean against the countertop or he might have fallen. Mrs. Finch was right about that.

"They should have been making certain she was taking her medication," Genevieve said. "In my training to become a foster parent, I learned that some kids put their meds under their tongue and spit them out later, especially their ADHD medications."

"Nobody expected a child who'd been through everything that Bailey Ann had would risk her life like that, especially after her new heart gave her a chance at having a normal one. She needs some psychological evaluations," Mrs. Finch said. "That's where I'm taking her today."

Collin tensed. "Where specifically are you taking her?"

"The child's ward of a psychiatric hospital. I have her packing now—"

"No!" Collin said. "She'll be terrified in a place like that."

"It's necessary," Mrs. Finch said. "What she did was so extreme. What happens if she doesn't get her way again? Will she deliberately sabotage her health until she gets what she wants?"

"I talked to her," he insisted. "She understands how dangerous what she did was. She won't do it again."

"I need to make certain of that," Mrs. Finch said.

Genevieve cleared her throat. "So what is this? Some kind of test? You'll see if she takes her meds away from him and if she does, she can come back to us?"

Mrs. Finch tensed. "I don't know. My supervisor and I will consider the psychiatrist's evaluation and make our determination on her placement."

Collin's heart rate quickened, his pulse racing. He was losing her. Just as he'd feared...

"THIS IS YOUR FAULT!" Bailey Ann cried as Mrs. Finch tugged her toward the front door.

Genevieve flinched, guilt weighing heavily on her because the little girl was right.

"This is your fault! You had to tell!" Bailey Ann shouted, tears streaming down her face.

Tears were streaming down Genevieve's, too. "I didn't mean for this to happen…" she murmured. She hadn't wanted Collin to lose her. She hadn't wanted to lose her.

Collin stepped around her. "Mrs. Finch, wait a moment please," he requested, his voice gruff.

The social worker stopped, her body stiff with resistance.

Bailey Ann threw her arms around Collin's neck. "I don't want to leave you, Daddy. I don't want to leave you!"

"Hey, hey," he said gently. "This isn't Genevieve's fault."

Bailey Ann's face tensed with displeasure and she glared at Genevieve over his head. "It is! I shouldn't have told her the truth!"

"Yes, you should have," Collin said. "You should always tell the truth. No matter what. I know you wanted to see me, but you put your health at risk."

"I won't ever again. I promise!"

Genevieve squeezed her eyes shut at the pain in Bailey Ann's voice.

"It's not just that," Collin said, still holding her gently. "Right now, the Morelys aren't allowed to take care of kids who have medical needs. That's not fair to them or to the kids who might need them. Do you see that?"

Though to some extent, Genevieve mused, they did deserve a mark on their record.

Tears trailed down Bailey Ann's face. "I didn't think about that…"

"You need to," Collin said. "I know you've been in this little world that revolves around you and your health, but there are other people out there, other kids like you who need good homes and need help—"

"I need you!"

"I need you, too," Collin said. "But we need to do it the right way. We don't want to play tricks or cause problems. That's not the right way to do things, especially when other people get hurt because of it."

Like the way Genevieve had hurt the Havens because she hadn't been straightforward about her relationship with her nephews and her concern for their well-being.

"I made a mistake like this," Genevieve said. And she knelt down next to Collin to face the little girl. "I was worried about Ian and Miller and Little Jake, and instead of finding out for myself how they were, I was being sneaky. I was asking other people to help me find out. And they got reported to CPS."

"CPS?" Bailey Ann asked. As angry as she was with Genevieve, she was still curious… probably just because it was about the boys.

"Child Protective Services," Mrs. Finch explained for her. She was watching this scene unfold closely.

"And they could have been taken away from the ranch, away from the Havens, and they might have even been separated," she said. "And I was wrong. I should have just been open and honest and they never would have had to worry." And she was going to push that adoption through as fast as she could to make sure they never worried again and that they had the security they deserved.

Bailey Ann deserved it, too.

"I made a mistake," Genevieve said. "Just like you did. Everybody makes them." She glanced up at Mrs. Finch. "It doesn't make us bad people…unless we don't learn from those mistakes. We need to always try to do better. To be better. But just because you made a mistake doesn't make you bad or wrong. It just makes you human."

Did the little girl understand what she was trying to tell her? She didn't want her blaming herself for this. Genevieve would much rather have Bailey Ann blame her. "You're a good girl," she said, as those tears continued to roll down her face, "and I love you very much."

Bailey Ann didn't say anything. She just closed her eyes and more tears rolled down her face. She probably hated Genevieve.

Genevieve stood up and stepped back, then turned away because she couldn't watch Mrs. Finch take the little girl out of the arms of the man Bailey Ann considered her father.

She braced herself as the door opened and closed. They were gone. And when she turned around, so was Collin.

She waited for a long while in that empty hallway, in that empty house, but he didn't come back. Bailey Ann wasn't the only one who blamed her. Apparently Collin did, too.

Genevieve had lost them both.

JESSUP GLANCED UP as the door opened. It was early for Marsh to come home. And Darlene, Sarah and her son were already here. Mikey was playing in the backyard while Sarah and Darlene made dinner.

He should have been doing something. For so many years he hadn't had the strength or the energy. But now, with his new heart, he was stronger. Healthier…

He jumped up now from the chair where he'd been reading and walked toward the front door. Collin was the one who'd opened and then closed it—with his back, apparently, since he leaned against it.

He was pale and shaky, like he'd seen a ghost. Like Jessup had felt for so many years. Like a ghost of himself. Of the father he should have been to his sons.

"Collin, what's wrong?" he asked with concern. "What happened?"

Jessup stepped closer, surveying his son for injuries. He looked fine except for his face. His expression of such…

Devastation. He'd only looked like that once before that Jessup could remember. When his mother had died…

No. Twice.

And when Cash had run off…

"You're scaring me," Jessup said. "What's going on?"

Collin blinked and roused himself, worrying now about Jessup. "I didn't mean to scare you," he said, his voice gruff. Almost as if he'd been crying.

Collin had always made it a point to never cry in front of anyone. Ever since he was a kid…

Jessup had figured at first that it was because he hadn't wanted his brothers to tease him about his tears. But even when they'd cried, he hadn't. It wasn't because he hadn't cared or he'd been too proud; it was because he hadn't wanted to worry anyone.

He wanted to take care of people, not have anyone take care of him.

That was why he'd become a doctor. Jessup knew all that. And he knew, too, that all those times he hadn't cried in public, he'd cried alone. Because Collin's voice had sounded then how it did now, raw and vulnerable, as he continued, "I just didn't know where else to go."

Jessup stepped forward and reached for his son, closing his arms around him as Collin gave into the sobs that wracked his body. He could barely understand what he said through his tears. But it sounded like, "They took her away. They took Bailey Ann away."

CHAPTER TWENTY-ONE

COLLIN HADN'T WANTED Genevieve to see him cry, so he'd just kept going after he'd walked Bailey Ann and Mrs. Finch out. He'd gotten in his car and driven off. And now he didn't know how to undo what he'd done...

With Bailey Ann.

Or with Genevieve.

Why hadn't he realized what the little girl had done? Why her body had been rejecting her new heart? He should have talked to her. No. He should have done what Genevieve had done. He should have listened.

Hopefully Genevieve hadn't listened to what the little girl had said in anger, how she'd blamed her. Genevieve already took the blame for too many things that weren't her fault.

Too many mistakes...

What she'd said to Bailey Ann was so much better than anything he or Mrs. Finch had told the little girl. Genevieve had done her best to make sure the little girl didn't blame herself for anything. She was an incredible foster mom. An incredible person…

An incredible woman.

She was his wife.

But that had only been for Bailey Ann. Now that Bailey Ann was gone…

It would have been awkward for him to go back to that house without the little girl. Without the reason he and Genevieve had gotten married in the first place…

But he had another reason now. He'd started to fall in love with his wife. And he missed her as badly as he missed Bailey Ann, and it had only been one night, one night spent lying awake in the den of his dad's rental house.

Jessup couldn't buy it yet, not until the insurance settled his house fire claim and the sale could close on the ranch. Collin wondered if settlements like this usually took so long. Was the insurance company investigating the possibility of arson? Of Jessup's involvement?

He couldn't believe it of his father. He had nearly died while he'd tried to find the nurse's son. His dad wouldn't have put anyone else in danger. He wanted to believe that Cash wouldn't have either. Cash had been so gentle with animals and with their mother when she was sick. But the Cash that had left their house had been so angry...

So full of rage.

Like Bailey Ann had toward Genevieve. He should have stayed after the little girl and social worker left. He should have comforted Genevieve. Instead he'd run home to his dad, to his comfort.

And he'd left Genevieve all alone.

And she was. She had no one.

He had his family. While he hadn't sought comfort from them before, somehow he'd always known they would be there when he needed them.

When Genevieve had needed someone, he hadn't been there for her. If he'd really been her husband, he would have been a lousy one. He needed to talk to her. To apologize...for his own behavior and for Bailey Ann's.

His cell vibrated in his pocket, startling him with the movement and the fact it hadn't died. He hadn't even plugged it in last night. He probably hadn't even brushed his teeth. After falling apart on his dad, he'd slunk away to the den and dropped onto the foldout bed. As exhausted as he'd been, he hadn't been able to sleep. Instead he'd kept imagining where Bailey Ann was, worrying that it was terrible and then wishing that Genevieve was there to force him to look on the bright side.

That the little girl needed to talk to someone, just as Dale and Jenny's kids had needed to talk to a child psychologist in order to deal with their parents' deaths. He'd been so concerned about Bailey Ann's medical care that he hadn't seen to her emotional and psychological care.

Mrs. Finch was doing just that. And chances were that she wasn't going to trust him with any care of Bailey Ann again. She might even move the little girl back to Sheridan so that she could see the specialists there.

His phone vibrated again, with a voice mail, and he realized he hadn't even answered it. He grabbed the cell from his pocket, anxious to see if it was Genevieve calling or Mrs. Finch. But it was the hospital.

He was needed for a consultation.

What about Genevieve? He should have called her and at least texted her. But she hadn't called or texted him either.

Had she needed him last night? This was why he hadn't wanted emotions to enter into their relationship. He never seemed to live up to what other people needed from him. He'd feared he'd end up hurting Genevieve, that she deserved more than he would be able to give. And his worst fears were coming true.

WHEN GENEVIEVE FINALLY gave up on sleep and rolled out of her bed the next morning, she felt the way Ian must have when that bronco had knocked him down.

Ian had just gotten a few bumps and bruises from his fall, though, whereas she felt like the thing had stomped all over her. She ached all over.

Mostly her heart.

All night she'd lain awake worrying about Bailey Ann and Collin. She'd only wanted to help them, but instead she'd hurt them.

Bailey Ann had been so upset with her. And Collin...

Obviously he hadn't wanted to be with her. He'd never come home last night. She'd lain awake all night with her head cocked, listening for any sound.

But there had been no creak of hinges, no

soft snap of a door closing. She'd been alone in the house—more alone than she'd felt in a long time.

Probably since she'd lost one of those babies she'd carried for such a short time.

This disappointment over losing Bailey Ann was nearly as sharp as the disappointment and devastation she'd felt when she'd tried to conceive. When, month after month, she'd found she wasn't pregnant. And then, when the IVF had worked, she'd lost the babies anyway.

But she hadn't been able to do anything about those losses. With Bailey Ann, maybe there was hope. She wasn't gone forever.

This time Genevieve could fight. As her foster parent, she had rights. She had to…

SADIE HAD GOTTEN another early morning call from Jessup. This time he wasn't angry with her. He sounded too upset and frustrated to be angry.

She understood how he felt—how much it hurt when one of your kids was hurting and you were no help. And he knew she understood because she'd felt that way about him so often; she felt that way even now.

Because she wasn't sure how much she would be able to help…

But she'd had to do something. So instead of going back to sleep with Feisty, who'd grumbled over the call, she'd gotten up and driven toward town. She didn't go to Jessup's, where Collin was staying. She didn't go to her grandson. He had Jessup and his brother and Darlene to support him.

Sadie went to the person who had no one.

Genevieve opened the door to Sadie and, her voice so soft and so much like Jenny's, said, "They're not here."

"I know," Sadie said. "That's why I'm here."

Tears pooled in Genevieve's blue eyes, rimmed by dark circles. She looked exhausted and vulnerable. But then she blinked back those tears and straightened her shoulders. "I'm not giving up."

"Good," Sadie praised her. "What are you not giving up on? Fostering Bailey Ann or your marriage?"

"My marriage isn't real," Genevieve said, but her voice cracked slightly. "What I need to fix is this situation with Bailey Ann. It was my fault Mrs. Finch took her away for that evaluation." Her voice cracked again, and she cleared it. "I have to make sure she comes back here after it."

"But Collin isn't here," Sadie said.

Genevieve sucked in a breath. "Did you talk to him? Do you know how he's doing? Does he blame me like Bailey Ann does?"

"No. His father called me," Sadie said. "And he didn't really understand what had happened. Just that Bailey Ann had been taken away. I don't know why. Did Mrs. Finch suspect the marriage wasn't real?"

Genevieve shook her head, and her tears pooled again as she told Sadie how the little girl had sabotaged her own health to leave her last foster family.

"You had to tell Mrs. Finch about that," Sadie assured her. "And her getting help is good. The boys needed that, and I wish we would have gotten it for them sooner. But it was so chaotic after the accident…"

Genevieve flinched, and her slim shoulders sagged even more with the weight of all that guilt she kept carrying. Sadie gripped those shoulders in her hands and turned her toward her.

"You didn't know," Sadie told her. "You

didn't do anything wrong, Genevieve, with your sister or with Bailey Ann."

The tears brimmed over and ran down her face. Sadie pulled her in for a hug. And Sadie wasn't really much of a hugger.

Genevieve clung to her for a moment before pulling back. "Thank you. Thank you for coming over to check on me. Thank you for caring."

"I don't think anyone cares as much as you do," Sadie said. The woman was a really good person. "You remind me so much of your sister." And her chest ached over that loss.

Genevieve smiled but shook her head. "It's the voice."

"It's the heart," Sadie said. "You both have big ones."

Genevieve's teeth nipped her bottom lip for a moment before she mused aloud, "Sometimes I wonder if Bailey Ann has Jenny's heart. She got it around the same time of the accident. But her surgery was in Sheridan—"

"All transplant surgeries for anyone in this area are done there," Sadie said. "The hospital here isn't set up for them. I've wondered the same thing. I like to know that something good could come out of something so horrible. I'm pretty sure that Jessup has Dale's heart."

"Oh… I'm sorry. I'm so sorry about Dale, too. I keep thinking of Jenny and the boys but Dale…" She shook her head. "I didn't know him. I didn't know my brother-in-law."

"He was so much like Jenny. If there really is such a thing as soul mates, they were it. It didn't matter how young they married, they would have made it for the long haul."

"Our parents were wrong," she said. "And they missed out on so much and keep missing out. Those little boys are the only grandkids they'll have."

"You won't have any?"

Genevieve snorted. "Not biological ones. And those are the only ones they'll consider theirs, just like my ex-husband. Some people don't understand that a child can be yours even if you don't share the same DNA. Collin understands that."

And Genevieve understood and cared about Collin. Why hadn't he stayed here with his wife?

"I'm going to fix this," Genevieve said. She lifted her chin. "I'm going to make this right for Bailey Ann and Collin."

"And what about what's right for you?" Sadie asked.

Genevieve shrugged. "It was always about them. I only agreed to help Bailey Ann." She sighed. "And instead I hurt her…"

"She's not the only one who got hurt," Sadie said.

"I know Collin is hurting."

"You are, too," Sadie said. But Genevieve only seemed to care about others, not herself. Somebody needed to love this woman like she deserved to be loved. Hopefully he already did; he just didn't know how to show it.

CHAPTER TWENTY-TWO

COLLIN WAS GRATEFUL that he'd had a reason to get up and out of the house. He was also grateful that he'd been able to help the person who'd come into the ER with what he'd thought was an anxiety attack.

It wasn't. And it could have been so much worse if his wife hadn't insisted on bringing him into the hospital. Fortunately Collin, with his interventional cardiology fellowship experience, was able to quickly assess and get the patient to the cath lab where he'd inserted a catheter and removed a blockage that could have killed the young husband and new father.

He was so glad to help that family. A real family, not like what he'd tried to cobble together. Genevieve didn't love him; he knew that. Love wasn't part of their marriage. Only Bailey Ann was and now she was gone.

His office door rattled, knuckles striking the wood. He glanced up from his desk and saw that those knuckles were swollen with arthritis but the hand, and the woman to whom it belonged, was strong. "I'd like a consultation, Dr. Cassidy," she said.

He shook his head. "You know I can't treat you anymore now that we know we're family."

Which was why he probably shouldn't have been treating Bailey Ann either, once he'd gotten so attached to her. Because she'd become family to him then and he hadn't been able to be objective with all of his emotions involved.

"I'm not here for a medical consultation," Sadie said.

He leaned back in his chair and arched an eyebrow. "My dad called you."

She nodded. "He's worried about you."

His stomach knotted. "I don't want to talk about this…" His throat already felt raw from last night, and he hadn't talked much. He'd cried instead. And he'd felt like he hadn't cried just for Bailey Ann but for all his other losses and disappointments over the years.

In some ways it had been cathartic. In other ways it had left him as raw as his throat. And vulnerable…

"I'm worried about you, too," she said. "I know how hard you studied and worked to become a cardiologist. I know you're not a quitter. So I don't understand why you're giving up now."

"Giving up?" he asked. "I have no rights to Bailey Ann."

"What about your wife?"

"Genevieve is really her foster parent," he said.

"She is going to fight for Bailey Ann," Sadie said.

"How do you know that?"

"I just talked to her," Sadie said. "She's determined. She actually thinks Bailey Ann might have her sister's heart." She cocked her head and studied his face. "Is that possible?"

He shook his head. "No. It's not Jenny's heart. Is that really what Genevieve has been thinking?"

"It's crossed her mind," Sadie said. "It's crossed my mind, too. The little girl just feels like she belongs with all of us."

"She deserves a family of her own," Collin said. "One that loves her for her." Not because of someone's body part they might have.

"Genevieve deserves the same thing," Sadie said.

He furrowed his forehead as the pounding in his skull intensified. "What do you mean?"

"Jenny talked about her big sister a lot," Sadie said. "She probably felt as guilty about Genevieve as Genevieve feels about her."

"Why? Everybody has said how sweet and kind and loving Jenny was." Which was maybe why Genevieve had thought Bailey Ann had her heart.

"She was. And she felt like it was her fault—the way her parents treated Genevieve. Her mom got pregnant with Genevieve in high school and dumped her on her grandparents so that she could live her own life. She probably would have left Genevieve there, but when she got married years later, her parents made her take her daughter back. It was as if nobody wanted responsibility for her. Nobody wanted her."

His gut wrenched with sympathy for her. "That's terrible. I knew it wasn't a good family situation, that her stepdad didn't really want her." But he hadn't realized that her mother and grandparents really hadn't either.

"That's why she wanted to help Bailey Ann," Sadie said. "Because she knows how it feels to have nobody want responsibility for you."

"I want responsibility for Bailey Ann," he said. But he wasn't sure he deserved it when he hadn't figured out what had really happened with her medications.

"What about your wife?" Sadie asked.

"She didn't want this to be permanent. She was just helping us out." While she might have fallen for Bailey Ann, he doubted she'd fallen for him. And even if she'd started developing feelings for him, he'd probably ruined his chances with her over how he'd left her after Bailey Ann had been taken away.

Sadie sighed and shook her head, as if she was disappointed in him. "Despite all your education and training, you just don't get it."

"Get what?"

"Life. Love. You've spent so much of time studying that you haven't spent much living, have you, Dr. Cassidy?"

He stiffened, getting defensive like he had whenever his brothers had teased him about never doing anything but studying and working. But they'd understood why; he wasn't sure that his grandmother did.

She walked around his desk and reached

down to lay her hand against his cheek. "Your father is doing well. And Bailey Ann, despite this issue, is doing well. You can stop worrying about everyone else for a bit, Collin, and worry about yourself. What do you want?"

"Bailey Ann." And Genevieve. He wanted his wife, too, but he was afraid to admit it, afraid that he didn't have a chance with her. She'd made it clear that she'd never wanted to get married again. He'd appreciated that she'd been willing to marry him anyway for Bailey Ann's sake, yet he found himself wishing that it had been for another reason. Wishing he'd been the man she'd married for love.

"Kids are wonderful," Sadie said. "But they grow up and move away. Or they run away before they grow up. They don't grow old with you. And you don't want to grow old alone." She moved her hand from his face, and she suddenly looked very old—her shoulders sagging, and the lines around her mouth and eyes deepening a little.

He thought she and Lem Lemmon were engaged. Had something happened?

"Are you okay?" he asked her with concern.

She nodded. "Yes. Just realizing that everything doesn't always work out how I intended…"

"Did you have a matchmaking scheme in mind when you referred me to Genevieve?" he asked.

"I did," she admitted. "But I realize now that throwing people together isn't enough… not if they're not willing to risk their hearts…"

Was she talking about him or Genevieve?

GENEVIEVE HAD GONE into her office, figuring that calls coming from a legal practice might bear more weight than calls from a scared foster mom. So she sat at her desk, calling Mrs. Finch and the psychiatrist and Mrs. Finch's supervisor, and she pleaded her case to every one of them.

She was just looking up the number for family court when her door creaked open. It was probably Hilda, who'd been very supportive this morning after acknowledging how tired Genevieve had looked.

She wasn't just tired. She was exhausted. Physically and emotionally. So when she looked up and saw that it was actually Collin standing in her doorway, she nearly groaned. If he was angry with her, she couldn't deal with that emotion right now, not on top of all the others pummeling her. "I'm working on trying to get her back," she promised. "I've been on the phone all morning…"

But she had no idea if Mrs. Finch had listened to her any more than she listened to Bailey Ann.

"Why?" he asked.

"Why what? We can't leave her in a psych ward or let them move her somewhere else…"

"No, I mean, why do you care so much?" Collin asked. "Is it because you think she has Jenny's heart?"

She sucked in a breath. "You talked to Sadie."

"So did you," he said. "I didn't realize you thought that."

She shrugged. "Just a couple of times in passing. I didn't think it was actually possible."

"It wasn't," he said. "She doesn't have Jenny's heart. But I know that someone got it who desperately needed it. A part of Jenny still lives on."

She sucked in a breath and nodded. "That's good."

"I hope that gives you some comfort," he said.

"I've accepted that I can't change the past," she said. "Like I told Bailey Ann, I can't make up for those mistakes that I made. I can just make sure I don't make them again."

"That's why you won't marry for love again? Because it didn't work out the first time?"

A bitter chuckle slipped out. "It more than didn't work out. It destroyed me. The IVF, the miscarriages, the disappointment…being the disappointment…" She was right; she was too full of emotions to deal with his right now. To deal with him at all.

She pointed toward the door now. "You can leave, like you did last night. The only thing we have in common is that we both care about Bailey Ann. You can question my reasons for caring, but that doesn't change that I care. Unless you'd rather I not get her back? Unless you'd rather she went to someone else other than me?"

Bailey Ann might not want to come back to her since she blamed her for all of this, just as Collin was probably blaming her.

"Genevieve, that's…" His throat moved as if he was struggling to swallow. "I didn't mean it like that…"

She shrugged as if she wasn't hurting as

much as she was. "We both know we were only together for Bailey Ann. So of course, you'd leave when she did. I didn't expect anything more from you."

She hadn't expected it, but she'd wanted it. She'd wanted his support. She wanted him. But clearly his only interest in her was to help him get Bailey Ann.

Suddenly very weary, she dropped into the chair behind her desk. "We can get this marriage annulled. We can end it now."

"Is that what you want?" he asked.

No. It was the last thing she wanted. But she also wanted to be wanted for herself, not for the babies she was supposed to give birth to or as a means to anyone's ends but her own. She wanted happily-ever-after; she wanted the love that Jenny had found with Dale.

She sighed. "You know... I'm still jealous of my little sister like I was when we were growing up. Even though she ultimately lost everything...even her life...she and Dale had it all."

Love was everything.

"Genevieve, I don't understand..." Collin murmured.

"No, of course you don't," she said.

"What do you want to do?" he asked.

She wanted to love and be loved, but she was done begging for it, like she had with her mom and stepdad, her grandparents. Even at the end, she'd begged Bradford as much as her pride had allowed.

"I want some time to think," she said. Because at the moment, all she could do was feel, and it was too much.

"Genevieve..."

She shook her head. "No. Please, just go."

He didn't argue with her. Didn't fight for her. He just turned and walked away like he had the night before when she'd needed him. Instead of coming together to support each other, he'd just left her alone.

She was sick of getting left.

Lem watched Sadie's face as she finished up her call. It had rung the minute she'd stepped inside his office, so they hadn't had a chance to even greet each other. And he'd missed her...even though he'd had dinner at her house the night before. But because he'd had a morning meeting, as Ben's deputy mayor, he'd left right after dinner. He didn't like leaving her anymore.

She clicked off her cell and closed her eyes and sighed.

"What's wrong?" he asked with concern. "Who was that?"

"Hilda Feltman from Genevieve's office."

He nodded. "Oh, so you have a source at Genevieve's office."

"Yes, and I don't like what she just told me. Sounds like Genevieve and Collin are done. She overheard them fighting." She shook her head. "And that's my fault. It's all my fault." A tear trailed down her cheek.

And Lem rushed around his desk to kneel in front of the chair she'd dropped into when she'd walked into his office. "Oh, Sadie…"

"Go ahead," she said. "You warned me. Go ahead and say I told you so."

"I love you," he said instead.

And she snorted, then laughed. "You never do what I expect you to do, Lem Lemmon."

"That's why you love me," he said.

"Yes, it is," she agreed. "Even like now, you're on your knees again after telling me when you proposed that was the last time you were getting down on the floor."

"I know you'll help me back up," he said. "Just like you did last time. And I want to help you, too, with Collin and Genevieve. But what I want to do most of all is to stop worrying about our families and just think of ourselves for once. I want to marry you, Sadie March Haven."

"You already proposed," she reminded him. "And I already accepted. Though technically I did propose first…"

"And I was a fool for not accepting right away," he said.

"You're proud. That's why I haven't…"

"Haven't what?" he asked.

"Haven't pushed for a wedding date."

He stared at her. "I haven't pushed for a wedding date because I thought you wanted to wait until Ben and Emily and Baker and Taye got married."

She snorted. "They're young. They have time. You and me… We shouldn't wait."

"I agree."

"I guess there's a first time for everything," she said with a chuckle.

"You know you always get me to come around to your way of thinking…" He chuckled now, remembering all the times she'd charged into city hall to confront him with something or other about the town. "Let's get married here or in town square," he said. "Like as soon as we can get the license and a tattoo artist booked."

She laughed. "You're serious about those tattooed rings."

"I'm serious about you," he said. "And I want everyone to know that. So will you marry me as soon as we can make it happen?"

She nodded. "I didn't want to push you, but I was hoping that you'd take the hint when I talked Ben into putting up the Valentine's decorations."

"Those were for me?" He was so touched.

"I am for you, Lemar Lemmon, and you are for me," she said. And she leaned forward and kissed him. "As long as we have each other, we can let the rest of them sort themselves out for once."

He touched her forehead. "Feeling okay, woman?"

"Never better," she said and kissed him again.

CHAPTER TWENTY-THREE

JUST WHEN HE'D thought he couldn't have made a bigger mess of things with Genevieve, he had. First he'd taken off the night before without saying a word to her. She'd probably thought he'd blamed her like Bailey Ann had.

And now he'd left her again. Sure, this time she'd told him to go. That she couldn't deal with him. That was why he'd walked out of her office and out of the practice. But now…

He stood on the street, watching the heart-shaped balloons and decorations flutter around in the slight breeze. It was as if it was all mocking him. As if love was mocking him.

He'd gone and fallen in love with his wife. And instead of fighting for her, for them, he had walked away again. She'd talked to him before about shutting down, and he realized now that was what he'd always done. He'd buried himself in his studies because it was easier than dealing with his fears over his dad's health and losing his mom and Cash.

He'd run away instead of dealing with his problems. Not that Genevieve was a problem…

The only problem was going to be if she didn't feel about him like he felt about her. If she hadn't fallen for him, too…

But he wasn't going to know until he asked, until he put his heart on the line first.

GENEVIEVE WONDERED IF she was going to need a new heart someday. Hers felt like it had been broken so many times, ever since she was a little girl, that she wasn't sure how long it would last.

She was smart not to risk it again. That had been her decision after her divorce. That had been the reason why she'd thought it so smart to just have a marriage of convenience, where there would be no messy emotions involved. No expectations. No disappointments.

But when Collin walked out of her office, that disappointment settled heavily on her again. She'd told him to go, so she had no reason to be upset with him. She should have been upset with herself.

She was the hypocrite who hadn't been open and honest with him like she'd promised they would be. She should have told him what she really wanted. A real marriage. She should have told him how she felt about him, that his kisses—even the innocent ones against her cheek—affected her. He affected her.

And his leaving had her putting her face in her hands and fighting to hold in tears, wishing that he would have fought for her...

For them.

A knock rattled her door. This time it had to be Hilda checking to see if she was okay, like she'd checked on her right after Collin had left.

She was actually very sweet. Like Sadie...

But Genevieve kept her face in her hands. She knew if she saw that look of concern and sympathy on Hilda's face that she would probably cry again. And she was already all cried out. Over Bailey Ann and over Collin.

"I'm fine," Genevieve said. "You don't have to worry about me."

"What about me?" a deep voice asked.

Collin.

He'd come back.

She tensed but lifted her face as he stepped inside her office again and closed the door.

"What about you?" she asked. She'd been worried about him last night; she'd known he was devastated when Mrs. Finch had taken Bailey Ann away.

"I'm not fine," he said.

"I'm sorry about Bailey Ann."

"That's part of it," he said. "I don't want to lose her. But I don't want to lose you either, Genevieve. I know this marriage isn't supposed to be real, but to me, it is. I have fallen for you."

She shook her head, unable to understand what he was saying. "You don't really even know me."

"We promised to be open and honest with each other," he said. "And I'm being open and honest. You impress me so much with your determination and your strength and your generosity."

She snorted. "Most of it's out of guilt."

"You shouldn't feel guilty," he said. "You haven't done anything wrong. But the fact that you do feel guilty proves what a good, caring person you are. You're so amazing that it's no wonder I've fallen in love with you."

"Really?" She couldn't believe it, couldn't believe what he was saying...

"I didn't realize what it was at first," he said. "I've never been in love before. So I didn't understand it, and I was terrified. I left yesterday because I was falling apart, and I didn't want you to see me like that."

"I know it hurt to have Bailey Ann taken away like that."

"It hurt you, too, and you were so strong for her, for me, but I couldn't do the same for you. I don't deserve you, Genevieve."

She sucked in a breath. "That's the way I've always felt, like I wasn't good enough to deserve love. That I wasn't enough."

"You're more than enough. You're everything," he said. "And even if we can't get Bailey Ann back, I don't want an annulment. I want you. Forever." He tensed then, as if bracing himself for rejection.

It was good that he'd braced himself because she jumped up from her chair and ran toward him to throw her arms around his neck, to hold him close, to hang on to him forever. "I love you," she said.

He stared down at her, as if in awe of the words. "I love you."

She and Collin were so much alike in how they'd dealt with their emotions, in how they loved, that it was no wonder they'd fallen in love. She'd found her soul mate in him. Or maybe Sadie Haven had found them for each other.

COLTON HAD FOUND a mobile tattoo artist for the ceremony. After all, the tattooed rings had been his idea. Now he just had to find his brother.

Grandma and his dad had told him about Bailey Ann, about how the social worker had taken her away from Collin and Genevieve a couple of nights ago. So he'd expected to find Collin burying himself in work at the hospital. But he hadn't been there.

He hadn't been at Dad's either. So Colton pulled his truck to the curb outside Genevieve's sprawling brick house. Collin's car was parked in the driveway next to her big SUV. Maybe they'd gotten Bailey Ann back. Feeling hopeful, for so many reasons, he ran up to the door and knocked.

Long moments passed. So long that he knocked again. Then he noticed the doorbell and rang that. Chimes played out inside the house. Just the sound of chimes, though.

Maybe they'd gone for a walk. He turned

away from the door, but then it creaked open. When he turned around, his mouth dropped open. Collin stood in front of him. His usually perfectly combed hair was tousled, and his face looked more relaxed than Colton had ever seen his twin.

"Are you okay?" Colton asked. "I heard about Bailey Ann being taken away."

"We're trying to get her back," Collin said, his expression tense.

Colton narrowed his eyes. "We?"

"It's not a marriage of convenience anymore," Collin said, and despite his concern for the little girl he loved, he grinned. Colton saw happiness there, too, which helped to temper his fears.

Colton had to believe, with Collin and Genevieve working together to get her back, they would win. They had to win.

"That's why I'm here," Colton said. "I'm supposed to get you to a wedding."

"I'm already married." Collin's eyes widened. "Wait, are you getting married?"

He shook his head. "Not yet. Grandma and Lem are getting married at city hall. And she wants us all there ASAP. I guess they figure at their ages, they don't want to wait another minute to spend the rest of their lives together."

"That will be a long time," Genevieve said as she joined them at the door. She looked like she was ready for a wedding in the dress she was wearing.

He grinned. "Grandma called you," he suspected.

She nodded. "She wanted to make sure we were all there." Tears glistened in her blue eyes. "All the family…"

Colton felt a twinge of regret for the doubts he'd had in the beginning about his sister-in-law. Clearly Grandma had been right about her and Collin. She was usually right about these things.

"Come on then!" he urged. "I have to make sure the tattoo artist gets there."

"The what?" Collin murmured.

But Colton was already heading back to his truck until a faint whiff of smoke stopped him. Reminded him…

Of the fire at the ranch. The lighter…

The destruction of not just the house they'd grown up in but their lives as they'd known them. But they'd gained more than they'd lost.

CHAPTER TWENTY-FOUR

COLLIN TRIED TO find a place to park, but the street in front of city hall was pretty packed. "We should have taken my car," he said. "It would have been easier to squeeze in somewhere."

"There," Genevieve said, her hand over his as she pointed him in the direction of a side street.

Collin turned and parked. Then he got out on the driver's side to go around and open her door. But she was already out and leaning in to the open back door. She pulled out something wrapped in a plastic dry cleaner bag, dangling from a hanger.

"What's this?" he asked.

She was already dressed in a soft blue dress that swirled around her legs when she walked. He was wearing a suit, too. They didn't need extra clothes.

"Sadie asked me to bring it," she said.

"Sadie can't wear anything of yours." His grandmother was six feet tall. Genevieve was probably only five feet four or five inches tall.

Those tears, that he'd glimpsed back at her house when she'd told him and Colton that Sadie had called, glistened in her eyes again. And his heart began to get that feeling again—a palpitation.

A flicker of hope…

Whatever was in that bag was too small for Genevieve to wear, too.

And he realized what she'd really meant back at the house. "She wants all her family here for her wedding…" he murmured.

"Go. Bring it to Lem's office on the third floor," she said. "He's getting ready there. They're getting married in Ben's office, since that was Lem's for a long time when he was mayor. And Sadie used to barge in and tell him how to run the town."

Collin chuckled. "Imagine that…" And he could. His grandmother was fierce. And somehow she must have pulled off what he'd thought impossible. She got Bailey Ann back. Maybe it was just for the wedding. Just for the day.

But for the moment, all that mattered was

seeing her again. "Come with me," he told Genevieve.

She shook her head. "You need a moment... just the two of you."

She slipped away into a big room where music played softly and he headed to the closed door with Lem's name on it. He was half-surprised it didn't say "Old Man Lemmon" instead since that was what most people in Willow Creek called him.

He raised his hand to knock, surprised that it was shaking slightly. It opened quickly and he was tugged inside—that strong hand, despite the arthritis, wrapping tightly around his. "Hello, Grandma," he greeted her. "Are you getting cold feet?"

"Not at all. I can't wait," she said. "For this." Then she urged him forward to the little girl who spun away from the woman doing her hair. Taye.

"Daddy!" she exclaimed. "Daddy! I missed you!"

He really needed that EKG; there was so much going on with his heart, so much love swelling in it. "Oh, sweetheart! I am so happy to see you!" He lifted her up, hugging her close.

She kissed his cheek and pulled back. "Did you bring my flower girl dress?"

"Genevieve did."

She peered around him. "Where's Mommy?"

"She thinks you're mad at her."

She blinked hard. "I was mean to her. I need to tell her I'm sorry and I love her so much. Where is she?"

He nodded. "She's in the room where the wedding is going to happen."

"Let's get you dressed and you can go see her before we start," Taye suggested.

"Only girl in the family, she's going to get this gig a lot," Sadie warned him.

"Is she?" he asked, his voice cracking a bit.

She nodded. "This isn't just for today."

"You got her back for us?"

Sadie shook her head. "Not me. Your wife did that."

"I am a lucky man," Collin said. Then he focused on his grandmother again. "No. Luck had nothing to do with bringing me together with Genevieve. It was all you."

She shrugged. She was wearing a long blush-colored dress in lace. It was so soft and feminine, so unlike Sadie, but she was different around Lem. She was so in love.

And because of her, so was Collin.

"Want to give me away?" she asked him.

"No. I intend to keep you forever," Collin assured his grandmother.

"I'll give her away," Jessup said.

"I'm sure you will," Sadie said with a chuckle.

Jessup hugged his mother. "I don't want to get rid of you."

"That's good," Sadie said. "Because I'm not going anywhere but down the aisle. Took Lem and I too many years to get here to not spend as many years together, driving each other crazy, as we can."

Collin had never met his grandfather. He'd only heard stories about Big Jake Haven. But there was something about Lem Lemmon, something that made Collin think the short little Santa-like man might have been his grandmother's true soul mate all along.

GENEVIEVE HAD FOUND a seat next to Becca on what was probably the Haven side of the room. Chairs had been put into rows on either side of a makeshift aisle. And some of those decorations from outside had found their way in here, like the balloons dangling from the ceiling. Her nephews, wearing those little white cowboy hats again, tried to reach the dangling strings of them. When they jumped to reach them, their hats slid down over their eyes. She chuckled at how cute they were.

"They're adorable," Becca said.

Genevieve smiled at her friend. "I'm surprised to see you here. I didn't know you and Sadie were that close."

"We're not," Becca said. "I'm kind of a plus-one."

Genevieve leaned forward and noticed the tall blond man sitting on the other side of Becca, next to the wall. Genevieve had left a few chairs open between her and the aisle for Collin and...

"Mommy!" a little voice exclaimed. And short arms wrapped around her neck, pulling her in for a hug.

Genevieve wrapped her arms around the little girl holding her close. "Oh, I missed you so much..."

"I missed you, too, Mommy."

"I thought you were mad at me," Genevieve admitted. That was why, when Mrs. Finch and her supervisor had authorized Bailey Ann to return to her care, she'd asked them to drop her here instead of right at her house. She'd wanted to surprise Collin, too, as much as he'd surprised her with his declaration of love.

"No. I know it's always the best to tell the truth and be open and honest," Bailey Ann said.

"Wow, you're one smart little girl," said the guy on the other side of Becca. He leaned around his date now. "How'd you get so smart?"

"From my mom and dad," Bailey Ann said, hugging Genevieve again. "This is my mom. She's a lawyer, and my dad is a doctor. A heart doctor." She touched her chest, but her scars were hidden beneath the lace and satin of her flower girl dress. "He fixed my heart."

He had fixed Genevieve's, too, opening it up for love again. For love to give and for love to receive.

"There's my daddy!" Bailey Ann exclaimed.

"You have to get back to Grandma," Collin said, "so they can get started. Can't start without the flower girl."

"Nope," Bailey Ann agreed as she rushed back down the aisle.

Collin dropped into the chair next to Genevieve, and he looked a little shaken. "I'm sorry

I didn't warn you," she said. "I just wanted to surprise you."

"With Cash?"

"With Bailey Ann," she said.

"But Cash is here, too," he said.

"Where?"

He pointed toward the man sitting next to Becca. Then he repeated her question to his brother. "Where have you been?"

"I've been here," Cash said. "In Willow Creek."

SADIE COULDN'T REMEMBER a time that she'd been happier, and it wasn't just because so much of their family was here. Jessup. His boys. Michael's boys. Dale's.

Even Livvy's brothers had made it to their wedding. And Cash…

The infamous Cash Cassidy. But he didn't call himself Cassidy. Or she would have known who he was all this time…

She would sort all that out later, though.

For now she just wanted to savor this day. To savor the moment she became Sadie March Haven Lemmon.

And the ring on her finger, tattooed on as an infinity symbol, would be there forever.

A testament of her love for the person she'd called an old fool for more years than he'd been old.

A person who'd challenged and infuriated her and always made her better. Those were the vows she spoke to him, and his were the same, about how she'd pushed him to be a better man. And how sometimes she'd just pushed him...

Just as she was pushing all of her great grandsons to find their soul mates, like she'd finally found hers in Lem even though he'd been here all these years.

* * * * *